## "We're not husba

You don't even know my name. You never once called me by name. You don't know any more about me than I do."

"You're making a mistake," Eden said.

"Yeah, I trusted you. That was my mistake. What I can't figure out is why you didn't call the cops last night when I stumbled in here. Why is that? What is it you're after?"

"Look, give me the gun, and we'll talk about it."

Until he knew differently, he had to assume Eden was his enemy, an enemy from whom he needed answers. But this was a dangerous place to try to get them. He needed somewhere that was safe until he figured out what to do. Where? That's when he remembered the painting above the fireplace.

He was getting out of here, going to that isolated houseboat on the river—and he was taking her with him.

Dear Harlequin Intrigue Reader,

Those April showers go hand in hand with a welcome downpour of gripping romantic suspense in the Harlequin Intrigue line this month!

Reader-favorite Rebecca York returns to the legendary 43 LIGHT STREET with *Out of Nowhere*—an entrancing tale about a beautiful blond amnesiac who proves downright lethal to a hard-edged detective's heart. Then take a detour to New Mexico for *Shotgun Daddy* by Harper Allen—the conclusion in the MEN OF THE DOUBLE B RANCH trilogy. In this story a Navajo protector must safeguard the woman from his past who is nurturing a ticking time bomb of a secret.

The momentum keeps building as Sylvie Kurtz launches her brand-new miniseries—THE SEEKERS—about men dedicated to truth, justice…and protecting the women they love. But at what cost? Don't miss the debut book, *Heart of a Hunter,* where the search for a killer just might culminate in rekindled love. Passion and peril go hand in hand in *Agent Cowboy* by Debra Webb, when COLBY AGENCY investigator Trent Tucker races against time to crack a case of triple murder!

Rounding off a month of addictive romantic thrillers, watch for the continuation of two new thematic promotions. A handsome sheriff saves the day in *Restless Spirit* by Cassie Miles, which is part of COWBOY COPS. *Sudden Recall* by Jean Barrett is the latest in our DEAD BOLT series about silent memories that unlock simmering passions.

Enjoy all of our great offerings.

Sincerely,

Denise O'Sullivan
Senior Editor
Harlequin Intrigue

# SUDDEN RECALL
## JEAN BARRETT

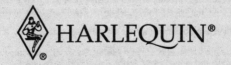

TORONTO • NEW YORK • LONDON
AMSTERDAM • PARIS • SYDNEY • HAMBURG
STOCKHOLM • ATHENS • TOKYO • MILAN • MADRID
PRAGUE • WARSAW • BUDAPEST • AUCKLAND

ISBN 0-373-22770-1

SUDDEN RECALL

Copyright © 2004 by Jean Barrett

This edition published by arrangement with Harlequin Books S.A.

® and TM are trademarks of the publisher. Trademarks indicated with
® are registered in the United States Patent and Trademark Office, the
Canadian Trade Marks Office and in other countries.

Visit us at www.eHarlequin.com

**Printed in U.S.A.**

## ABOUT THE AUTHOR

If setting has anything to do with it, Jean Barrett claims she has no reason not to be inspired. She and her husband live on Wisconsin's scenic Door Peninsula in an antique-filled country cottage overlooking Lake Michigan. A teacher for many years, she left the classroom to write full-time. She is the author of a number of romance novels.

Write to Jean at P.O. Box 623, Sister Bay, WI 54234. SASE appreciated.

## Books by Jean Barrett

HARLEQUIN INTRIGUE
308—THE SHELTER OF HER ARMS
351—WHITE WEDDING
384—MAN OF THE MIDNIGHT SUN
475—FUGITIVE FATHER
528—MY LOVER'S SECRET
605—THE HUNT FOR HAWKE'S DAUGHTER*
652—PRIVATE INVESTIGATIONS*
692—OFFICIAL ESCORT*
728—COWBOY P.I.*
770—SUDDEN RECALL*

*The Hawke Detective Agency

# CLASSIFIEDS

# CAST OF CHARACTERS

*Eden Hawke*—She is prepared to risk anything to get her son back, including the man without a past.

*Shane*—He is on the run and with no memory. Can he trust the alluring P.I., or is she another threat to him?

*Tia*—Eden's friend is worried about her.

*Nathanial*—Is Eden's son still alive? If so, what became of him after he vanished three years ago?

*Roy*—The caretaker is unwilling to tell what he knows.

*Harriet Krause*—The lab technician is frightened. What is she hiding?

*Bruno and Boris*—Whatever their actual names might be, the two brutes are both dangerous and desperate.

*Lissie Reardon*—She is prepared to sacrifice everything, including her life.

*Charles Moses*—Eden had once loved him, but now he's her enemy.

*Irene Moses*—The daughter of Sebastian Jamison is as shallow as she is beautiful.

*Claire Jamison*—What family secret is Sebastian's elegant but ruthless widow determined to protect?

*Estelle and Victor DuBois*—They are valuable friends, but how far are they willing to go to help Eden and Shane?

To my good friends Bev, Jane and Kathy. You're the tops.

## ACKNOWLEDGEMENT

A special thank you to Judy Scrimpsher, R.N.,
for sharing her medical knowledge.

# Chapter One

Whatever it was, it was vital. Something he had lost and had to recover before it was too late. That part was clear, though nothing else was.

He wished his head would stop hurting. If only he could achieve that much, ease the throbbing inside his skull, he was certain he would remember just what it was he was trying to find.

Then a new thought struck him. Maybe it wasn't a *something* from which he had been separated but a *someone*. Could that be right? Yes, he was sure of it now. Someone was waiting for him, someone who needed him. Or was it the other way around? Was *he* the one in need?

In his confusion he wasn't absolutely certain of anything, only that he had to get there. Wherever *there* was. He was so disoriented he had no idea what this place was or how he'd gotten here. Neither the hour nor the weather were his allies.

It was late, sometime in the middle of the night. He could sense that much. And there was water off to his right. A river, he thought. He could see lights on the other side, and more lights off to his left. Between them was this strip of darkness along which he had been wandering. For how long he didn't know.

A parkway, he decided. That was the explanation for the grassy strip. He was alone and on foot along some city parkway. A wind blew off the river, cold and wet, pelting him with needles of rain. He wasn't dressed for the weather. Drawing the collar of his light jacket up around his neck, he turned and moved away from the biting exposure of the broad river.

That's when he realized that more than his head was hurting. His whole body was sore, aching with the effort of each step. Had he been in an accident?

He came to a wide boulevard where the traffic at this hour was light. On the other side were the glowing lights of what looked like a convenience store, one of those places that never closed.

They would have aspirin in there. If he could get some aspirin inside him, relieve the stabbing inside his head, he was confident his brain would find the answers he was searching for.

He shuffled across the thoroughfare, and into the store. The light was dazzling after the darkness outside. It took him a moment to adjust to the glare. Then he saw that the store was deserted except for him and a young attendant at the checkout counter talking on her cell phone.

He found the aspirin at the rear of the store. There was bottled water nearby. He took both the aspirin and a bottle of water up to the checkout.

"Customer," the attendant said into her phone. "Gotta go."

She ended her call and turned her attention in his direction. There was a startled expression on her face when she looked at him. It puzzled him for a second, and then he remembered how wet he was from the rain. He must look as if he'd fallen into the river.

He placed his purchases on the counter and reached for his wallet in his back pants pocket. There was no wallet, not in that pocket or anywhere else on him. Had he been robbed? The young woman was staring at him.

"Sorry," he muttered. "Forgot something."

He left the aspirin and water on the counter and retreated

down one of the aisles. When he was out of sight of the checkout area, he stopped and searched again through all his pockets, trying not to panic, trying to understand.

But there were no funds on him anywhere, not in his pants, his shirt or in his jacket. No money, no credit cards and no identification. Nothing at all.

In desperation he clutched at the sides of his jacket. And that's when he felt it. Something deep down inside the lining. His hand plunged again into the lower left pocket, this time finding a tear in one corner. His fingers dug through the opening, fished around, and finally closed around two small rectangles of thick paper.

Not concerning himself with how they had gotten there, whether they had slipped down into the lining by accident or whether they had been deliberately concealed there, he hoped only that they would tell him who he was and what was happening to him, if not why. He withdrew his discoveries.

One was a photograph of a young, solemn-faced boy. He didn't recognize the child, and there was no writing on the back. There was printing on the other rectangle. A dog-eared business card. Hawke Detective Agency, it said. Under that, beside the emblem of a golden hawk, was a name and address. Eden Hawke, 99 Mead Street, Charleston. There were also a phone number and an address.

None of it triggered any memories. None of it meant anything to him. But it was all he had, and he suddenly knew that he had to go to the address on this card. That it must be the place he was seeking, and that there was someone there waiting for him.

A phone. He remembered seeing a pay phone in a corner at the back of the store. He had no money to place a call, nor any wish to make that kind of contact. No desire to do anything but reach that address. But first he had to locate it. Public phones were accompanied by city directories, and directories had maps in them. A map that could tell him how to get to 99 Mead Street.

Providing, that is, this was Charleston he was in and not some other city far away. And why didn't he know? Never mind, he promised himself as he moved down the aisle toward the phone. It would all get sorted out.

There was a display of sunglasses with a small mirror at eye level, to see what the glasses looked like on you. He caught a glimpse of himself as he started past the display. Coming to a stop, he peered into the mirror, shocked by his image.

No wonder he was in pain and that the attendant had been jolted by the sight of him. The unrecognizable face that stared back at him looked like a battleground. One eye was bruised and so swollen it was half shut, his bottom lip split open, a raw wound on the bridge of his nose, blood smeared on his cheek.

Something had happened to him out there all right. Something very bad. No time to wonder about it. Later. He had to get to Mead Street.

Backing away from the mirror, he went on to the phone. A directory was attached to it by a chain. The cover under the heavy black binding told him what he needed to know. He was in Charleston, South Carolina. The street map inside the directory provided him with the location of Mead Street.

He would need the map. Tearing it out of the directory, he folded it and placed it in his jacket pocket along with the business card and the photograph.

He had to get out of the store before that attendant got nervous and called the cops. Maybe she already had. He didn't want the police, didn't consider asking the attendant for help, either with medical assistance or directions. He wasn't sure why, but instinct told him there was a potential danger in this situation that he had to avoid.

He left the store, head lowered, and went out into the wild blackness of the night. There was a street sign on the corner. He read it and then checked the map under the streetlight. Mead Street was twelve blocks from this corner.

Not far, but light-years away in this weather and in his condition. But he would manage it. Somehow.

It was a struggle. The wind had risen again, blasting rain into his face. In several places he stumbled over limbs that the storm had torn from the trees. He fell once and fought the temptation to just lie there and forget he must be oozing blood and that every step was agony. Picking himself up was an effort, moving on an ordeal. But he did it.

There were few people out in this weather, and at this hour the traffic almost nonexistent. A cab did pass by. If only he could have hailed it. He couldn't. He had no money for a taxi.

There was another car that made him melt into an alley. A police cruiser. He didn't know why he should fear it, but a sense of self-preservation had him blindly doing just that. He wasn't challenged, which meant they probably hadn't spotted him. The cruiser turned the corner and disappeared.

He emerged from the alley and went on, driven by an urgency he didn't understand. He was worried, too. Worried that he wouldn't make it, because both his head and his leg were hurting like hell. He was limping badly and so weak and dazed that he had trouble with his bearings.

Where was he now? How far had he come? He wasn't sure, but it looked as if he was in an historic district. There were rows of vintage houses, most of them shuttered and all of them crowded to the edges of the brick sidewalks.

Mead Street. He saw the sign for it by the gleam of an old lantern on a post. He was almost there. Dragging himself along the length of the street, he searched the numbers and came at last to ninety-nine.

With a white frame and a narrow face, it was one of those Charleston structures known as a single house. The kind with a fanlighted door at one end of its front wall that opened onto a piazza at the side of the building. He didn't know how he knew this, but it seemed that he did.

There was a brass plate on the door and sufficient light from a nearby street lantern to permit him to read it. He was so spent by now, so light-headed from his exertions, that he almost passed out when he leaned down from his considerable height to peer at the lettering. Steadying himself, he focused on the plate. Hawke Detective Agency, it said. He had come to the right place.

Why he should trust a private investigator any more than the police, he didn't know. And what made him think anyone would be here at this hour?

They were questions for which he had no answers. Nor was his mind functioning with any clarity. His head was swimming now. There was only one clear emotion inside it. Relief.

He didn't bother knocking on the door or looking for a bell, both of which might be loud enough to draw attention to him out here on the street. He didn't want to risk that. Instead, he reached for the knob and turned it, and since the door was actually a gate and not really a door at all, it was unlocked. Just as he had figured, it opened on a piazza that overlooked a storm-littered garden at the side of the house.

Then he was inside and the door closed behind him. Inside and mercifully safe.

There were a door and windows off the front of the piazza. Probably the agency's office. The windows were dark. But at the rear of the piazza, where the house turned in a right angle, were lighted windows. He staggered toward their welcoming glow.

He didn't make it. Halfway along the piazza, his body finally betrayed his determination. Although it felt as though he was collapsing in a silent slow motion, he must have toppled with a crash. Because as he lay there, helpless on the wet bricks, a door banged open and light spilled onto the piazza.

There was the sound of hurrying footsteps, a little cry of alarm, and then he sensed someone kneeling beside him, caught the whiff of a fragrance. A feminine scent that was warm and comforting. Something that made a man want to sink into its sweetness.

He lifted his head and just before he slid into unconsciousness, he managed to plead in a strained, husky voice, "Am I home?"

HE WAS CONSCIOUS again but still so disoriented he was only dimly aware of his surroundings. What was this place? A bedroom apparently, since he felt a firm mattress under him and a warm quilt drawn over his prone figure.

But it was hard to be certain of that since the room was in almost total darkness. The only source of illumination was a thin strip of vertical light, which was the result of a door left slightly ajar somewhere on the other side of the room.

All right, he was in a bedroom. But whose bedroom, and where? He wanted to believe it was his own room, that he belonged here. But he couldn't be sure of that either.

He hated his confusion. Hated this state of helplessness that prevented him from...what? He didn't know, but it nagged at him. There was something he was supposed to do, someone he was supposed to see, but he couldn't recall what or who.

And then he heard it. The sound of voices drifting through the crack where the door was ajar. Two people engaged in a conversation out there in another room. Voices so low that he couldn't make out their words, only their tones. One of them intense, earnest. The other calm but equally insistent. *Her* voice.

He recognized it now, remembered its reassurances to him. As soothing as her hands on him, as silken as her scent. It was all right then. If she was here, close by, then he was safe. He could forget all the rest, worry about it later.

He was so damn sore and exhausted that he needed to

do just that. The voices droned on and then faded altogether as he drifted back into unconsciousness.

"YOU CAN'T DO THIS, EDEN. It's wrong. The man should be on his way to the E.R., not stretched out back there in your guest room."

Eden watched as her friend and neighbor from the apartment upstairs placed her medical supplies back in her bag. There was an expression of pronounced disapproval on Tia's delicate Asian face.

"He's not at risk. Didn't you say it yourself when you patched him up? That someone with a body that fit wouldn't need a hospital to recover?"

"Well, I shouldn't have said it. I'm a nurse-practitioner, not a doctor, and if there should be any complications—"

"Then I'll see to it he has whatever attention is necessary."

"When?" Tia demanded, revealing a form as dainty as her features when she came to her feet. It was a figure that belied her strength. Tia had demonstrated that robustness, a result of her work with patients twice her size, when she had helped Eden bear her midnight visitor into the guest room where he had been stripped and examined, his wounds treated. All of which Tia had handled skillfully, if unwillingly.

"As soon as he tells me what I have to know," Eden promised her.

"Let the police question him then. You should have called them right away."

"And see him taken away?" Eden shook her head obstinately. "No, I won't risk losing this opportunity. I won't trust hearing what he has to say from anyone but him personally."

"Eden, this is reckless. The guy could be dangerous. Probably *is* dangerous. Stumbling in here out of nowhere like that, no identification on him, absolutely nothing to suggest who he is or where he came from."

"He won't hurt me."

"Why? Just because at the moment he's too weak to be a threat?"

"No, because my instincts tell me this is a decent man. Couldn't you hear it in his voice?"

"What I heard were a few mutters that didn't make sense. But what I *saw* worries me. Those injuries aren't the result of some accident. I think he was beaten, *brutally* beaten. And I'll tell you something else. He has several old scars on his body, a bad one on his right leg."

"I noticed."

"Then those scars should have told you this is someone with a history that might not be so good and that you shouldn't have him here. Come on, Eden, you're thinking with your emotions, not your head."

"Wouldn't you if you were me and this brought him here?" Her hand went out to the table beside her and snatched up the business card she had found in the jacket of his pocket. *Her* business card. "And *this*." Her other hand closed around the photograph that had accompanied the business card. She could feel the painful longing deep inside her as she gazed down at it. "Nathanial, Tia. He was carrying a picture of Nathanial."

Tia's face softened at the mention of Nathanial. "Honey," she pleaded gently, "be reasonable. Having red-gold hair and a pair of lavender-blue eyes, distinctive as they are, doesn't make him Nathanial. He was what when he was taken? Less than two years old, right? It's been almost three years now, and kids change a lot. The boy in that photo could be anyone."

"It's Nathanial," Eden insisted fiercely. "I *know* it is!"

*Because you want it to be.* That was what the expression on Tia's face told her. She knew what her friend was thinking, what all the sympathizers had thought and refrained from saying since Nathanial's disappearance. That too much time had passed, that she would never recover him, that Nathanial was probably dead.

Let them think it. She knew better. Nathanial was still alive. She had never stopped believing it in all the agonizing weeks after his disappearance, in the months and years that had followed. She had never dared permit herself to believe otherwise, haunted as she was by his loss, frustrated as she was that none of the efforts of the professionals, including her own, had produced any results. But now... Oh, yes, *now*.

"He's a link to Nathanial, Tia. Whoever he is and whatever brought him to my door, he's a link to Nathanial. And however rash you think I'm being, I'm not letting him leave until he tells me what I want to know."

"You're vulnerable as long as he's here. You realize that, don't you?"

"I'm a mother, Tia," Eden reminded her. "I'll do anything to find my son. *Anything.*"

Tia sighed softly. "Yeah, I guess I can understand that kind of desperation. I just hope you know what you're doing." Medical bag in hand, she moved toward the door to the piazza and the outside stairway to her apartment. "The painkiller should have taken full effect by now. My guess is he'll sleep the night through, but if he should wake up and you need me—"

"I won't hesitate to call you," Eden promised, following her friend to the door to see her out.

"I'll come down tomorrow to check on him. Oh, damn, I just remembered. Quinn is picking me up first thing in the morning. We promised to spend the day with his parents down on Seabrook Island, and if I cancel—"

"Don't cancel. Go, and stop looking at me like that. It's not as if I'm entirely on my own. The Davises are just across the garden."

Tia went, though reluctantly and with last-minute instructions about the patient, which she followed with a promise to phone Eden in the morning before she left with her boyfriend.

Eden was relieved when she was finally able to close and lock the door behind her upstairs neighbor. She shouldn't have been relieved. She was all alone now with a man she knew nothing about, a stranger who had arrived out of nowhere in the middle of a wild night. There was everything about him to make her apprehensive, but her only fear was that he wouldn't be able to tell her what she would give her soul to know.

She stood there for a moment in the stillness of the apartment, listening to the sounds of the wind and the rain outside. Then she crossed the parlor and went into the guest room to look in on her patient.

The light from the door she left open was sufficient to reveal the man who lay there, undisturbed by her entrance. She stood beside the bed, gazing down at him, remembering the body concealed now by the quilt that covered his length. It was a tall body, and though it had suffered, it was solidly built, with powerful shoulders, lean hips and long legs. A body that had been conditioned for—

What? She had no way of knowing. That was as much a mystery as the rest of him, including his square-jawed face. "Hard to tell," Tia had observed when she'd been working on that face, "but there could be something worth looking at under all this battering."

Restless, he stirred briefly, muttering something in his sleep before he became quiet again. Whatever it was, Eden was unable to understand it. Nothing he had murmured since collapsing on the piazza had been intelligible. Except for those first three words. "Am I home?"

She didn't know what, if anything, he had meant by them or why at the time she had been so moved at hearing them. *Am I home?*

Eden mentally embraced those words now, clung to them, because only this way, remembering their poignancy, could she go on convincing herself that she was not making a terrible mistake by keeping this man in her home.

## Chapter Two

Eden loved her adopted city. Charleston had so many things to offer, the climate being one of them. Even in midwinter like this, the weather was generally mild. Having grown up in Chicago, she appreciated that.

Last night's frigid temperature had been an exception. But this morning, early though it still was, the thermometer had climbed to a balmy level that had prompted her to open the door to the garden where the sun was already drying the soaked and sagging vegetation.

Eden could hear the tolling of the bells from Charleston's historic churches summoning worshipers to Sunday services. It was another thing she enjoyed about the city. Not this morning, however. She was too anxious to be soothed by their restful sounds drifting through the open doorway as she waited for the coffeemaker to finish brewing.

The phone on the kitchen wall rang. She picked it up, knowing it would be Tia, knowing, too, what her friend would immediately ask. She wasn't wrong.

"Is he awake yet?"

Eden was careful to keep her concern out of her voice. "He's still sleeping, but after what he must have gone through that's to be expected, isn't it?"

"Maybe. You check his vital signs like I showed you?"

"Yes. They're normal."

"You want me to come down?"

Eden heard an impatient sound in the background and realized that Tia's boyfriend was there and not happy about an offer that would delay them. "That's not necessary. I'll give him another hour, and if he isn't conscious by then, I'll wake him myself."

"And if you can't revive him—"

"I'll call an ambulance. Look, don't worry. I can handle it. Just go and enjoy your day."

Eden's certainty evaporated when she hung up. She was back to wondering again, asking herself the same question that had troubled her since she had last looked in on her patient. Could he have a serious head injury, and was she denying him the treatment he needed by keeping him here?

It was the thought of Nathanial that kept her from reaching for the phone again. Smothering the threat of guilt, she glanced at the coffeemaker, saw that the brew was ready and poured herself a steaming mug. The first few sips steadied her.

Mug in hand, she headed once more for the guest room. Spreading the door inward, she stole quietly into the room. Her silence this time was unnecessary. He was awake.

Apparently sensing her presence, he turned his head on the pillow and gazed at her from a pair of deep brown eyes that were more alert than she would have expected, and far more unsettling. There was something positively intimate in the way they held her gaze.

"Hello," he said, his voice slow and raspy.

Eden held the mug in front of her, as though she were gripping a weapon. Swallowing nervously, she made the effort to address him with a casualness she was a long way from feeling. "Good morning. How do you feel?"

He frowned, considering her question for a moment before answering her in that husky voice. "Like an eighteen-wheeler rolled over me. I seem to be aching in places I didn't know I had."

"Your head?"

"Not inside, but—" He broke off to raise one of his

hands to his head. His fingers began to explore the wounds
on his face. He looked puzzled when they encountered the
bandage across the bridge of his nose. "Your work?"

Eden shook her head. "No, Tia's from upstairs. She's a
nurse-practitioner."

"I'll have to thank Tia."

"You'll have to wait to do that. She left for the day."

He nodded thoughtfully. "I don't remember Tia. Is she
one of our friends?"

Eden thought it was an odd thing for him to say. He
sounded normal enough otherwise. In fact, he was in a far
better state than she could have hoped for, but she experienced a moment of uneasiness. If he was still dazed, not
entirely lucid, it could mean he had sustained a head injury
after all.

He was looking at her as though waiting for her reassurance. "Well, she's my friend, anyway. Are you sure you
don't have anything like a headache? Or some dizziness
maybe?"

"Not this morning, no."

She fought the need to ask him about Nathanial, why he
had been carrying a photograph of a child she was convinced was her son along with her business card, both of
which were tucked now into her purse for safekeeping. But
an interrogation like that would be insensitive when his
well-being had to be their immediate concern. Her urgent
questions would have to wait.

"Does that mean you did have a headache last night?
That you experienced dizziness?"

"I suppose so," he said vaguely.

"You had quite a lump on the back of your skull. The
swelling went down after Tia applied ice packs."

"That's good."

He didn't seem troubled by any of it, but Eden was beginning to be worried for him. How could he be so blithe
about everything? His behavior under the circumstances
didn't seem altogether rational. "Do you remember last

night at all? How you found your way here and passed out on the piazza?"

"Sure I do. I had a hell of a time getting here."

"What happened to you? How did you get those injuries?"

"I can't tell you that."

"Why?"

"Because I don't know."

"What do you mean, you don't know?" Eden's uneasiness was beginning to deepen into alarm.

"I remember everything from the time I found myself wandering out there beside a river, but not before that."

"Nothing?"

He pondered her earnest question for a few seconds and then shook his head. "Afraid not."

"What about before last night? You must remember something."

He thought about it again. "Sorry. It's all a blank."

Eden stared down at him, shaken by the realization of his condition. He had no memory. No past. "Are you telling me," she asked him slowly, "that you don't know who you are? That you're suffering from amnesia?"

He lifted his head from the pillow, his wide mouth offering her a smile. It was a smile that was both reassuring and unexpectedly sensual. "Don't worry about it. Now that I'm back, everything will be fine. You can tell me all about us, everything I need to know. I'll listen, and it'll come back to me. Even exactly what happened to me last night. That coffee smells good," he said cheerfully, indicating the mug she was clutching. "Do you think I could have a cup?"

He couldn't know it, but he had just given her exactly what she craved at this moment—an opportunity to escape his presence long enough to recover from her astonishment, to collect her bewildered thoughts.

"Of course," she said.

Eden fled from the room. It wasn't until she reached the

kitchen that she realized her hand bearing the coffee mug was trembling. She set the mug on the counter and drew a steadying breath before making an effort to deal with her confusion.

He had amnesia. That was frustrating enough right there, because if he couldn't remember who he was, how could he possibly tell her anything about Nathanial? Even more puzzling, he had somehow gotten the idea into his head that they knew each other, that she could tell him all about himself. She couldn't begin to imagine why.

What was she going to do about him? The answer was an obvious one. If he needed professional help, and it was beginning to look as though he did, then she had an obligation to surrender him to the people who were equipped to handle this kind of thing. Except she couldn't bring herself to do that. Not just yet. Not until she tried to find some way to unlock his memory.

*Because you* are *professional help. That's exactly what a private investigator is supposed to do, deal with people's troubles.*

She was arguing herself into something that was morally questionable, and she knew it. But she couldn't help herself. She had to have those answers about Nathanial.

Her patient was waiting for his coffee. She filled a mug, then hesitated. Did he take it black or white? With sweetener or without? No way of knowing if he even remembered that much. She put the mug on a small tray and placed a spoon, sugar bowl and container of milk beside it.

He presented a disturbing sight when she returned to the guest room with the tray. He had propped himself up against the headboard in her absence, displaying an expanse of naked male flesh he seemed in no way self-conscious about.

Eden had viewed that hard body last night when she and Tia had examined him and attended to his injuries. But that had been an impersonal thing. Now, though, with him awake and aware of her standing there…

She tried not to gape at the powerful chest whose allure was not diminished by its several scars as she set the tray on the bedside table. Ignoring the sugar and milk as though they didn't exist, he reached for the mug and brought it to his mouth. She watched him drink the coffee in eager gulps. There was something strangely mesmerizing in the way his Adam's apple bobbed in his strong, corded throat as he swallowed.

"Ah, that's better," he said, lowering the mug. Leaning toward her, he sniffed the air, then demanded abruptly, "What is it?"

"I beg your pardon?"

"The scent you're wearing. I don't remember that either, just the whiffs of it I caught last night when you were helping me and my thinking how much I liked it. Something floral, huh?"

"Lily of the Valley."

"Nice," he said, putting the mug back on the tray.

Before she could back away from the side of the bed, he reached out, wrapping his big hand around her own hand and dragging it up to his face. Turning it over, he buried his nose into the back of her wrist, inhaling deeply.

"Yeah, *very* nice," he growled softly.

Eden was so startled that she failed to react. Failed to stop him when his bold mouth covered the place where his nose had been. He planted a warm kiss on her wrist, the tip of his tongue caressing its vulnerable pulse point. The action was so unexpected, and so instantly tantalizing, that a jolt of electricity raced up her arm. Gasping, she snatched her hand away from his provocative assault.

He chuckled. "What's the matter? Can't a man nuzzle his own wife?"

"What did you say?" she whispered.

"Nothing, just that I was appreciating how my wife smells." He laughed again. "Among other things."

Eden stared down at him, so stunned that she was speechless. This was incredible, much more involved than just his impression they knew each other. He thought he was her husband! That they were actually married!

*Tell him. Why aren't you telling him?*

Eden didn't know what was holding her back from immediately and emphatically correcting his mistaken belief. Or was it that she didn't want to know, because a remorseless little voice was already telling her that she could take advantage of this situation? Unthinkable! How could she even consider it? And yet...

"Do you suppose I could have some breakfast to go with this coffee? I'd fix it for myself if I remembered where things are."

Eden managed to find her voice then, shaky though it was. "Do you think you're well enough to eat?"

"My insides tell me I am." Demonstrating his rapid recovery, he swung his long legs over the side of the bed and eased himself to his feet. To her relief, he kept the quilt wound around his hips. "See? Perfectly steady. Now, if you could point me to my clothes..."

She nodded in the direction of the adjoining bathroom. "In there. I laundered and folded them for you."

What if he asked for a change of outfit? Clothing he hadn't been wearing last night? What would she tell him? But he accepted her choice without question.

She watched him, making certain that he was capable of reaching the bathroom without her assistance. When the door closed behind him, she picked up the tray and retreated from the bedroom.

Her brain couldn't be any more numbed than his had been as she moved around the kitchen, preparing a breakfast of scrambled eggs and toast, trusting that he wouldn't expect cereal instead. Or, for all she knew, steak and potatoes.

*Am I home?*

The words he had uttered last night before passing out on the piazza floor made sense now. He'd been convinced he had fought his way home to his wife and was safe. All the rest were clear as well. The way he had looked at her so intimately, his thinking he was supposed to remember Tia, grasping her hand and kissing it like that. Those made sense, yes, but nothing else did.

Man and wife. How could he think it? What in his jumbled mind had led him to such a fantastic conclusion?

*And you're planning to make use of it, too, aren't you? That's why you haven't told him the truth. You see this as an opportunity.*

All right, so it was wrong of her to let him go on thinking she was his wife, even cruel. But the temptation was too strong for her to resist, because his assumption that she was his wife meant that he trusted her. Trusted her fully. And only if he continued to trust her would he willingly share with her whatever he knew about the photograph she had discovered inside his jacket.

Only for a little while, she promised herself, silencing the guilt that was gnawing at her conscience. Just long enough for her to tap into whatever memory he might still possess, and then she would set him straight. She *had* to know.

"I think I'm ready for action again."

Eden swung around at the sound of his deep voice behind her. Her first thought when she caught sight of him standing there in the doorway was how appropriate his declaration was. He'd meant it as a simple assurance that he was feeling better, but no adult female with functioning vision could have failed to put a spin on his words. He was that impressive, with the kind of athletic body meant to be wrapped around a woman.

He definitely knew how to fill a pair of jeans to maximum effect. She hadn't noticed it last night, but the cut of both those jeans and his shirt were western in character. She recognized the style because of her brother, Roark, who lived and worked in Texas. There was something else she observed. His skin was bronzed and his brown hair streaked in front to shades of blond, like a man who has been exposed to a desert sun. Did they mean nothing, or were they clues to his origin?

"Sit down," she instructed him. "Breakfast is almost ready."

He started toward the table she had been setting at one end of the parlor, when she noticed what the trailing quilt had concealed in the bedroom. He had a faint but definite limp.

"Your leg," she said, voicing her concern over what she assumed was another of last night's injuries. "If you're in pain, then maybe you shouldn't be on it. Maybe you should have stayed in bed."

He stopped midway across the room and gazed down in puzzlement at the leg to which she referred. "I don't have any pain in my leg," he said. "What are you talking about?"

"Nothing," Eden assured him, suddenly remembering that Tia had directed her attention last night to an old scar on his right leg. Then his slight lameness wasn't the result of any recent injury but something that had happened in the past and become so much an accepted part of him he was no longer aware of its existence, particularly now when he had no memory of its cause.

After he'd settled himself at the table, she went back into the adjoining kitchen. When she returned with eggs and toast, she found him gazing with interest at his surroundings. She knew he was seeing for the first time all the elements of the parlor that she so loved—the delicate molding that had suffered scuffs and marks over the decades, the cracked but elegant marble surround of the fireplace, the worn boards of the polished floor.

But, of course, he didn't know that he'd never viewed any of these things before. It was painful to watch him struggling to renew a knowledge he had never possessed. So painful that she was tempted then and there to tell him the truth. But, remembering Nathanial, she held her tongue.

"The painting," he said, his gaze settling on the framed

scene above the fireplace. "Do I know that place? Where is it?"

"It's a watercolor of the houseboat that—" she'd been about to say *I* but corrected herself in time "—we keep up along the Ashley River."

"For weekend getaways, you mean?"

"Yes, something like that."

He nodded thoughtfully. "I like it. It looks quiet and peaceful."

"You'd better eat before your breakfast gets cold." She seated herself across from him.

He started to pick up the glass of orange juice beside his plate and then hesitated, frowning over it as if he wasn't sure whether he liked orange juice. And if he didn't, would he wonder why his wife had given it to him? This deception was proving to be more difficult than she'd anticipated, Eden realized. Any little mistake could arouse his suspicion, cost her his trust, which was a good reason not to waste time going after the answers she wanted.

Apparently deciding the orange juice was acceptable, he drank it. She waited just long enough to permit him to help himself to scrambled eggs before she led into her cautious interrogation. "Do you have any recollection yet of what happened to you last night?"

"Afraid not. Aren't you going to eat?" he asked, noticing that she had nothing in front of her but her coffee mug.

"I had something earlier. No clue at all then about last night?"

"I've been thinking about it, and I figure I must have been beaten and robbed. Whoever the punks were, they got away with my wallet and everything in it." Something occurred to him then, and he glanced at her quickly. "You report this to the police?"

"Not yet, but we should, don't you think?"

"No," he said, a sudden sharpness in his voice, which he amended with a softer "Let's wait a bit and see if I can remember anything useful to give them."

Was it her imagination, or did the idea of the police worry him? "Were you missing anything else?" she asked, hoping he would recall the photograph in his jacket.

"Keys. I must have had keys, and I suppose they took those, too. Did I have a car with me?"

It was a question Eden answered with an elusive, "The car is safe in the alley." No lie. Her car *was* parked in its usual spot behind the house. "You were on foot."

"Why was I out there?"

*That's exactly what I was hoping you could tell me.* Again her reply, out of necessity, was an evasive one. "You had some business. Maybe it had to do with this."

She had brought her purse to the table. She extracted the photograph from it and passed it to him across the table. Holding her breath in anticipation, she watched his face for a reaction as he took the picture and studied it carefully.

"They didn't get this," he said slowly, a faint grimness in his voice.

"You remember it then?" she said tensely.

"Yes. The photo was in my jacket along with your business card." He looked up, meeting her searching gaze. "Who's the little boy?"

Eden managed to hide her deep disappointment. "You don't know?"

He shook his head. "Is the kid someone I'm supposed to remember?"

Hoping a name would make a connection for him, Eden considered telling him that she believed the boy in the photograph was her son, Nathanial. But she wasn't ready for this step just yet, to risk the volley of questions that would be certain to follow such an admission.

"It seems that you should, since you were carrying his photograph. Look again," she urged him. "Maybe if you try hard enough, he'll start to look familiar to you."

Lowering his gaze, he reexamined the photo. Once again she watched him closely, studying his face for a revealing expression. She couldn't be sure, but his features seemed to slowly tighten into something that was guarded, something so automatic that he might not even be aware of it.

"What is it?" she pressed him.

He didn't answer her. Something else had captured his attention, something that had apparently registered in his peripheral vision. Suddenly alert, his gaze swung in the direction of the window that overlooked the piazza and the garden beyond.

"Who's that?" he demanded.

Eden had been far too focused on her objective to be aware of anything outside. But now, head turned, she discovered a rotund figure in the garden busy filling a large basket with the debris from last night's storm.

"Our neighbor, Skip Davis," she said mildly. "He's a retired navy officer. He and his wife share the garden. That's their house on the other side."

"Oh." He seemed to visibly relax, but seconds later he asked Eden, "Could you adjust the blinds? The light hurts my eyes. Guess it's a leftover from last night's headache."

"Of course."

She got up and went to the window, redirecting the light and in the process eliminating any view of the garden. She knew that his request had been an excuse, that the presence of Skip Davis out there disturbed him in some way.

The interruption lost her the opportunity to question him further. When she got back to the table, prepared to resume their session, he had lost interest.

"The face means nothing to me," he said, placing the photograph on the table and dismissing it. "I'll try again later, okay?"

Frustrated though she was, he left her no choice. If she pushed him too hard, he might close up altogether. She had to be patient if she was going to stand any chance of acquiring what was locked in his mind. But it wasn't easy, particularly when those brown eyes with the golden lights in them kept casting looks at her as he went on with his eggs and toast. Looks that were as warm and tender as a

pair of hands stroking female flesh. They were also un-
nervingly possessive.

"Why do you keep on looking at me like that?" she
challenged him, returning the photo to her purse for safekeeping.

"I just want to be sure."

"Of what?"

"That it isn't my imagination I have damn good taste in
wives."

This had gotten risky, like that moment in the bedroom
when he had fondled her hand. It was time to bring an end
to the scene before it got out of control.

Eden changed the subject by indicating his plate. "Have
you finished?"

"Yes, and the eggs were great, just the way I like them."
He grinned at her outrageously. "Not that I'd know, of
course."

Refusing to fall in with his playful, and she feared sexy,
mood, she came to her feet and rounded the table. "I'll
clear up then."

But when she reached for his plate, he caught her high
around the waist and drew her down onto his lap, snugging
her tightly against the hard wall of his chest. Alarmed by
his increasing familiarity with her, she stiffened in his embrace.

"This isn't wise."

"You're not going to deny your husband a chance to
show his wife how much he appreciates the breakfast she
cooked for him, are you?" he teased.

"I am when he's been hurt and in no condition to fool
around like this."

"Sweetheart," he whispered, his voice at her ear raspy
and seductive, "I may have a black eye and a lip that's
still tender, but I guarantee I'm recovered enough for a little
cuddling."

She felt the stubble on his unshaven jaw as he slowly
rubbed his cheek against hers, felt his warm breath mingle

with hers. It was a highly charged situation, one that shook her with the sudden realization that she was susceptible to it. In another few seconds he would swing her around and, sore lip or not, fit his mouth to hers. She would taste him, perhaps even welcome his tongue on hers.

The whole treacherous business was made worse when she moved on his lap with the intention of getting to her feet. Her action aroused him. She could feel his hardness strained against her as his arm shifted in order to hold her more comfortably, grazing the side of her breast, searing her. Eden panicked.

"I don't want this!" she commanded sharply. "Let me up!"

He went very still. A long moment passed, and then the arms that had been embracing her relaxed and dropped away. Eden scrambled off his lap and turned to face him. What she saw had her heart lurching inside her breast.

His mood had altered completely, revealing an entirely different facet of him. This was not the good-natured man who had awakened in her guest room with a smile. He had changed into someone harder, colder. She could see that change in the way his mouth had tightened and in his eyes that were regarding her suspiciously. Eyes that suddenly seemed dark and stormy.

There was something else that dismayed her. Something she had failed to anticipate until his arms had secured her on his lap, until his mouth had threatened to meld with hers. On some level she was afraid to define, she had wanted him to kiss her. It was a threat she could trust no more than the man who went on sitting there staring at her silently.

Making an effort to defuse the volatile situation, Eden began to load their dishes onto a tray. "I'll just rinse these off and stack them in the dishwasher," she said lightly, as though nothing had happened, as though there was no strain between them so intense it almost crackled.

Wanting to get away from him, needing a moment alone

to decide on a course of action, she picked up the tray and retreated into the kitchen. But when she reached the sink, she knew he had followed her. She could feel him behind her.

Turning around, she discovered him stationed in the doorway, looking big and intimidating. He was still watching her, not with admiration this time but with a narrow-eyed, speculative gaze. There was something instinctively professional in the way he stood there measuring her, making her wonder all over again just who and what he was.

"Why don't you lie down and rest," she suggested. "You need to rest."

"Later," he said, and there was no note of gentleness now in his tone.

Eden turned back to the sink and began to rinse the dishes, knowing that Tia had been right and that she had made a serious error in judgment in her blind determination to learn about Nathanial. The man she had so eagerly taken into her house was not dependably harmless and therefore manageable. He was, in fact, potentially dangerous.

She acknowledged that now. It wasn't just because of this sudden toughness in his manner either. There were other things. Things which, as a trained investigator, she should not only have been observing all along but also suspecting. Things that ought to have warned her.

Eden didn't ignore them now. His nervousness about reporting whatever had happened to him to the police. His uneasiness with the presence of Skip Davis in the garden. Skip, who with his naval background, might be perceived as a figure of authority and therefore a possible threat. And, most damning of all, the realization that, since he had been carrying a picture of Nathanial, he could in some manner be responsible for the disappearance of her son.

She could sense his eyes still on her, and she knew that she didn't dare to confront him. Couldn't risk telling him that they weren't man and wife for fear of how he might react. There was only one thing she could do and which, had she not been such a desperate fool, she would have done at the very beginning. She had to report his presence to the police, had to get him out of her house. But how, without igniting whatever it was that she was convinced was simmering inside him?

SHE WAS A FRAUD. He understood that now. She hadn't liked being on his lap, had plainly not wanted him to touch her. This, together with a flash of insight that had more to do with old instincts rather than any actual memory, had finally warned him something was wrong. That this woman wasn't what she'd been pretending to be.

No wedding bands, either on her finger or his. That small evidence alone should have alerted him of her deceit. Why hadn't he observed this before? Why, instead, had he believed in her? Believed in her so strongly that he'd convinced himself he belonged both to her and this place? Had he in his confused state needed a safe refuge so badly that he could have so easily deluded himself?

Or, he wondered, examining her as she loaded the dishwasher, had he been beguiled by something else? Like a pair of pure blue eyes and a mane of lustrous dark hair? A full mouth and a tall, alluring figure? Or maybe a nature that had seemed warm and caring from the start.

Any of these could have been responsible for his fantastic illusion. And none of them mattered. Not now when he knew he had made a serious mistake in coming here, that he couldn't trust this woman who had been willing to let him think she was his wife. Why? What did she want?

His mind was searching for an answer, seething with the frustration of his plight, when she finished with the dishes and crossed the kitchen, intending to return to the parlor. He continued to stand in the doorway, blocking her path.

"Let me by," she said.

She stood so close he could smell the scent he found so tempting. Lily of the Valley. He looked down into her face, noticing the slight depression at the tip of her piquant nose. Noticing, too, that she wore a purposeful expression.

"Why? Where are you going?" He hadn't meant the question to sound harsh, but that's the way it came out.

"To my office."

"It's Sunday. Offices aren't open on Sundays."

"I need to check my answering machine for messages."

That sounded reasonable enough. He moved aside in the doorway.

She slipped by him, caught up her purse from the table, and crossed the parlor toward a closed door on the other side.

"If you won't lie down," she called over her shoulder, "then at least sit down. I'll only be a minute."

She went into her office, closing the door behind her. He stood there for a few seconds, and then a warning went off inside his head. Why had she taken her purse with her? Why had she shut the door? Danger!

He crossed the parlor as swiftly as his game leg would permit, bursting into the office. He found her standing behind her desk, the phone in one hand and her other hand poised to dial. She shot him a startled look that told him she knew *he* knew the truth about them.

He was at the desk in a flash, snatching the phone out of her hand before her finger could punch the buttons. Slapping the receiver back into the cradle, he faced her accusingly.

"You were calling the cops, weren't you?" He couldn't let her turn him in to the police. Couldn't end up being held. Although he realized now the urgency that had driven him to her door last night was all wrong, he was still convinced there was something he must do, someone he had to reach.

"I was returning a client's call."

She was lying. He could see it in her eyes, along with her fear. "We're not husband and wife, are we?" he challenged her. "You don't even know my name. You never once called me by name. You don't know any more about me than I do."

She didn't answer him. She looked increasingly nervous, and that's when he saw it. On the desk in front of her was a small key, which explained why she had taken her purse into the office with her. She must have removed the key from her purse to unlock—what?

Yes, the top drawer in the desk. It was still slightly ajar, as though she had closed it hastily with his sudden entrance. She'd noticed the direction of his gaze. Her hand swooped to the drawer, yanking it open, reaching for what was inside.

Something kicked in, old instincts and skills that had him sensing he'd handled this kind of thing before. Whatever it was, it served him well in this instance. He shoved against her, throwing her off balance. Before she could recover herself, he had taken possession of the semiautomatic in the drawer. The pistol felt familiar in his grasp.

He had to admire her. As frightened as she had to be, she faced him defiantly. "You're making a mistake."

"Yeah, I trusted you. That was my mistake. What I can't figure out is why you didn't call the cops last night when I stumbled in here. Why is that?"

She didn't answer him.

"What is it you're after?"

"Look, give me the gun, and we'll talk about it."

Until he knew differently, he had to assume she was his enemy. But she was an enemy from whom he needed answers. "Oh, we're going to talk."

"Not until you lock the gun back in the drawer, and if it makes you feel better you can hang on to the key. At least do that much."

He had no intention of surrendering the pistol. He might need it. "Be quiet," he ordered her roughly. "Let me think."

He wanted answers all right, but this was a dangerous place to try to get them. They were in the city with cops close by and neighbors all around. Neighbors like that guy out in the garden. He needed somewhere that was safe, removed from the threat of people while he figured out what to do. Where? That's when he remembered the painting above the fireplace.

He knew now what he was going to do. He was getting out of here, going to that isolated houseboat on the river, and he was taking her with him.

# Chapter Three

She had a full bottom lip that made her mouth sultry. Had the circumstances been otherwise, he would have been tempted to explore that inviting mouth with his own. But right now his only interest in her lower lip was how it trembled with emotion as those wide blue eyes of hers stared at him in disbelief. He had just informed her of his intention.

"You can't," she objected.

"This says I can." He waved the pistol in front of her nose.

"You don't want to do this," she attempted to reason with him. "Aside from the fact that forcing me to go with you constitutes kidnapping, there's nothing for you to gain by taking me along."

"What do I want to do instead, Eden? Borrow that car of yours out in the alley, have you cheerfully promise me you won't call the cops while I run for it? Assuming, that is, I have a reason to run."

Her silence told him she realized any further argument in that direction would be useless. They both knew he couldn't leave her behind, couldn't trust her now out of his sight.

"It's a houseboat, isn't it, Eden? Well, you and I are going to play house on it while you tell me everything I want to know, and maybe before we're through I'll be able to decide just what the hell is going on. Oh, don't worry. Nothing is going to happen to you. Providing,'' he added, his voice slow and raspy as he leaned in close to her, ''you behave yourself.''

''Look, I can help you if you let me. I *will* help you, but not this way, not—''

She got no further. They were interrupted by a male voice calling out to her from the direction of the parlor where she had left the door open to the piazza.

''Eden, you in there?''

''It's Skip Davis from next door,'' she whispered.

''Answer him. Tell him you'll be there in a minute.''

''I'll be out in just a second, Skip.'' She lowered her voice again. ''Now what?''

''Get rid of him. Whatever he wants, tell him you're busy and you'll talk to him later.''

''And what if he caught a glimpse of you and wants to know who you are?''

''Tell him your long-lost husband is back from the dead,'' he said, unable to keep the sharp edge of sarcasm out of his voice. ''You ought to be able to convince him of a little lie like that. You had me believing one.''

There was more than just fear in those blue eyes now. There was also healthy anger.

''Get going,'' he ordered her before she could express that anger. ''Make it good. And, Eden?'' She paused on her way to the connecting door, looking back at him reluctantly. ''Be careful. We don't want anyone getting hurt.''

She nodded, understanding him, knowing he had the pistol and that he would be listening and watching from behind the office door. Leaving the office, she crossed the parlor, greeting her neighbor who waited in the open doorway.

Through the crack, he could just make out the heavy figure of the retired naval officer, hear him as he asked Eden to join him and his wife for lunch. There was a pause after the invitation was issued. He tightened his grip on the pistol and tensely wondered if she would do or say anything to alert her visitor.

But to his satisfaction, she was too smart to make this kind of mistake. She probably figured he was so desperate he wouldn't hesitate to use the pistol at the first sign of a threat to him. Let her go on thinking just that. He would be safer that way, and so would she.

"I'm sorry, Skip. I wish I could, but I have to work. I'm afraid Sundays are no exception when clients come to me with troubles that won't wait."

He had to give her credit. She couldn't be anything but nervous, and yet she sounded cool and without a concern. She also managed to convey in that simple reply an explanation for him, should her neighbor have detected his presence, as well as a reason for her later absence.

He was relieved when her neighbor accepted her excuse and departed, and she closed the door after him. But he was far from ready to relax. The sudden appearance of the navy man justified his decision, making it more imperative than ever that he remove them from the scene.

He waited to make certain Eden came directly back to the office before he turned his attention to her purse on the desk.

"What are you doing?" she challenged him sharply, as he appropriated the purse and began to investigate its contents.

"Looking for a breath mint. You never know, I might get lucky later on. Man and wife, remember?"

"That's low."

"Is it?" He lifted his gaze, coldly meeting her angry eyes. "So, just how virtuous were you being, sweetheart, when you didn't correct me? When you let me go on believing we were married?"

"That was wrong of me, I know, and I apologize for it. But I had a vital reason, and if you'll just let me explain—"

"Later," he cut her off. "Right now I have some vital business of my own."

He found no weapons in the purse, nothing that she could turn against him. There was a cell phone, and this he removed and tucked into his pocket. Making sure that her wallet held an adequate supply of cash and that the purse contained her keys, he handed the bag to her.

"Now what?" she demanded, hugging the bag to her breasts.

He didn't answer her. His mind was busy with a mental list, checking off the preparations for this flight to her houseboat. Once again, he was aware of old skills. Training from his unknown past that urged him to be thorough, to cover all the necessities before he went into action. He didn't understand this instinct, but he was grateful for it.

"This friend of yours upstairs—Tia. She have an answering machine?" He remembered Eden telling him Tia was out for the day.

"Yes."

"Call it. Leave a message for her. Tell her you're going to be gone for a couple of days on a case. That everything is fine, including the patient, and she isn't to worry about you. You'll explain everything when you get back." It wasn't the most brilliant of remedies to a potential problem, but it would have to do. He just hoped her friend would be satisfied by it. "No details, Eden, and make it convincing."

He handed her the receiver and stood close beside her as she dialed, ready to grab the phone away from her if she tried to communicate any warnings. But again she was wise enough to do just as she'd been told. In a calm voice, she delivered the concise message he had instructed.

Of course, she wasn't calm at all underneath that composed exterior. Her lower lip continued to betray her. It was still quivering when she hung up and faced him. He didn't blame her. He'd be shaken himself if someone was holding a gun on him. Well, he had no choice about it.

Damn, but she had one sweet mouth, as appealing as

those pure blue eyes framed by thick, dark lashes. Were the lashes real? he wondered.

"Do you have to stand so close?" she complained. Her voice was low and breathless, as if his nearness was robbing her of air. As if she was suddenly and unwillingly as aware of him as he was of her.

But his awareness of her on any sensual level was a mistake. He reminded himself that her blue eyes were not guileless and that her sweet mouth had lied to him. He stepped back away from her, forcing himself to be practical again.

"You keep any personal essentials at this houseboat? Some extra clothes for yourself, that kind of thing?"

"Yes."

"Then we don't need to waste time while you pack a bag."

He was anxious to get out of here without understanding why. What was he running from? The police? Did the cops want him for something so bad that his mind, unable to deal with it, had shut down on him? The possibility worried him.

Or was it a much darker enemy that had his insides in knots? Someone he had to elude at all costs? An enemy for whom Eden Hawke might be working? Having her business card and the photograph of the boy, both of which had been a link that had brought him to her, didn't make her a friend. He realized that now. Understood that she could be as treacherous as that generously endowed body of hers.

"Let's go," he ordered her gruffly, gesturing with the pistol in the direction of the parlor.

She preceded him from the office carrying her purse.

"Where's the jacket I was wearing last night?"

"There," she said, indicating a coatrack near the door.

"Get it."

She snagged his jacket from the hook and a light coat for herself, draping them both over her free arm as she led the way through the kitchen to the back door that opened onto the alley.

"Wait," he said, when she'd unlocked and opened the door.

He moved in front of her to check the alley in both directions. It was empty except for a dark green Toyota.

"Car keys," he commanded.

She fished the keys out of her purse and passed them to him. He unlocked the Toyota, saw her settled behind the wheel, and rounded the sedan to install himself in the passenger seat. Only then did he return the keys to her.

"All right," he said, buckling his belt, "let's roll. And, Eden?"

"What now?" she asked, starting the engine.

"Don't surprise me. Make sure it's your houseboat that's our destination. And if for any reason we get stopped, I'm your husband, remember. Your *loving* husband."

She glared at him, but she offered no objection. Not when he reminded her of the consequences if she tried to trick him by patting the hard lump that was the pistol hidden beneath the jacket slung across his lap.

The houseboat, he thought as they swung out of the alley onto a side street. Only that wasn't where he needed to go. It was somewhere far more important than that. This was what had driven him last night, the conviction it was urgent for him to reach something or someone. If he could remember just who or what it was…

WATER AND church steeples. They were what came first to Eden's mind whenever she thought of historic Charleston.

The water was everywhere in the shapes of the broad harbor, countless inlets, tidal marshes and the Ashley and Cooper Rivers flowing on either side of the peninsula that embraced the original city. Clustered within its core, with their soaring spires, were Charleston's famous churches, majestic Georgian structures outside whose doors basket makers offered their wares to passing tourists.

Radiating from this nucleus was a maze of lanes that boasted a wealth of traditional architecture with a strong West Indian influence. Narrow streets like Eden's, where the air was scented with camellias and an exchange of Gullah could be heard by the strolling vendors from the sea islands.

It was a rich, wonderful culture, and Eden was never immune to it. Until this morning. She was far too angry to be aware of sights, sounds or smells as she navigated the Toyota through the Sunday traffic. Her current anger was directed not at her silent companion but at herself.

How could she have been so overconfident, so naive to totally misjudge this man? She was a private investigator. That meant she was supposed to be able to read people accurately, tell the good from the bad. She hadn't. Not this time, not even when Tia had cautioned her against permitting her emotions to get in the way.

Nor had she been resourceful enough to manage any warnings for either Skip Davis or Tia. She had messed up all around and deserved to be angry with herself.

Trapped. Trapped with a man who plainly regarded her as his enemy. What now?

Stopped at a traffic light, she stole a glimpse at his profile. His features were rigid, uncompromising. And dangerous.

He turned his head and looked at her. Something tugged at her insides. She wanted to believe it was nothing but fear and was worried it might be more than that.

"The light's green," was all he said.

*It's not too late,* she told herself as they proceeded through the intersection. *You can start being the P.I. you're supposed to be. Convince him you're not his enemy. Your survival could depend on it.*

"Will you let me explain now?" she asked him, making her voice as persuasively pleasant as she could.

"I don't want to hear it."

"But—"

"I said no. Why should I believe you? Why should I believe anything you tell me? Just be quiet and let me think."

It was no use. He was not going to listen to her. Not, anyway, until they reached the houseboat. But if there was any way to prevent it, she couldn't let him take her there. The houseboat was isolated. She would be all alone with him in a lonely place. Anything could happen.

Help. She needed to seek help, but she had to be careful how she managed it. Trying something reckless, like alerting a passing police cruiser of her plight, was out of the question. Not when he had that gun in his lap.

But her situation wasn't entirely hopeless. She did have one promising means of rescue, providing she could make the opportunity to use it. Not yet, though. A glance at the fuel gauge told her she would have to wait a bit. Until then, she tried to forget the desperation of the man seated beside her, tried to remember instead that he was still a link to Nathanial.

Charleston was also a city of bridges, and they crossed one of its major spans over the Ashley River a few minutes later. Then, with the peninsula behind them, came the slow crawl through the urban sprawl of the modern city.

Reaching the river road, they traveled inland, following the winding Ashley River through a region of ancient live oak, groves of palmetto, and all the other less familiar vegetation of the lush low country. As the miles passed, Eden kept her eye on the fuel gauge.

Now, she thought.

"We need to stop for gas," she informed her companion.

He leaned over to check the gauge for himself, breaking his long silence. "How far is it to the houseboat from here?"

"Far enough that we'd arrive on empty. Anyway, if you plan on us staying there long enough to eat, then we need a few essentials. Milk, bread, that kind of thing. We can get them, along with the gas, at a convenience store just up the road here.''

"All right," he agreed.

There was a tricky, tense moment when they arrived at the convenience store and pulled up in front of a pump. He insisted on taking the keys from her again before either of them got out of the car, then challenged her when she started to open the back door on her side.

"What are you doing?"

"I want my coat. I'm cold."

"Feels like summer to me."

"It's February, and I don't care what the temperature is. I'm still cold. I imagine being scared has something to do with that," she said sarcastically.

"Have it your way. Just hurry up."

Eden breathed with relief and removed her coat from the back seat, where he had allowed her to place it before leaving Charleston. His own jacket was still with him. It hung over one of his arms, where it continued to hide the pistol under its folds. He stood beside the pump and watched her fill the gas tank after she slipped into her coat.

"You pay for the gas before we shop for groceries," he instructed her as they entered the convenience store. "Just in case we have to make a fast exit."

He was being thorough, Eden thought. Except there was one thing he had overlooked. He had failed to check the pockets of her coat.

The store was empty of customers other than themselves. He stayed close at her side to make sure she didn't try to signal the attendant as she paid for the gas.

Now comes the hard part, she thought when they came away from the counter.

"I need to use the bathroom," she said.

"That can wait until we get to the houseboat."

"No, it can't. I'm sorry, but being scared makes me more than just cold."

He swore under his breath. "Okay, where is it?"

She led the way to the far end of the store where the single, unisex rest room was located off an alcove. Its door stood open, the light inside already on.

"Wait," he said, moving in front of her to check out the interior, presumably to make certain there was no other exit or a window that would offer her a chance to escape.

"Will you please hurry?" she urged him, wanting him to be convinced it was an emergency.

There was another bad moment when he turned his head to gaze at her speculatively. Did he suspect something?

"Maybe I ought to go in there with you," he said.

"You wouldn't!" But she was afraid he might do just that.

"Then just make sure you behave yourself in there. When I check afterward, which I intend to do, I don't want to find any distress message scrawled on the mirror. And don't lock the door behind you either. I'm going to be standing right here in this alcove just outside, and if I hear the click of that lock…"

He left the rest unsaid as he moved his jacket aside to finger the pistol tucked now into the waistband of his pants. He was telling her that attendant or no attendant, he would shoot off the lock if she tried to barricade herself inside.

When Eden hesitated, wondering if he actually meant his threat, his broad shoulders lifted in a little shrug. "If you're not sure about the lock, then I think I should go with you."

"No lock," she promised him.

Before he could insist on some other precaution, she scooted past him into the rest room, swiftly closing the door behind her. Damn him. She had counted on locking herself in, but now she would have to risk her action without that security.

There had been no opportunity to investigate the pockets of her coat, either back in Charleston or outside at the gas pump. He had been much too observant for her to take that chance. But now, placing her purse on the sink's counter and hoping her memory was reliable, she plunged her hands into the deep pockets of the coat.

To her relief, her probing fingers closed around a flat, compact instrument at the bottom of the right-hand pocket. Thank God, she hadn't been wrong. The phone was here where she had placed it after last using it.

Eden's mother, who was the accountant for all the Hawke detective agencies at the home office in Chicago, had complained that Eden's purchase of a second cell phone was excessive. She had withdrawn her objection when Eden explained that she was forever either misplacing her cell or forgetting to keep its battery charged. And since a P.I. often had to rely on a cell phone, a backup was essential.

Grateful for her carelessness that had made an extra phone necessary, Eden withdrew the instrument and flipped it open. Now, if only she hadn't gone and drained its power again… Ah, good, she had a strong signal and a full battery. She was in business.

With a worried glance at the closed door, she flushed the toilet and turned on the faucet at the sink, counting on the sound of the running water to muffle her voice. Then, extending the phone's antenna, she started to punch in a rapid 911.

The nine was all she managed before the rest-room door burst open. Her heart sank at the sight of him. Covering the space between them in two swift strides, he snatched the cell phone out of her hand. His face was like a storm. A savage one.

"You were cold, huh?" he thundered. "The hell you were!"

He was talking about her coat. That was why he had charged into the rest room. It must have suddenly occurred to him out in the alcove that he had neglected to investigate her coat.

That he would have thought of the coat at all at this stage startled Eden. Just who was this man, anyway? No one

ordinary, certainly. Not when he was so careful not to overlook any potential threat to him. That smacked of a dark
history, maybe even a violent one. Just what was he involved in, and how serious was her own jeopardy because
of it?

"What do you do?" he growled. "Collect the damn
things?"

Switching off the instrument, he thrust it into his pocket
where it joined the phone he had seized earlier from her
purse. Then, tossing his jacket on the floor in order to free
both his hands, he advanced on her slowly. The look on
his face said he meant business.

Eden backed away from him until she had nowhere else
to go. She was pinned against the sink. He towered over
her, a daunting figure.

"You have any more surprises in that coat, Eden? Something I should be worried about?"

Before she could stop him, he was pressed up against
her, his arms on either side of her, his big hands plunged
into her pockets. She could feel the heat of his fingers probing the depths of both pockets. There should have been
nothing personal in that search, but there was. Eden found
it difficult to breathe.

"Guess not," he said.

Swallowing, she managed a cool "If you're through."

But he was in no hurry to withdraw his hands. They
remained in her pockets, making an intimate contact with
her hips through the fabric. His eyes were on her face, a
seductive gleam in them. He inhaled slowly, deeply.

"Lily of the Valley, huh?"

Her fragrance still intrigued him. And her lower lip.

"It's quivering again, Eden," he said, his voice husky.

He was leaning into her so closely she was aware of the
stubble on his square jaw, the heat of his hard flesh. This
time he did slide a hand out of her pocket, lifting it to the
level of her face where the slightly rough pad of his thumb

lightly stroked her bottom lip. Eden felt a slow flame coiling deep inside her.

"Take your hand away," she commanded, her own voice turning hoarse.

"You wanted to play husband and wife. So, all right, we're playing husband and wife."

"Stop saying that!"

"Maybe you'd like my mouth here instead of my thumb. Would you, Eden?"

She'd had enough of his steamy games. Whether he was formidable or not, she refused to be intimidated any longer. "You've satisfied yourself there's nothing else in my pockets. Now back off. And count yourself lucky I didn't try to grab my pistol out of your waistband." She had considered such an action, but as quick as his reflexes were, that could have resulted in a struggle in which one of them might have been shot.

Motivated by her threat to recover her gun, he stepped away from her. His eyes never left her face. "If you had the gun, would you use it on me?" She didn't answer him. "Maybe you think I'm some kind of monster. I'm not. At least I don't think I am."

"Then what are you? Just an innocent victim?"

"It's possible."

"If you believe that, then why don't you turn yourself in to the police? Tell them as much as you know and let them sort it out."

"That's a plan. Except if it turns out I'm a wanted man—" He shook his head. "Uh-uh, I'm not bringing the cops in on this. Not until I know what's going on and why."

"So, instead, you're going to go on playing the tough fugitive who kidnaps women at gunpoint."

"And makes their lips tremble in tempting ways."

Eden angrily tightened her mouth. It was a defensive reaction, and he didn't miss it. He smiled. A sardonic smile.

"You know," he drawled, "if I wanted to, I think I

could make that mouth of yours do a lot more than just tremble. And not by using my thumb, either.''

"You might have lost your memory, but you're not suffering from a loss of ego, are you?'' The awful thing was, she feared there was some truth in what he claimed and that she would have to guard herself against it.

"Could be you're right,'' he admitted. "Only we don't have the time to test your theory.'' Leaning down, he recovered his jacket from the floor. "We've still got that shopping to do. Come on, let's go make that attendant out there think you and I are the happiest married couple in South Carolina.''

THE HOUSEBOAT WAS exactly what she had wanted when she'd bought it a little over a year ago. A quiet getaway far enough removed from the city to guarantee her absolute privacy whenever she needed a few days' retreat between difficult cases.

But now, looking at the gray houseboat moored at the end of its short pier, Eden regretted the remoteness of the place. There were no neighbors within hailing distance, just the thick vegetation along the shore and the softly flowing river with its reedy shallows where the herons fished.

She was aware of the man who followed closely behind her along the narrow path from the car, bearing their sack of groceries. She was alone with him in this seclusion, not knowing what he intended to do with her. It was a situation that unnerved her on every level.

He, however, was satisfied by the isolation. She could see it in his face when they reached the door of the houseboat, and she turned to him as he spoke to her.

"You've got electricity, huh?'' he said, noticing the wire stretched from the pole on shore to the side of the houseboat.

"Yes, all the comforts of home,'' she said, unlocking the door and spreading it open.

He held out his hand. Knowing what he wanted, she laid

the keys on his palm. He was making certain that she wouldn't try to escape in the car.

"Inside," he directed her.

She looked at him again when they were inside and the door was shut behind them. His gaze was making a fast survey of the place. It was a simple arrangement. A narrow living room in the center, a tiny kitchen off one end, and at the other end a single small bedroom and bath. All of it was comfortably but plainly furnished in the warm colors that Eden favored.

"Nice and cozy," he observed. "Just the sort of setting that makes a man think of, oh, I don't know. An intimate weekend with his wife, maybe?"

The houseboat had never seemed cramped to her before. It did now, as if there wasn't enough room to contain both of them. But Eden refused to let him see how that worried her. Or to respond to his mockery on the subject of a marriage that had never existed. She had more vital matters on her mind.

"Now can we have that talk?" she asked him.

"Later," he said brusquely, dumping the sack and his jacket on the bar between kitchen and living room.

"But you told me—"

"I said *later*."

He had spotted the portable TV in the bookshelves. The clock on the VCR that accompanied it registered the time as just a minute past twelve. He lost no time in settling on the sofa, the remote in his hand.

"You're going to watch television?"

"It's noon. There should be a news broadcast."

Eden understood his sudden interest then. He was eager to learn of any accident or crime that might offer him a clue to his identity. Leaving him perched on the sofa, knees spread as he leaned earnestly toward the screen, she went into the kitchen area to put away the groceries.

She listened to the broadcast as she fixed sandwiches and poured them glasses of milk. Like him, she hoped to hear

of something to which they might connect him, but there
was nothing promising in any of the reports.

She brought him his lunch. They ate in silence, his attention focused on the news. And all the while, Eden was
conscious of him, wary of his possible danger to her. She
remembered he had tried to assure her he wasn't evil, and
last night her instincts had been convinced he was a decent
man. But how could she trust any of that when he was
driven by a desperation neither of them understood?

Well, she was desperate herself, as only a mother could
be. She managed to restrain that desperation through the
entire lengthy newscast of both local and national events.
But by the time the program wrapped up without results
for him, she'd had enough. She wanted answers, and she
no longer cared how much she might be risking herself to
get them.

Opening her purse, Eden removed the photograph and
business card she had found in his jacket last night. His
gaze was still fixed on the television screen when she came
to her feet and inserted herself between the sofa and the
bookshelves.

"Look at them," she commanded, facing him with determination as she placed the photo and card on the coffee
table in front of him.

He glanced down and then up. "Again? I thought I told
you back in Charleston—"

"I want to know how you got them. Do you remember
at least that much?"

"No."

*"Try."*

"What do you think I've been doing since I opened my
eyes this morning? When I wasn't worried about what you
were going to try next, that is. And why are you so interested in that picture?"

Eden was prepared at this point to plead with him. "I
have a good reason. The best reason in the world. It's because—" She stopped abruptly, realizing that, unless some-

one was able to address an individual by name, an appeal somehow lacked strength. "Look, if you and I are going to spend any time together—"

"Ah, now you want to spend time with me?"

"I didn't think I had any choice about that. You were the one who forced me to come here." She was getting angry again. That wasn't the way to reach him. "The point is," she went on, her voice softening, "you don't have a name because you don't know who you are. So what am I supposed to call you?"

His gaze drifted away from hers. There was a long silence between them. Had the windows been open, she might have heard the gentle lapping of the waters against the pier, a sound that would have soothed her while she waited tensely for his answer. But the windows remained closed, and the only sound in the houseboat was the TV, which droned on behind her.

She looked at his face. Except for a slight discoloring around the eye that had been bruised and swollen shut last night, what had to be a tenderness in the lip that had been split open, and the bandage that still covered the bridge of his nose, he was healing rapidly.

There was strength and character in that face. She could see it in the square shape of his jaw, the fine radial lines at the corners of his observant brown eyes, even in the small mole high on one beard-shadowed cheek. That it was also a face with sensual qualities, to which she was regrettably susceptible, Eden preferred not to think about.

A lean face, too, like the rigorously conditioned body that carried it. Solid and athletic, even with that limp. As though it had been trained for a specific purpose.

And again the question gnawed at her. Who was he?

"Him," he said without expression, nodding in the direction of the TV behind her.

Puzzled, Eden swung around to face the set. There was a movie playing on it now, a classic old western. She couldn't remember its title.

"*Shane,*" he said. "You can call me Shane."

Eden recalled the story now. Shane was its hero, a mysterious loner who had arrived out of nowhere. No past, no other identity beyond that single name. Shane. It was perfect. Like the character in the movie, the name suited him.

"Shane it is, then," she said.

He nodded, satisfied. "Now let's move on to another name. The kid in that picture. You know who he is, don't you? Or at least you think you do. Who is he?"

Eden caught her breath, then released it in an emotional rush. "His name is Nathanial. Where is he, Shane? What have you done with my son?"

# Chapter Four

He could feel himself scowling as he stared up at her. He didn't like this. Didn't like it one damn bit. He already had a few small problems of his own, and now she'd gone and dumped this latest surprise in his lap.

Her kid? The boy in the photograph was her kid?

"Answer me, Shane."

Though he had chosen the name himself, hearing her call him by it seemed odd. Because, of course, Shane couldn't be his real name. But a man had to have some identity, and he supposed this one sounded as good as any. He accepted the name, slipping into it with ease. What he couldn't accept was the look of accusation on her face.

"You're asking me, the man without a memory? And if I did have a memory, what makes you think I'd have any knowledge of your son?"

"You were carrying his photograph along with my business card. There has to be a connection, and I intend to learn what it is."

"That why didn't you call the cops last night, when I staggered in out of nowhere? And why did you let me think I was your husband? So you could use me?"

"All right, maybe I was taking advantage of the situation, and I suppose that was wrong of me."

"You bet it was wrong. A hell of a lot wrong, in fact."

"And I'd do it again," she vowed fiercely. "That and much more if it meant finding my son."

Shane plowed a hand through his hair while she continued to stand over him wearing that expectant look in her eyes. He didn't know what to say to her. "So what are we talking about here? A kidnapping?"

"Whatever it was, Nathanial was taken. I don't know who took him or why, just that he's gone."

"I know you're a P.I., but isn't this something the cops should be handling?"

"They were handling it. Without results."

"How long has the boy been missing?"

"He was nearly two years old when he disappeared."

"Wait a minute, the kid in this photo—" He leaned forward to gaze at the picture on the coffee table. Red-gold hair and eyes that were lavender blue. A handsome child, but no two-year-old. "This boy must be five years old, four at the least."

"Nathanial vanished almost three years ago. And don't tell me he isn't alive, because the photograph proves that he is."

"Three years is a long time when you're that age. Kids can change so much that—"

"Don't say it, because I don't want to hear that either. It is Nathanial in that photo. I *know* it is."

"And I was carrying his picture, and that's supposed to mean something. Assuming you're right, and this is your son."

"It *does* mean something. It has to. There was a reason why you had the photo and my business card, why you came to me like that."

"Maybe, but what do you expect me to do about it?"

"Help me to learn that reason."

"Look, I'm sorry your kid is missing, but how am I supposed to help you when I can't help myself?"

"If we could unlock your memory, then we'd be helping each other."

She continued to gaze at him with that anxious, hopeful expression in her blue eyes. It was a look that twisted his gut. He couldn't take it anymore. Surging to his feet, he crossed the room and stood looking out at the river with his back to her, hands shoved into his pants pockets.

Shane. He regretted the name now. It conjured up too strong an image of the movie hero he had borrowed it from. Did she have some sudden, misguided notion that he was going to turn out like that hero? A drifter riding in out of nowhere to save the day?

Hell, he was no hero. He was nothing more than a poor, frustrated lout who couldn't recover his own memory, never mind a kid who had vanished three years ago.

But there was something he couldn't ignore. Not after Eden's emphatic reminder. The photograph *had* been in his possession, supporting her conviction that his path must have crossed in some inexplicable manner with the boy she was convinced was her son.

*Someone he had to reach.*

Last night's urgency that had driven him to Eden's door came back to him. But what if it hadn't been Eden he'd needed to reach? What if it was the child? *Her* child? Too fantastic.

Still, he couldn't deny her argument. He wanted his memory, she wanted her son. Find the one, and it was possible they would find the other.

He looked over his shoulder. She continued to stand between the TV and the sofa, hands clasped in front of her as she waited for his decision.

"I'm not saying yet that it's worth a shot. I'm just saying maybe it is. One thing, though," he went on solemnly. "What if it turns out I had something to do with snatching your kid? That I'm the bad guy in this scenario?"

It was a possibility that already haunted him, but he didn't tell her that. She had to take him as he was, without the assurances he was incapable of giving her. She understood that.

"I have no choice but to take that chance. Look, my proposal isn't as hopeless as it sounds. I *am* a private investigator, remember."

"Uh-huh."

"Meaning, I suppose, that you don't think I can be a very good one, or I would have found Nathanial long ago. Believe me, I tried in every way. But there was nothing to go on. Absolutely nothing. Until now."

Shane looked again at the river. "Is there a path along the riverbank?"

"Yes."

"Then suppose you and I walk it, because I'm going to need some more convincing."

He was restless, wanting to get out of the houseboat. And by the look of the area, there wasn't much risk of them encountering anyone. He figured Eden would immediately agree to his suggestion, but when she didn't answer him, he turned away from the window to learn the reason for her hesitation.

He found her eyeing the pistol that was still stuck in his belt. So she still didn't trust him, was worried by what might happen to her if she went out there in that wilderness with him while he was armed. He guessed he couldn't blame her. He'd been pretty hard on her.

"The gun isn't loaded," he said, taking the weapon out of his belt and placing it on the bar. "I removed the clip after you went into the rest room."

"Yes," she said. "I guess I should have known you wouldn't let me get that close to the gun if there was the chance I could have used it."

He shrugged. "I didn't want anyone getting shot, and as long as you believed it was still loaded…"

"I'd do what you wanted," she finished.

He could see by the look on her face she was aggravated he'd been so confidently able to control her with an unloaded gun.

THE PATH, spongy in places from the previous night's rain, was bordered so thickly by tangled growth it reminded

Shane of a jungle, making him wonder if he'd ever had any experience with a tropical rain forest. Still, the path was wide enough to permit them to stroll side by side along its length.

They weren't out of sight of the houseboat, when Eden, eager to win his cooperation, asked him, "What do you want to know?"

"Let's start with Nathanial's father. Where is he?"

"Dead."

"I'm sorry."

"No, it's all right. I never knew him. Never even met him, in fact."

Shane broke step to gaze at her in confusion.

"I know," she said. "That doesn't make sense. Maybe I'd better explain everything from the beginning."

He nodded, prepared to listen to her as they moved on through a grove of tall slash pines.

"Charleston wasn't always home to me, Shane. I grew up in Chicago. My mother and father are still there operating the home office of the Hawke Detective Agency."

"There are branches?"

"Six of them in different parts of the country, including mine and the original one in Chicago. The other four are staffed by my brothers and sister."

"Your whole family are private investigators?"

"In the blood, I guess, which makes what I did understandable, if not very smart."

"And that was?"

"I went and fell for another P.I. who was in Chicago on a case. I thought what we had was real. Real enough, anyway, that I followed him back to Charleston. We were going to run an agency together, raise a family."

"And the dream went sour," Shane guessed.

"I won't go into the details. Let's just say I learned in time that he liked women. *Lots* of women. In the end, he moved on, and I stayed. I no longer loved him, but I did love Charleston by then.'' She interrupted her story to apologize to him. ''My whole history isn't what you wanted to hear, is it? But I just thought if you were going to understand what happened…''

''If I get bored, I'll let you know. Go on.''

''I made a life for myself in Charleston. Opened the agency, bought the houseboat, made friends.''

''Everything but that family to raise, huh?''

''And I wanted that. My brothers and sister were all having babies, everyone around me seemed to be having babies, and…well, I wasn't.''

Turning his head to gaze at her, Shane thought he could understand her need. It wasn't easy to define, but there was a nurturing quality about Eden Hawke. He had experienced it last night when she had cared for him so solicitously. She had a woman's body, too. The kind of lush body that, among other things, made a man think about her in terms of bearing his children.

Hell, where had that come from?

He must have had a strange look on his face, because she was looking at him in puzzlement. ''What?'' she asked.

''Nothing. You were saying?''

''That I wanted to be a mother. But without the complications of marriage and a husband.''

''An issue of trust,'' he said perceptively, wondering how he had learned to be so observant. ''Or weren't you saying in so many words that, after the boyfriend, you were disillusioned in that area?''

''I suppose so,'' she admitted. ''Oh, I knew what all the arguments were against single parenthood, but I felt I had a lot to offer a child. Believe me, I did agonize over the subject. Examined it from every angle, even considered adoption. But I wanted a child of my own, which is why in the end I decided on a donor.''

''A sperm bank?''

''At a fertility clinic in Charleston, yes.''

"And the outcome was Nathanial."

"He was the love of my life, until—"

Her voice cracked. He stopped on the path beside her to give her a chance to collect herself, wondering if she would be able to go on. He knew she had to be suffering her loss all over again.

They had paused where honeysuckle vines sprawled over a little spit of land that extended into the river. In the summer the air here would be fragrant with honeysuckle blossoms. But in this season there were only the odors of the river and the moist earth, a pungent blend of moss, decaying vegetation and the swampy smell of the reeds that grew in the shallows.

"You don't have to do this," he said.

"Yes, I do," she insisted, resuming her story as they continued along the path. "There was a playground in the park across the street from the day-care center Nathanial attended. The little ones loved it when they were taken there almost every afternoon."

"And on one of those afternoons?"

"It was like lightning. One minute Nathanial was there in that playground with all the other kids in his group, and in the next he was gone."

"And no one saw anything?"

Eden shook her head. "The day-care staff was always very careful, but they'd been distracted by a little girl's nosebleed. When that was under control, they realized Nathanial was missing. If he'd wandered off, none of the kids had noticed it. They'd all been gathered around the nosebleed."

She didn't need to tell him of the frantic hours that must have followed, hours that had lengthened into days, then weeks. He could imagine it all. The search, the questioning of every possible witness, the failure to produce any results. And a mother's ceaseless torment.

"It was bad," she said, as though sensing the direction of his thoughts. "You hear all the stories about a parent's worst nightmare, and they're true. But what no one ever tells you about is the terrible anger you experience. Anger with the media who write things about child predators and how the victims rarely survive, anger with the police when they tell you there's nothing more they can do, and, worst of all, anger with yourself because you failed to protect your child. Especially in my case. I was a P.I., and no matter what efforts I made—and believe me, I made them all—I couldn't find my own son."

"What about your family? All the other Hawke P.I.'s?"

"They went to the wall for me, every one of them. Were even able to get several promising leads that the police hadn't discovered. There was one in particular, a woman who was sighted in Seattle with a little boy matching Nathanial's description. But the trail went cold. They were all of them dead ends."

"Anything with Nathanial's biological father?"

Eden shook her head. "Records at sperm banks are absolutely confidential. All the pertinent data of the donors, their characters, histories of health, that kind of thing, are made available to the mothers, but the actual identities are withheld."

"But under the circumstances…"

"Exactly. Mine was a special case, so the court was able to subpoena the record. They wouldn't release his name to me, but they did tell me he'd died in a boating accident without ever being aware of Nathanial's existence. He was a young artist, the only surviving member of his family, so he'd left no one behind."

"In other words, another dead end."

She nodded.

They stopped again, this time under the canopy of an ancient live oak festooned with long scarves of Spanish moss. There was an impassive expression on Eden's face as she watched a snowy egret skim over the surface of the river, but Shane knew that behind that expression were emotions that seethed.

Lost in those emotions as she was, he didn't think she was aware of him. But when he shifted his weight from one leg to another, she glanced down at his right leg. The one that was responsible for his slight limp.

"If it's bothering you," she said in concern, "and you'd like to turn back—"

"Forget the leg," he said, an edge of annoyance in his voice. "It isn't bothering me, and, no, I don't know how I ended up with the scars or the limp."

She was silent again, one of her hands fingering a strand of Spanish moss that trailed down near her shoulder. After a moment she gave voice to those intense emotions roiling inside her.

"I suppose every mother in my situation refuses to believe her child is dead, and I was no exception. I never gave up hope. *Never.* But it wasn't easy. You have this aching void after they disappear. This awful emptiness that won't go away. So you try to fill it by wondering where they are and what they're doing at that moment. And if they're safe and happy. Yes, as awful as it is, you want them to be happy, even if they aren't with you."

She was tugging now at the Spanish moss, an unconscious action that expressed her deep anguish. Shane didn't want to listen to her. It tore his guts out listening to her.

"Never a day went by that I didn't think of him," she confessed. "I'd think how I was missing out on all the changes that kids go through at that age. The ways their minds and bodies grow. If he had any memory of me. Somehow that was the worst. Because it was likely that at two years of age he would soon forget all about me. And if that was true—"

She dragged so hard at the strand of moss that it came away from the tree. She looked at it in her hand and then up at him.

"Sorry to go all emotional on you like this," she apologized, her voice quavering as she turned to him. "It isn't easy for me to talk about Nathanial."

Oh, hell, there were tears in her eyes now. He didn't know how he was supposed to deal with that. But somehow he did. Somehow he found himself reaching out to her, his arms wrapping around her.

She didn't oppose his action. In fact, she surrendered to it with a sigh of gratitude, dropping the moss and allowing herself to be drawn snugly against his length. He knew she no longer considered him an aggressor to fear and mistrust. Not in this moment, anyway, when he offered the comfort she so badly needed. When it didn't matter that he was still a stranger who might in some way be connected with the disappearance of her son.

An act of compassion. That was what it was supposed to be, and at first that's all it was. Shane held her and murmured some awkward nonsense intended to soothe, his hands gently stroking her back.

He didn't know when it changed. Maybe when he became aware of how perfectly she fit against his chest, how right it felt for her to be there. So right that he wondered fleetingly what it would be like to be her husband for real. Suddenly he was conscious of her softness, her tantalizing warmth and womanly scent. And of his longing to taste her.

Eden must have sensed that change herself. Her head lifted from where it had been nestled under his chin. The pure blue eyes that searched his face were wide and moist, her mouth parted. An invitation? Shane wanted to think so. Wanted to join his mouth with hers, sink his tongue into that sweetness.

Another part of him yearned to be buried inside a more tender area. He ached with that raw need. The swollen evidence of it was something she couldn't mistake. An insanity, the whole thing, and she knew it even if he didn't.

"We can't do this," she implored.

She was right. Things were complicated enough as it was. They'd only be worse if a surrender to lust got added to the mix. But it wasn't easy to let her go, to withstand the urge to let his hands slide along the sides of her enticing breasts as she stepped away from him.

"Now what?" he asked her.

"I was hoping you could tell me. That, having heard my story, maybe you—"

"Could tell you mine? I wish I *could* return the favor, but nothing you've said triggers a recollection, if that's what you were hoping for."

"Then you haven't remembered anything yet? Anything at all?"

"Nothing," he said flatly.

"Well, look—"

She paused to swipe the backs of her hands across both of her eyes, ridding herself of any remaining tears. In the process she shed the vulnerable mother and became again the professional P.I., all earnest business.

"I think it's time," she continued, "that we had help with this. We need to consult a therapist, someone trained in dealing with amnesia. That means going back to Charleston."

Shane didn't hesitate. "No, and don't suggest it again."

Though he might not understand his refusal, he instinctively knew he couldn't risk either Charleston or a professional therapist. There was danger in that kind of exposure. But dangerous for who? Himself? Or someone he was shielding?

Eden apparently understood the wisdom in not arguing with him about the idea. She regarded him in a long, speculative silence. Shane had the sudden, uneasy feeling of being a specimen under a lab microscope.

"I don't like it," he said.

"What?"

"Whatever you're thinking."

"It was just something I was remembering. About this woman who lives in the village down the road. Her name is Atlanta Johnson."

"And?"

"She's a hypnotist."

Shane understood immediately what she was about to suggest. "Uh-uh, forget it. No way am I going to be a subject for some local witch doctor."

"She doesn't practice that kind of thing. She's a professional and a very effective one. I've seen her in action, Shane, and her sessions have helped people. She even cured someone I know of a smoking habit."

"Yeah? She ever cure anyone of amnesia?"

"I don't know, but if she's willing, it's worth a try, isn't it? Maybe under hypnosis, she can plug you into your memory."

How could he turn his back on a prospect like that when the frustration over this void inside his head was eating away at him? It wasn't just a matter of wanting his memory back but of needing it. Because he couldn't shake his mounting sense of urgency, of time running out. But there was one thing that concerned him about Atlanta Johnson.

"Can we trust her?"

"She claims that anything she hears from a client she keeps strictly to herself, and I believe her. She's like a doctor in that respect."

"Then let's go for it."

"Uh, there's just one thing," Eden said as they started back to the houseboat where, with luck, they would not only reach the hypnotist by phone but secure an emergency appointment with her.

"What's that?" he asked suspiciously.

"I don't want you to be put off by it, but Atlanta is… well, just a bit of a character."

AN UNDERSTATEMENT, Eden realized, recalling her casual warning with a sheepish glance at Shane when Atlanta Johnson arrived that evening. The look on his face as the mammoth woman with a mop of orange hair waddled through the front door of the houseboat was one of classic surprise.

Garbed in a pair of stretch pants that barely accommodated her, a silk blouse in an explosion of colors, and clanking with jewelry, Atlanta definitely qualified as a character. And that was only visually.

The first words out of her mouth were a cheerful, "You got anything to eat, girl? I've got to have energy for a job like this."

That had been a good half hour ago. Since then, Eden had watched Shane's impatience deepen while their visitor consumed a considerable portion of the refrigerator's contents. This had been accompanied by Atlanta's nonstop complaints about the less savory members of her vast family.

Shane was no longer impatient. He rested now on the sofa, eyes closed, all signs of strain gone from his face. Having satisfied herself with what the refrigerator offered, Atlanta had gotten down to business. In a matter of minutes, she'd had Shane in a deep trance.

The hypnotist, however, was in no hurry to follow up on her impressive performance. She was currently working on a chocolate bar she had discovered at the bottom of her capacious carryall.

"Should he be left like that?" Eden wondered. "Shouldn't you—"

"He's all right. Let him settle in for a bit, get hisself comfortable with things, so to speak. It works better that way."

Eden hoped so. Shane certainly looked peaceful enough at this moment, she thought, casting an anxious glance in his direction from the chair she occupied near the sofa.

She couldn't deny to herself that her glance was also a frankly admiring one. They had visited a discount store out on the highway that afternoon in order to buy him some essential toiletries and several changes of clothes.

He had shaved and showered before Atlanta's arrival. With the bandage removed from his nose, leaving a raw spot that was already fading, and his whiskers scraped away, Shane no longer had the look of a tough desperado. But even in repose like this, his face was still a bold one, with strong, appealing features that stirred her senses.

Flutters. She had flutters inside her stomach that shouldn't be there. She tried to tell herself they existed only because she was worried this experiment might be a mistake. But she couldn't totally convince herself of that.

Balling up the wrapper from her chocolate bar, Atlanta parked her bulk on the stool in front of the sofa. There was a candle burning on the low table beside her. She had used its flickering flame, along with her melodic voice, to induce Shane's hypnotic state. Ready now to begin, she blew out the candle. But before she leaned toward her subject, she turned to Eden with a solemn caution.

"Girl, you don't get yourself set here for something that maybe won't happen. He went under quick enough because he wants his memory back. But that don't mean what's deep inside is willing. And if it ain't willing, then it's not gonna give up what it's holding on to."

Eden nodded her understanding.

Atlanta returned her attention to her subject and proceeded to demonstrate that she knew her business.

"Shane, are you with me, hon?"

"Yes," he murmured, eyes still closed but aware of her voice directing him.

"That's good. That's real good. Now I want you to rest easy and cast your mind back. Go back two weeks."

They had agreed beforehand that, unless it proved necessary, they would not try to regress his memory to his early years.

"Are you there, Shane?"

"Yes."

"Tell me where you are."

Atlanta waited, but there was no answer. "What's happening?" she urged.

Silence.

"Is something happening, Shane? Tell me what it is."

"Beth," he said.

"Beth who?"

No answer.

"Is Beth with you?"

"She's gone. I've lost her again. Lost her before, and now this time…"

"What, hon?"

"Don't know."

"Where did Beth go? Where do you think she went?"

"Don't know," he repeated stubbornly.

It isn't working, Eden thought. He's resisting. His mind is blocking it out, maybe because the memory is so awful. Or maybe because there's some danger associated with it. Atlanta must have decided the same thing, because she tried another approach.

"If that's not such a good time, hon, we won't stay there. Won't go forward either until you're ready. Let's go back some ways before Beth. Maybe to a better time and place. Go back now to nine months ago. Are you there, Shane?"

"Yes."

"Where are you?"

Eden was prepared for another silence and was surprised when this time he identified his surroundings.

"In the jungle."

"What jungle?"

"Can't tell."

Or won't tell, Eden thought, listening tensely to the exchange.

"What's happening in the jungle, Shane?" Atlanta coaxed. "Can you see it?"

There was a pause during which Eden held her breath. Then slowly and haltingly, he began to describe the situation.

"Rain. Never stops raining. Always wet. And hot. Heat and bugs. My men are complaining, but orders are orders. Be glad when it's over."

"What, Shane?" Atlanta probed. "When *what's* over?"

"The operation. Free the hostages, only—"

He stopped. Eden, watching him intently, could see that he was disturbed. A muscle in his jaw began to twitch.

"What's going on there now, Shane? What are you and the other men doing?"

"Working our way through the jungle. Going to the rendezvous. I don't like it. Something is wrong. I can feel something is wrong."

"You tell me what's wrong, hon. Tell Atlanta."

"Ambush. We've walked into an ambush." Shane's body went taut on the sofa, his voice expressing rage and excitement. "The bastard betrayed us! *Get down! Take cover!*"

*He's fighting a battle,* Eden thought, experiencing his agitation along with him. *He's living it all over again.*

"There's gunfire! One of my men is down! *Vinny!*" he shouted. *"Vinny, watch out!"*

Eden couldn't bear the pain in his voice, the way his body was twisting now from side to side, as if in a desperate effort to dodge a hail of bullets.

"I've got to get them out of here before we're all wiped out! I've been hit, but I've got to get my men out! Do you understand? *Now,* before it's too late…"

Eden could stand to witness no more of his anguish.

"He's suffering!" she cried. "Take him out of there! *Please take him out!*"

Atlanta bent forward and placed a reassuring hand on Shane's arm. "It's all right, baby," she said, her voice low and soothing. "You can leave that place. You don't have to be there anymore."

His face and body slowly relaxed, became quiet again. Eden's own body went limp with relief in the chair.

"No more of this," she said with determination. "The session ends here."

Atlanta sat back and gazed at her soberly. "You sure of this, hon? We got yet to learn what you both asked for. His real name, what happened to him in the here and now that lost him his memory.''

''I don't care. I'm not putting him through any more. Take him out of the trance.''

''Always better for them to come out of it in an easy manner.'' She leaned again toward her subject, planting a posthypnotic instruction in his mind. ''You stretch out on that sofa now, Shane. You go to sleep for a bit, and when you wake up you're gonna feel fine. Real fine.''

Shane obeyed her, sinking into a deep slumber. Satisfied by his serene state, Atlanta gathered up her things. ''He'll be all right. He'll maybe remember what he said while he was under, maybe not. Depends on how tight he's hanging on to that past of his. But you call me if you need me.''

Eden assured her that she would, paid her, and accompanied her to the door. Atlanta turned to her before leaving.

''Yeah, he'll be all right,'' she repeated, ''but maybe you won't.''

''What do you mean?''

Atlanta's gaze slid in the direction of the sofa across the room, then focused again on Eden. ''You listen to me, girl,'' she said severely. ''I've been around and know some things. Yeah, he's one sexy devil, but if you go and keep that man over there…''

''What?''

''He's gonna do things to you. Things that are gonna squeeze the life out of your heart and soul. Maybe worse after the violence we heard him speak of. So you watch yourself with that one. You hear?''

# Chapter Five

Eden tried not to remember Atlanta's parting words to her as she watched over Shane from the chair near the sofa, waiting for him to waken. But she couldn't stem the disturbing thoughts that swarmed into her mind.

The man stretched out on her sofa, the man Atlanta had warned her about, was a stranger to her. As close as they had become in just a matter of hours, and admittedly they had, he was still a stranger. One, it seemed, who had at least one violent episode in his history. Maybe more. How that might be connected with Nathanial worried her.

But, stranger or not, she and Shane needed to trust each other if they were going to solve the mystery of his past and find Nathanial. That trust wasn't going to be easy for either one of them. Not when it turned out that both she and Shane had been taught by painful betrayals in their pasts not to trust.

There was another treachery at work here—her growing attraction to this man. It could only get in the way, complicate the issues that were already problems enough in themselves.

Problems like *Beth*.

Who was she, and what did she mean to Shane? Someone significant in his life probably, a woman who might be waiting for him somewhere even now.

But Eden didn't want to think about Beth, whoever she

was. Nor did she want to examine her reason for resisting the subject of the mysterious Beth. All she longed for was to have Shane wake up.

A moment later, as though responding to what she willed, his eyes opened. Turning his head on the pillow she had provided for him, his gaze found her in the chair.

"How do you feel?" she asked, leaning toward him. Hoping, in spite of Atlanta's reassurance, that his trance wouldn't leave him dazed.

"Surprisingly rested." He lifted his head, his eyes searching the room. "Where's Atlanta?"

"Gone."

"Then the session is over with? I actually went under?"

"Yes."

"Was it a success?"

"Do you remember what you told us?"

"Nothing." He sat up and bent toward her earnestly, his hands planted on the knees of his parted legs. "It was a disappointment, wasn't it? I can see it in your face. Didn't I give you anything useful?"

"Not much, but maybe it's enough to trigger your memory." She told him about Beth. He was silent for a moment, his mind seeking a conscious recognition. Then he shook his head.

"The name means nothing to me. What else? There must have been something else."

Eden hesitated, hating to take him back to that jungle and the horror he had experienced there. But he deserved to know.

"There was more," she said, and she told him all the rest.

Shane said nothing when she finished relating the episode in the jungle as he'd described it. Uneasy with his silence, she ventured a speculative, "Do you think this is how you ended up with the scars and the limp?"

He shook his head, indicating he didn't know.

"It could have been the result of some kind of military

operation,'' she suggested. Or, she thought, not wanting to say it, something totally nefarious. ''Do you suppose you might have been a member of a Special Forces unit? Is that possible?''

Again, he was silent.

''Shane,'' she pressed him anxiously, ''talk to me. Does any of this suggest anything, open up your memory at all?''

''No.''

He was lying to her, she thought. She could tell, because the muscle in his jaw was twitching again, just as it had when he'd relived the scene in the jungle for them. And his face wore that same grim, guarded expression.

''You're not telling me the truth,'' she said. ''If nothing else, you *do* have a conscious memory now of that mission.''

''No, not a memory of the actual images,'' he admitted. ''Just the…''

''What?''

''The shadows of them. It's like I'm seeing the shadows of them.''

But those shadows, even if they had yet to make any sense to him, were enough to shatter his self-control. Shuddering with the sudden anguish they evoked, he hunched over, his head in his hands.

''Oh, God, what has any of this got to do with you and your boy? Or with me? Just who the hell am I, Eden, and what have I done?''

It was the plea of a wounded man, and whatever the consequences, Eden couldn't ignore his need. She went to him at once, kneeling on the floor between his parted legs. Willing to share in his despair, but refusing to let him surrender to it, she reached out to him, holding his big hands in her own.

''We'll learn who you are, Shane. I promise you that somehow we will. We'll put it all together, and give your life back to you.''

He lifted his head, his potent brown eyes with the golden

lights in them meeting hers. "And yours, as well," he said, referring to Nathanial in a hopeful, husky voice.

The promises they exchanged were reckless ones. As reckless as what followed them. Clearly needing more than her verbal comfort, needing her physical one as well, Shane abandoned all restraint. Before she could object, or even decide if she should object, he had freed his hands from hers. The action permitted him to reach down and gather her into his arms.

Eden found herself dragged up between his legs and clasped against his hard body, caught in a fierce embrace that involved his muscular legs holding her like a vise and his hands now framing her face on either side of her head. His mouth that swooped down on hers was just as demanding, just as eager in the kiss it delivered.

It was a wild kiss, all hot and hungry. And she didn't try to stop him, didn't want to stop him. Not this time. This time she welcomed the male aroma of him in her nostrils, the virile taste of him in her mouth. She not only welcomed his passionate assault, she returned it with an equal ferocity.

Both of them by now had lost all control, any shred of reason in this sensual storm that consumed them. It lasted until Shane's hands, which had left the sides of her head and were clamped to her hips, pulled her tightly against his groin. She felt the rigidity of his awesome arousal. Heard the aching groan from him that accompanied it.

And that's when the shadow of the unknown Beth came between them, descending like a sword whose sharp edge was a cruel reminder that Shane might belong to another woman.

Realizing they had gone too far, Eden flattened her hands against his chest, pressing against him to communicate her wish to be released. He let her go, and she sat back on her heels and gazed up into his sober face.

She waited for a moment, giving them both a chance to recover before she spoke to him softly. "This isn't the answer, Shane."

He nodded, and she knew he understood her. Realized that if they had any chance of succeeding in their quest, their energies needed to be focused on recovering his memory and not on each other. Neither of them mentioned that other barrier.

*Beth.*

His embrace had not been a tender one, but a gentleness asserted itself now. "Did I hurt you?" he asked her. "I didn't mean to hurt you."

Ironic, Eden thought. Considering the intensity of their kiss, it was his bottom lip, suffering from a cut when he'd arrived at her door last night, that should have been hurting. But he hadn't complained.

"No," she said, "you didn't hurt me."

Not physically, anyway, she thought. But emotionally she felt battered. That's when she remembered Atlanta Johnson's warning to her. And feared it was already too late.

SHANE THOUGHT about blaming the sofa for his sleepless state. But the sofa was comfortable, even if it wasn't quite long enough to accommodate his full height.

No, it wasn't the sofa. It was the woman behind the closed door of her bedroom who was responsible for his restlessness as he lay in the darkness. Or, more accurately, his longing to be inside that bedroom with her.

Considering his situation, Shane knew that his yearning was madness. How could he want her like that, have any *right* to want her, when all afternoon and evening he'd been haunted by the thought that he might actually be to blame for the abduction of her kid?

An unspeakable possibility, but then if it wasn't true, who had taken Nathanial and where had the boy been all these years? And if Shane did have any hidden knowledge of him or had somehow ended up with the kid, what had he done with him?

In the morning, a weary Eden had promised him before

retiring for the night. In the morning they would decide
what to try next to restore his memory and learn those
answers. But as racked by frustration as Shane was, tomorrow morning seemed a hell of a long way off.

AN INSISTENT VOICE awakened her. Eden's eyes opened to
find Shane leaning over her bed. His presence in her bedroom didn't alarm her, but the expression on his face did.
He looked tense and grim, a man ready for action.

"What is it?" she demanded, struggling up against the
headboard.

"There's a cop car out there just pulling into the driveway."

She saw his gaze slide in the direction of the bureau. On
its surface rested one of her two cell phones he had appropriated yesterday. The other phone was still in his possession, but he had given this one back to her so she could
make that call to Atlanta Johnson. She knew immediately
what must have occurred to him.

"I did not call the police," she informed him emphatically. "And, no, I don't have any idea why they're here."

"We don't have time to argue about it. That cop must
already be on his way to the door."

"I'll get rid of him," Eden said, swinging her legs over
the side of the bed and reaching for her robe on a chair.
"You stay in here out of sight."

She could see this instruction didn't agree with Shane.
He wasn't a man to let a woman face a threat to him while
he cowered behind a bedroom door. But wisdom overcame
male pride. He accepted her plan with a reluctant nod.

There was a knock on the front door as Eden, struggling
into her robe, left the bedroom, closing its door behind her.
What had brought the police to her houseboat? Had Atlanta
Johnson, worried about Shane's presence here, alerted
them? No, she didn't think the hypnotist's code of ethics
would permit her to betray them like that. Then why—

The knock sounded again as Eden reached the door, unlocking it and pulling it back to reveal a young sheriff's deputy standing on the pier in the early-morning sunlight. He was a local officer. She had seen him before around the village. It would have been difficult not to notice him. He was very good looking.

"Ms. Hawke?"

"Yes."

"Sorry to rouse you like this, but if I could just have a word with you..."

He looked at her expectantly, and she knew he was waiting for her to invite him inside. There was a sharp breeze off the river, and he probably wanted to escape its chill. On the other hand, he could just be looking for an excuse to check out the interior of the houseboat. To deny him entrance would be to risk his suspicion. Eden couldn't afford that.

"Come in," she said, moving aside in the doorway.

"Nice place," he said, casting his gaze around the living room after he'd stepped inside and she'd closed the door behind him.

"Thank you. How can I help you, Officer?"

"You have a friend back in Charleston. Name of—" He consulted a small notebook in his hand. "Tia Wong."

*Tia?*

"She phoned our office and asked us if we would just stop by and look in on you to be sure you're all right," the officer explained. "She'd been calling around trying to locate you and then had an idea you might have come out here to your houseboat."

"But why—"

"She got worried about you, Ms. Hawke. Said she'd been trying repeatedly to reach your number and could never get an answer."

The cell phones, Eden thought. Shane had turned off both of them when he'd taken them away from her. And though the one had been turned on again for the call to Atlanta, Eden had afterward switched off its power to conserve its dwindling energy. She'd been much too wrapped up in the situation here to consider that Tia might try to reach her.

"Your friend have any reason to be so worried about you, Ms. Hawke?"

*Had* Tia told the sheriff's office about Shane? Was that why the deputy was here? No, Tia must have held back on that. Otherwise, the deputy would be asking her a whole lot of other questions. There was nothing to be alarmed about.

Or was there?

The young officer was now eyeing something both she and Shane had forgotten about when the sheriff's cruiser rolled up the driveway. Shane's jacket was hanging over the back of a chair. It was plainly a man's jacket, much too large for her. When the deputy looked around again, his gaze settled on the closed door to the bedroom. He knew she wasn't alone.

This could be trouble.

Eden acted fast, providing an explanation that was familiar to her by now. "My husband returned unexpectedly from an extended business trip. That's why we came out to the houseboat, to share some quality time together. We had the phone turned off so we wouldn't be interrupted."

The deputy accepted her explanation with an understanding smile.

"I should have told Tia he was home," Eden added. "She's very protective of me when he's away."

"Call her," the officer suggested, closing his notebook.

"I will," she promised, seeing him to the door. "And thank you for checking on me."

Shane emerged from the bedroom at the sound of the cruiser retreating down the driveway. The look on his face was not a happy one.

"Were you able to hear everything?" she asked.

"I heard." He muttered an obscenity that expressed his

frustration. "It looks like I'm no safer out here from the risk of the cops than I was in Charleston."

Eden watched him as he went to the window. There was a brooding quality about him as he stood there looking out at the river, broad shoulders hunched, hands buried in his pockets.

"That being the case, then…"

She paused, wondering if he was listening to her. But after a moment he swung away from the window and gazed at her perceptively.

"I can see it in your face," he said.

"What?"

"The look that says, 'It's time for me to be a private investigator.' All right, what are you recommending?"

"That we go back to Charleston and retrace your route that night. Every step of the way from your first awareness of wandering out there in the storm until you arrived at my door. Hypnosis didn't work to trigger your memory. Maybe this will."

He was silent again while she waited anxiously for his decision, maintaining her belief that her recovery of Nathanial depended on this inscrutable man.

"You're right," he said. "There are no answers for either one of us in this place. If we're going to learn anything, we have to start in Charleston where it began. Only, if it turns out I am wanted by the cops—"

"We'll deal with that problem when, and if, we have to. But if you are ever challenged… Well, there is maybe a way to reduce that risk."

"Being?"

Eden hesitated, unable to believe what she was about to propose. "The deputy who was here," she went on, "he accepted your presence without question when I told him you were my husband."

"So he did. Is that what you're suggesting then, Eden? That we go on posing as husband and wife?"

She could see it now, the unmistakable glint in his eyes.

Damn him, he was enjoying this. "Forget it. It's a bad idea."

"Actually, it isn't. That cop might have demanded some ID."

"Which you wouldn't have been able to produce."

"Exactly. Instead, he went away satisfied."

"Because I passed you off as my husband."

"And could again in a sticky situation. Yeah, I like it. I think I'm even getting comfortable with the idea. And since we've already had some practice in that direction…"

Eden was beginning to wish she had kept her mouth shut. This arrangement could end up presenting more problems than solutions. But she wouldn't retract her offer to play his wife, not if that's what it took to recover her son.

Before Shane could have any more fun with the situation, she escaped into the bedroom to shower and dress, leaving him to fix their breakfasts. While she was there, she called Tia. Eden told her friend just enough about what had been happening to satisfy her. Fortunately, Tia was getting ready for work and had no time to demand details. All she really wanted to hear was that Eden was safe.

*But just how safe am I with any of this?* Eden wondered an hour later as they followed the road back to Charleston. It wasn't as if she feared the man at her side would physically harm her. But though she no longer worried about that, there were other concerns.

She remembered how, back there in the houseboat when Shane had announced the arrival of the sheriff's cruiser, he had entertained a suspicion she had called the cops. However momentary that suspicion had been, it was an evidence of his struggle with trust. And there was her own lingering mistrust of him. She couldn't forget he had abducted her from Charleston. Did that make him capable of having abducted Nathanial?

Just as though he had sensed her nagging misgiving in this direction, Shane turned to her, his manner sober now. "Are you sure you want to do this?"

*Stop it, Eden. You have to trust him. Both of you have to learn to trust each other if this investigation stands any chance of succeeding.*

"Yes, I'm sure," she said, and she meant it.

Only there was something else connected with her safety. She thought about it behind the wheel of the Toyota. Thought of the young deputy who had called at the houseboat and how handsome he was. But his looks had in no way interested Eden.

She wished she could say the same about the man beside her. He wasn't handsome, not in the conventional way. His face was too craggy for that. It didn't matter, though. He didn't need to be handsome. He had sex appeal. A lot of it, and she was entirely too aware of it.

And that, Eden thought, stealing a glance at him, wasn't safe for her. Especially when they were playing man and wife.

*It's for convenience's sake,* she reminded herself sharply. *That's all this marriage is. Not real, just a masquerade to facilitate our investigation.*

Eden had the uneasy feeling she was going to have to go on reminding herself of that. Frequently.

SHE FELT LIKE a mother watching her child take his first awkward steps. Wanting him to succeed. Resisting the urge to help him. Knowing he had to do this on his own.

Eden experienced all of these emotions as she and Shane worked their way on foot from her front door back along the twelve blocks he had traveled the night before last. Their progress was a slow one, partly because of his limp but mostly because she wanted him to have sufficient time to assimilate the sights and sounds along the route. Any one of them could stir a vital recollection.

Holding her silence when she longed to ask him whether this experiment was in any way useful wasn't easy. But it was necessary. She didn't want to short-circuit his sensory process.

However, Eden doubted he would have heard her eager questions. Shane seemed to be almost as much in a trance as when Atlanta had hypnotized him. He moved in a kind of robotic state, his head swinging mechanically from side to side, gaze darting here and there.

It was a little scary, like walking beside a machine scanning for something. Which, of course, was exactly what Shane *was* doing. He was looking for his memory.

"That's where I ducked into the alley to avoid the patrol car," he said woodenly.

A little later on he indicated: "Here's where I fell down."

And finally: "There's the convenience store across the street."

They had covered the entire twelve blocks by now and stood on the edge of the parkway where he had found himself wandering that night, the cars whipping past them on the boulevard. Eden could no longer hold her tongue. Fearing their effort was a failure, she was about to ask him if he had recovered any scrap of memory at all, when he abruptly left her side and moved rapidly ahead of her along the parkway. Catching up with him, she could sense his sudden excitement. A glance at his face told her that he was being bombarded with images.

"What is it?" she demanded. "A breakthrough?"

He didn't answer her. He kept walking, his gaze searching the area. He was limping noticeably now, and that worried her. The twelve blocks had tired his leg.

"Let's sit down and rest," she said, motioning to a nearby park bench that overlooked the river.

She could see that her suggestion irritated him. He was the kind of man who didn't want to admit his strength might in any way be hindered by his limp. But he didn't argue with her. They settled side by side on the bench.

"Flashes," he said. "What happened to me that night is starting to come back in flashes."

"Take your time," she encouraged him. "Don't force it.

Let the bits and pieces come through at their own rate, and we'll piece them together as we go."

It was good advice, Eden felt. But even as she gave it, she had to restrain herself from rushing him for a knowledge that might mean everything to both of them. She could see that Shane, too, was impatient, that he was fighting for the memories of that night.

"It's all a little muddy, but I can see myself in a car. I'm alone in a car and driving somewhere. I don't know where, but it's dark and raining, and I'm out on this highway. It must be late. There's hardly any traffic on the road."

"Do you know where you were coming from?"

"No."

"What about the car? Do you think it was your car?"

He shook his head. "I have the feeling it was a rental I picked up somewhere and was maybe on my way into the city."

"The airport," she said. "You could have arrived at the airport and hired a rental car."

"Makes sense. What happened afterward doesn't."

"Tell me."

"I was forced off the road by another vehicle."

"Couldn't it have been an accident? It was dark, after all, and with the rain—"

"No," he insisted. "It was deliberate. I'm positive it was deliberate. I lost control of the car. Crashed into something off the road. Lost consciousness."

"And when you came to?"

"Don't know. Except I don't think I was in the car anymore."

"Try to visualize it, Shane. Try to see yourself there, just as you did when you put yourself inside that car."

She watched him as he made a concentrated effort to recall the scene.

"A room?" he asked himself slowly. "Yeah, that's

right. I'm in this room somewhere. I'm tied to a chair. They've got me all trussed up and tied to a chair."

"Who?"

"Three of them. There are three of them. A couple of mean brutes who look like they should be called Bruno and Boris and this little weasel of a guy. They must have searched me when I was out, emptied my pockets. All my stuff is dumped there on the table. Everything but the picture and the business card." He laughed harshly. "The bastards didn't get those."

"Why?"

"I think…yeah, I think at some point I must have managed to wiggle them down inside the lining of my jacket."

"What happens next?"

"The two brutes send the little weasel outside. They don't want him to hear when they question me. They want something. They keep asking me over and over what I did with him."

"*Him?* Are you sure it's a *him*, Shane, and not an *it?*"

"Did I say *him?*"

"Yes."

"I guess that's right then. They want to know where he is, and when I can't tell them, or won't tell them, they work me over. The bastards work me over."

The image of Shane being beaten, along with her memory of his battered condition when she had found him on the floor of her piazza, sickened Eden. And angered her, as well.

"I'm no longer in that room now," he continued. "They're dragging me outside, dumping me into the back of a van. No, wait, it isn't a van. It's a panel truck, and it's seen better days. The little weasel is driving it, and one of the gorillas is up front with him telling him where to go. They didn't get what they wanted out of me so they're taking me someplace else. It's going to be another interrogation when we get there, I guess."

"Do you know where that is?"

"No, I didn't hear."

"Go on."

"The other bastard is riding in the back with me. They think I'm unconscious again, no threat. But I'm only playing at being out. I wait for my chance. There's an old bike pump over in the corner. It's peeking out from under some burlap on the floor near where I'm lying. He doesn't see it, but I do. I wait for my chance when his back is turned, and then I grab it. He goes down without a sound, and I'm out of there when the truck slows for a corner. The two up front never know I'm gone."

"And then?"

"The parkway, I suppose. That's when I must have found myself out here on the parkway."

"With everything a blank."

"Total."

Any part of the long trauma he had suffered could have been responsible for the amnesia that had resulted, Eden realized. The crash of his car, the beating he had received, his leap from the back of the truck. Or all of them together.

"If you remembered this much," she said, "maybe you can remember the rest. What about before that night? Anything?"

"Not a clue."

"How about your name?"

"It's still Shane."

Frustrating, she thought. For both of them, judging by the expression on his face. She tried something else. "Those men must have known who you are if they took you like that. How did they address you when they questioned you?"

"With language you don't want to hear. Look, Eden, it's no use. If names were used, either mine or theirs, they didn't stay with me."

Eden took a deep breath and released it slowly in an effort to temper the excitement that had been building in her ever since Shane had spoken of his captors' demands.

"You were headed toward the city, carrying the photograph and my business card. Were you coming to see me? Is this *him* they kept asking you about Nathanial? Is it, Shane?" She leaned toward him earnestly.

He looked at her, and he said nothing. He didn't have to. She could see it all in his eyes. The same questions that haunted her must be haunting him since he'd dredged up those fragments of memory from his subconscious. Questions like: Did he have Nathanial? If so, how did he get him? What was he doing with him, and why do those men want him? And where is Nathaniel now?

They were questions without answers, because his mind was blocking out all the rest. Why? Was it guarding something so terrible that it was using amnesia as a shield?

*Nathanial. I want to know where he is, too. I want my son back.*

This was no good. Surrendering to a mother's desperation wouldn't get them the answers. Not when he was as tortured as she was by his inability to provide them. It would be much more useful for her to forget she was a mother and turn to her P.I. skills.

"It's all right, Shane. For now, we'll go with what we have. Let's go back to that panel truck. Can you recall anything more about it? License plate, name on the side?"

"Negative," he said regretfully.

"The place where they held you. Visualize it again." This time he closed his eyes. She watched him hopefully. "Tell me what you see."

"Shabby. The place is run-down. Uh, it's…it's a motel room."

"How do you know?"

"There's everything there that says it's a cheap motel. And there's a sign out front. I see it when they haul me out to the truck. Hear the sound of surf, too. The beach must be nearby. Hold it. I can see the name on the sign now. The Jolly Mariner. Oh, yeah, that's it. The Jolly Mariner."

His eyes opened. They looked at each other eagerly. This is what they had been seeking. A name. A place to begin their search.

"I think you and I are going to pay a visit to the Jolly Mariner," he said.

Eden read a grimness in his tone, as if he couldn't wait to get his hands on the men who had brutalized him. She wasn't sure she cared for that idea. Tangling like that with a trio who might be armed, and were certainly dangerous, could risk the recovery of both his memory and Nathanial. Not to mention their lives.

"Maybe it's time we went to the police," she said.

"No cops," he insisted.

He still feared the police then. It was something that worried her, but she wasn't going to argue with him about it. Not now when at last they had a definite lead. "We'll start with the Jolly Mariner then," she agreed. "It's a long shot, but maybe we'll get the answers there we need. There's just one problem, though."

"Being?"

"Where *is* the Jolly Mariner? There are beaches everywhere in the Charleston area and all of them with dozens of motels."

"There's got to be a way to locate it."

Eden nodded. "The Internet. I think that's our best method."

Minutes later, they were able to hail a cab, which sped them back to Eden's place. Once inside her office, she put Shane online at the computer while she settled behind her desk with the phone.

There were several car rental agencies at the airport. She tried them all, hoping to learn Shane's identity by asking if one of their vehicles might have been recovered from the scene of an accident and, if so, who had rented it. But none of them would discuss what they regarded as confidential information. Nor did Eden want to press them, fearing they would contact the police, even though she didn't give them her real name.

"No luck," she reported after she'd exhausted the list. "You?"

"I've got it!" Shane said triumphantly. "The Jolly Mariner is at Folly Beach."

Eden looked over his shoulder at the listing on the screen. "I know it. It's on Folly Island, south of Charleston."

Within minutes, they were on the road again and headed away from the center of the city. They didn't talk. Eden's mind was on the traffic and reaching their destination.

They were still weaving their way through the urban sprawl when Shane ended the silence with an abrupt "Pull over."

Startled by his command, she glanced at him in dismay. "What's wrong?"

If Eden hadn't learned by now just how forceful this man could be when the occasion demanded it, she learned it now.

"Damn it, just stop the car, will you?"

# Chapter Six

A driver blew his horn in anger as Eden whipped across the lane in front of him to reach the curb. She didn't blame him. She had risked a collision in order to comply with Shane's urgent command. That she had obeyed it instantly and without question was an indication he was a man used to giving orders. And that could also mean he had served as an officer in some branch of the military.

Coasting into a parking space against the curb, she threw the gear into Park and turned to him. "This had better be good."

"The store back there on the corner," he said, jerking his thumb over his shoulder.

Eden twisted around in her seat. "It's a pawnshop."

"Right."

"And that's your emergency?"

"We need it."

She was totally perplexed by now. "What could we possibly need from—"

"Wedding rings. If we're going to make this marriage of ours look convincing, then we ought to be wearing wedding rings. Come on."

Eden felt this might be taking their masquerade to unnecessary lengths, but Shane gave her no opportunity to argue about it. He had already unbuckled and was sliding out of the car. She had no choice but to follow him.

The pawnshop had a large selection of wedding rings in all sizes and designs. It troubled Eden that so many people could be desperate enough to pawn their wedding rings. But she didn't comment on this as Shane carefully examined them, rejecting any that had engraving inside. After trying them on, they settled on a pair of plain, matching gold bands.

Shane took possession of the rings after Eden paid for them. "Uh, isn't the idea for us to wear them?" she asked as they came away from the shop.

"Right."

He gave her one of the rings. Eden looked at it. "This is yours."

"I know." He turned and faced her on the sidewalk where they had paused. "I thought it might be nice if we placed the rings on each other's fingers. Just to sort of seal our arrangement to work together."

Eden felt something turn over inside her.

"A temporary deal, of course," he added.

"Naturally. Uh, you don't expect us to exchange some kind of vows, too, do you?"

"I guess we don't have to go that far."

He held out his hand. Eden hesitated and then placed the ring on his finger. If he had ever worn a wedding ring before, there was no telltale sign of it on his finger. Not that this was proof of anything.

She experienced a little jolt when he took her own hand, holding it warmly for several seconds before he slowly slid the ring over her finger. He took far more time with the action than he needed to. It was disconcerting to feel how easily the gold band settled into place on her finger. As if it belonged there.

It was equally disconcerting when Shane leaned down and brushed a kiss over her mouth. "The bridegroom's prerogative," he said in a deep voice that sent a shiver dancing along her spine.

This husband-and-wife thing was getting to be more

emotionally complicated than she'd anticipated, Eden thought. And far too provocative.

LESS THAN AN HOUR later they crossed a bridge over the Folly River and entered the resort district of Folly Island.

"I've seen more life in ghost towns," Shane observed as they rolled along the deserted beachfront.

"Come back in summer," Eden said, "and you'll find the place choked with traffic. What's the address again?"

"It's 3211 North Ocean Avenue. We've got some distance to cover yet."

Which meant the Jolly Mariner was not in the high-rent district, Eden thought. Not that she expected it to be, considering Shane's description of the motel.

They continued along the oceanfront where many of the facilities were closed for the season. Those that were still open had few visitors. And that, she realized with a shudder, made it an area where you would be reasonably safe from interruption while you beat a man senseless.

The Jolly Mariner bore this out when they finally reached it just beyond a golf course empty of players. Eden pulled past the sign into the parking lot and turned off the engine. They sat there in silence for a moment, checking out the situation.

Long and low, painted a faded blue and with shaggy, overgrown crape myrtles emphasizing its seedy look, the Jolly Mariner was the kind of motel that got guests only after the better inns were filled.

"Not very jolly, is it?" Shane remarked. "Or encouraging."

Eden knew he was not referring to the condition of the motel but to its aura of absolute vacancy. There was not a soul in sight, and the drapes at all the windows were fully closed. What could they hope to learn here? Those men who had seized and held him were certainly not hanging around.

"Still…" he said, unbuckling and reaching for the door handle.

He didn't need to finish. She knew what he meant. They had to try.

When she joined him outside the car, Shane was checking the semiautomatic to be certain it was in readiness should they need it. He probably would have returned her pistol to her if she had asked him, but he seemed to feel more secure keeping it in his possession. Besides, the way he handled the weapon, with complete confidence, assured her she was in the care of a professional. One of the guys in white hats. She hoped. After all, they had yet to learn what he was.

Satisfied, Shane tucked the weapon into the back side of his waistband where he could easily reach it just under his open jacket. "Stay behind me," he instructed her as they started for the office located at the center of the motel.

Eden was a trained P.I. who knew how to handle herself in the event of trouble. She should have resented his take-charge attitude. But she didn't, and now wasn't the time to ask herself why.

She could hear the dull boom of the surf on the shore across the avenue as they cautiously approached the office. Eden was glad of her jacket. There was a cold wind off the ocean.

"Locked," Shane said after trying the door.

What had they expected? The motel, without any hope of business, was obviously closed for the season.

"There," he said, that familiar grimness in his tone as he nodded in the direction of a room three doors away. "That's the room where they held me. I'm sure of it."

The room was no more promising than the others, its window closed and drapes pulled. Eden was convinced that even if they broke in, they wouldn't find anything useful. Besides, her gaze had been attracted to something much more interesting.

There was a huge magnolia at the far corner of the long

building. Through the thickness of its glossy foliage, she could just make out the white metal of a vehicle parked behind the tree.

"Maybe we're not alone here," she said, drawing his attention in that direction.

Shane looked and nodded. "The truck they used was a light color. Could have been white. Let's investigate."

They did, again with caution. When they reached it, the unoccupied vehicle proved to be an old panel truck, most likely the one that had been used to transport Shane. If there had ever been lettering on its sides, it had been painted out. Quite possibly to prevent identification, because even the truck's license plate had been plastered with mud.

From this angle Eden could see that the motel was L-shaped. While Shane walked around the truck, trying its doors, all of which were apparently locked, she gazed nervously down the length of the building's side wing. Maybe the truck had been abandoned in this spot after serving its purpose. Maybe not. And if any one, or possibly all three, of those men *were* still here and even now lurking inside one of these rooms, watching them from behind a drape...

"I don't like this," she said. "What if they're here and armed? I know how you feel about it, but don't you think it's time we called—"

Shane held up one hand, silencing her. "Hear it?"

She listened and did hear it. There was the repeated clang of metal against metal, muffled by distance. It came from somewhere behind the motel.

"Sounds like somebody doing repairs," Shane said. "Let's go find out just who he's working for."

"Shane—"

"Maybe you ought to wait here."

She'd been about to suggest the police again, but there was no point in doing that. He was determined. So was she. "And leave you without backup? I don't think so. Just be careful, huh. For all we know, this guy is lethal with plumbing tools."

Shane led the way again, moving down the length of the side wing with its ranks of identical outside doors. Although he didn't remove the pistol from his waistband, his hand was back there, ready for a quick draw. The banging was louder as they reached the corner and rounded the back side of the motel. It stopped suddenly, replaced by a string of muttered curses.

The source of this frustration was revealed to them when they neared the angle where the two wings of the motel were joined. Situated on a concrete platform in the ell was the bulky compressor for a central air-conditioning unit. A figure in stained coveralls was crouched beside it, hammer in hand.

Aware of their approach, he glanced up at them. The sun was behind them. They couldn't have been much more than silhouettes to him. "Place is closed for the season, folks."

"That's funny," Shane said cheerfully, closing in on him, "because it was open just the other night. One of the rooms here was, anyway."

The man peered at them. Eden watched an expression of recognition travel across his thin face. The hammer dropped out of his hand, clattering on the cover of the compressor that lay beside the unit. She guessed who he was when he got to his feet, licking his lips and backing away from them. This had to be Shane's little weasel.

He looked exactly like a skinny weasel, with a twitching nose and a pair of beady, frightened eyes that darted from side to side, seeking escape. But trapped in the ell as he was, there was nowhere for him to run. He made a stab at it, though, dodging to his left.

That's when Eden learned that Shane in action was impressive. He was on the little weasel like a wolf pouncing on his next meal. Hand locked around the throat of his catch, Shane pinned him against the wall of the motel.

"Tell you something interesting—" Shane paused, his gaze dropping briefly to the name stitched in red thread on a breast pocket of the coverall "—Roy. The other night

when you boys dragged me in here like that, I was unconscious. You must have figured I wouldn't have a clue who
grabbed me or where I was. Same for when you hauled me
out. Only you figured wrong, Roy. See, on that second trip
I wasn't unconscious, only playing at it, which is why I
had a glimpse of the motel's sign out front. Now, that's
interesting, right?''

"Man, you're making a big mistake."

He squealed like a little animal, too, Eden thought.

Ignoring the objection, Shove shoved his face close to
the twitching nose. "Tell you something else, Roy. My
wife here was real upset when you sent me home to her all
battered and bruised like that.''

"W-wife?" Roy said stupidly.

"Wife, Roy. As in this.''

Shane held his left hand up to Roy's face, displaying the
newly purchased wedding band, as if to test its believabil-
ity. Or maybe, Eden thought, just because he was having
fun again with their masquerade. He was forever choosing
the worst moments for that.

"So, Roy, what are we gonna do about making her feel
better?''

"I don't know, man, I don't know." He tried to squirm
away, but Shane's right hand clamped around his neck continued to hold him against the building.

"Sure you do, Roy. You can start by telling us all about
those two buddies of yours.''

"I don't know who you're talking about. Honest, I
don't.''

Shane looked him up and down. "You're what, Roy?
Owner of the Jolly Mariner? Nah, that's not right. More
like the caretaker and maintenance man. Except there
wouldn't be enough work for you in a dump like this. My
guess is that you service some of the other motels in the
area, too. Wonder what all their owners would say if they
knew you were hiring out their rooms for some really nasty
stuff? Things like the other night.''

"Man, have a heart," he pleaded, his voice a squeaky whine by now. "You don't know those two guys. They're mean as snakes. They'll kill me if I talk."

"Or maybe I could beat it out of you. Like they tried to beat information out of me. What do you think, Roy?"

Shane's hand slowly tightened on the caretaker's throat. Alarmed that he would strangle the man, whose eyes were bulging now with terror, Eden started to go to him.

"Stop!" Roy gasped. "I'll tell!"

"That's better." Shane relaxed his grip, but he didn't remove it. The caretaker continued to hang there against the wall in his grasp. "Your two friends, Roy. Who are they?"

"I don't know. No, that's the truth, I swear. I never saw 'em before that night, and they wouldn't tell me their names. Come up to me in this bar where I hang out. Wanted to use me and my truck and a room here for a couple of hours. Willing to pay big, but no questions asked."

"So you went along with the idea?"

"Man, I needed the money. But I never knew what any of it was about, not who you were or why they snatched you like that or what they wanted out of you. Hey, they sent me out of the room when they got around to questioning you, remember?"

"What happened to my husband's things they took off of him?" Eden asked. "His wallet, for instance?"

"I don't know, lady. I guess they kept them. I never saw the stuff again after I left the room."

"But you do know where they were taking me after we left here," Shane insisted. "You were driving. They had to have given you directions. We went to Charleston. Where in Charleston, Roy? Give me a name, an address."

The caretaker hesitated. Shane's fingers began to tighten again on his scrawny neck.

"Some woman's apartment," Roy babbled. "Krause, I think her name was. That's right. One of 'em said to the other that you needed to see Harriet Krause, and maybe then you'd talk.''

*Harriet Krause.* Hearing the name shocked Eden. She remembered it, knew who the woman was. But this wasn't the moment for dealing with that recognition.

"The address, Roy," Shane reminded him.

"Bahama Street—301 Bahama Street."

Shane looked questioningly over his shoulder at Eden. She nodded, indicating to him that she knew the street and how to find it. His gaze rested on her face for a few seconds, and then he turned back to the caretaker.

"I'm going to let you go now, Roy, but you're gonna be real good. You're not going to tell anyone we were here, because if you do…''

"DO YOU THINK your threat was enough to keep him quiet?" Eden asked Shane when they were back inside the Toyota and on their way to Charleston.

"Who knows? He's certainly not going to open his mouth to the cops, but if he was lying about not having anything more to do with that pair who hired him…''

"Then, even at the risk of you looking him up again and using him as—a punching bag, was it?—he could contact them about us. Providing, I suppose, they made it worth his while."

"Yeah, we already know Roy can be bought. We'll just have to hope he was telling the truth."

There was something Shane needed to ask Eden. Something he had been wondering about ever since the caretaker had given them the address and he had turned his head and saw the startled look on her face. But he waited until they were a safe distance away from the motel to frame his question.

"This woman, Harriet Krause. You recognized the name when you heard it, didn't you? Or was it the address?"

"Was I that transparent? It was so unexpected I suppose I was. No, it wasn't the address. It was her name."

"You know her?"

"There was a Harriet Krause who was a lab technician at the sperm bank I used. That is, if she's still there. She worked in the clinic where Nathanial was conceived." Her eyes left the road just long enough to seek his own gaze. To communicate to him the intensity of the emotions she must have been experiencing ever since the caretaker's revelation. "Do you see what that means, Shane?"

Shane was afraid that he did. The photograph he had been carrying, the brutal interrogation that had cost him his memory, the intention to confront him with this Harriet Krause—they were all a connection that could no longer be denied. "Yeah, I do. I'm involved somehow with your son."

Just how serious his involvement was scared the hell out of him. Could he have been responsible for the disappearance of Nathanial? Known where he was all these years? Was he even now concealing him?

Eden gave voice to his fears. "That's why those men grabbed and questioned you, isn't it, Shane? God knows why, but it's Nathanial they want. And they're convinced you know where he is."

There was an edge of accusation in her tone. He didn't blame her. Maybe it was all true. Maybe he was no better than Roy, a part of some rotten scheme for a mercenary purpose. Which didn't make the urge he was feeling in this moment in any way reasonable. But it was there. *Strongly* there.

He wanted to ask her to stop the car so that he could take her in his arms, comfort her in her distress. Hell, face it. He wanted to do a lot more than that. He wanted his mouth on hers, his tongue caressing her trembling lip, his nostrils inhaling her warm, womanly fragrance. Wanted to fill his hands with her breasts. Not to mention a few other things he wanted to do with her.

*Was I that transparent?* That's what she'd asked him. Was she? Or was it that he was just able to read her so accurately, sense her moods? As if she actually was his wife, he thought, glancing at the wedding band on her finger. And that feeling made no sense when he hadn't known her two days ago, when their relationship could be measured in mere hours.

Physical or emotional, whatever the explanation for his longing, his timing was all wrong. He suppressed his urge by turning to a practical matter.

"This is Monday, Eden. A workday. It's not very likely we'll find this woman at home."

"You're right. I think we'd better start by checking with the clinic to learn if she's there. We'll need a phone directory for the number. Look for a quick stop."

They found one shortly after crossing the bridge to the mainland. Purse hanging from her shoulder, Eden went into the building while Shane filled the car with gas. She was back within minutes bearing a plastic sack in one hand and waving her cell phone in the other.

"I called while I was inside," she reported. "We're in luck. Not only does Harriet Krause still work there, they told me she went home early to nurse a cold. Oh, and I paid for the gas when I bought these."

"What is it?" he wondered, eyeing the sack.

"Lunch."

It was long past midday, and they hadn't eaten since their early breakfast at the houseboat. Shane welcomed the contents of the sack. They munched on fruit and cheese-filled crackers as they sped toward Charleston.

Eden was silent at the wheel. A worried kind of silence. They were nearing the city when she spoke.

"About those men. If they're still in the area and desperate to get their hands on you again…"

"Yeah, it could mean trouble."

"It isn't just the risk of them hunting for you, bad as that is. It's not understanding why they want you and how Nathanial may figure into it. What's it all about, Shane?" she pleaded.

He wished he had answers for her. He didn't. "Let's hope Harriet Krause can explain everything for us."

And revive his memory in the bargain, Shane thought. Because, although the woman's name meant something to Eden, it meant absolutely nothing to him.

IT WAS MIDAFTERNOON when they parked in front of 301 Bahama Street. The address was located in the historic area three blocks in from the harbor front. Harriet Krause's vintage building was similar to Eden's. Only, in this case, it was a double house. Like Eden's, it had been converted into apartments. The mailboxes out front informed them that Harriet Krause's apartment was on the second floor.

There was an outside stairway at the back of a deep piazza. Shane, leading the way, hesitated at its foot. He was suddenly reluctant to see this woman, fearing what she had to say. By now, he wasn't just wondering, he was convinced that he was implicated in some way with Nathanial. Or, anyway, the boy Eden believed was her son. How?

Would Harriet Krause tell him? Would she ask him what he had done with the boy in the photograph? Demand to know where he had hidden him? Accuse him of holding the child against his will? Maybe for ransom? That's what Shane didn't want to hear. That's what he didn't want to learn about himself.

"What is it?" Eden asked him.

"Nothing," he said, steeling himself to face the truth, no matter how bad it was. Alert for action should Harriet Krause not be alone in her apartment, he climbed the stairs ahead of Eden.

There were two apartments off the landing at the top. Cards beside the doors identified the occupants. Harriet Krause's was on the left. Eden knocked, and they waited. There was a peephole. Shane sensed a moment later that they were being checked through it. The door was unlocked then, drawn back a few inches on a security chain.

"Yes?" A woman's hoarse voice spoke cautiously through the crack.

Shane let Eden do the talking.

"Ms. Krause, I'm Eden Hawke. Do you remember me? I was one of the clinic's clients about six years back."

There was a lengthy pause before she replied. Shane had the impression it was an unwilling reply. "I remember. What do you want?"

"Could we talk to you for a few minutes? Please, it's very important."

Harriet hesitated again before asking suspiciously, "How did you know I was here?"

"I called the clinic. They told me you'd come home with a cold."

"Then you should know I'm not in any state to have visitors. Come back when I'm feeling better."

We should have expected this, Shane thought. If she's involved with those two gorillas, she *would* refuse to see us. But Eden wasn't prepared to back off.

"We could do that," she said, "except this really can't wait. It's about my son, Ms. Krause, so I think, if you won't talk to us, I should go down to the clinic and tell them what I've recently learned. I think your employers might be interested in hearing it."

Shane already admired Eden on a number of levels. But here was a new one. They had no actual knowledge of Harriet Krause being in any way connected with Nathanial beyond his conception, which made Eden's subtle threat a bold gamble. Damn, if it didn't work.

"All right," Harriet said. "But there is something I need to ask you before you come in. Are either of you wearing a fragrance, a strong aftershave or perfume? I have trouble tolerating them in a closed room, and feeling as I do, anything like that would be particularly bad."

Shane shook his head.

"Me neither," Eden assured her. "I do sometimes wear perfume, but not today."

Satisfied, Harriet nodded. "Hang on, then."

She closed the door in order to remove the chain. Eden and Shane exchanged glances that said: *Looks as if Harriet Krause has a reason to be worried, and not just because of strong fragrances, either.*

If she was hiding something, though, her face didn't show it when she opened the door fully this time and admitted them into her small, rather dim apartment. It was a long face framed in thinning, untidy hair and with a pink nose that was presumably the result of her cold. She was wrapped in a floor-length, terry-cloth robe.

A pair of narrowed eyes rested on Shane. *Does she know about me?* he asked himself. *Or is she just wondering who I am and what I've got to do with any of this?* Eden enlightened her with no more than a brief introduction.

Harriet nodded. "You'd better sit down," she said, indicating a pair of easy chairs. She settled on a flowered sofa facing them. There was a box of tissues on one of the cushions. She reached for a tissue and dabbed at her nose. "Now, what's this all about?"

This was Eden's turf, so Shane let her handle this one.

Eden leaned earnestly forward in her chair. "You're aware from the investigation at the time, Ms. Krause, that my son vanished three years ago. You probably also know that in all this time I was never able to discover what happened to him. But last Saturday night…"

Shane listened silently while Eden went on to concisely relate everything that had happened since he had turned up on her piazza. He also watched Harriet. There was no emotion on her face, but she had several tissues in her lap now. Her nervous fingers were busy shredding them one by one.

"I don't see what any of this has got to do with me," she said, when Eden had finished explaining why they were there.

"Those men were bringing Shane to your apartment, Ms. Krause. They must have had a reason for that."

"I don't know them. I can't imagine why they might have been bringing this man to me."

"It looks like we're wasting our time here, then," Eden said to Shane. "I guess we'd better do what we should have done all along and take this to the police."

Harriet sent a look of appeal in Shane's direction. He answered it with a smile and a little shrug.

"I should warn you, though," Eden said, "that the caretaker at the motel is prepared to name you if it comes to a police investigation."

Harriet was more than uneasy now. She was plainly scared. "Wait," she said, as Eden started to get to her feet.

"Yes?" Eden asked, her tone as casual as it had been with her lie about the caretaker.

"It's true that I don't know these men, I swear. But if I help you by telling you what I do know, then you have to promise me—"

Shane decided it was time for him to speak up. "No promises," he said sharply. "Let's hear what you have to say, and then we'll decide what comes next."

Harriet looked undecided. She also looked miserable, probably more from their presence in her apartment than her cold. Shane watched her glance down and discover that the shredded tissues in her lap were useless. Taking a fresh one from the box at her side, she blew her nose.

"It's either tell us," Shane pressed her, "or tell the police."

Harriet made up her mind. "All right," she agreed. Tossing the crumpled tissue into a paper bag at her feet, she cleared her throat. "There are four apartments at this address. Two up and two down."

And what's that got to do with anything? Shane wondered.

"There used to be a fifth apartment," Harriet continued. "Out back in this little building that was a kitchen in the slave days. It's not occupied now. Well, it's not much of an apartment, but it was all Lissie and her boyfriend could afford when they lived there.''

''Lissie?'' Eden asked, looking as puzzled now as Shane was.

Harriet nodded. ''Lissie Reardon.''

*Reardon.* The name surfaced in Shane's mind with the speed and brilliance of a strobe light.

## Chapter Seven

Shane tried to hang on to it. But before he could make any sense of it, the memory was gone, sinking back into the maddening blackness of his subconscious.

Eden was staring at him. She must have realized he'd just experienced another connection. Shane shook his head, indicating that the flash of memory, if it could even be called that much, had buried itself again before he could understand it.

If Harriet Krause had noticed, she didn't make any remark. "Lissie and I got to be close friends," she went on. "Kind of funny since we were such opposites, but I liked her. She was this free spirit, which is why I guess she fell for an artist. Not a very good artist either, in my opinion, but Simon was sure serious about it."

"An artist," Eden realized, looking suddenly tense. "Nathanial's biological father was an artist."

Harriet avoided her gaze. There was a loose thread on the sleeve of her robe. She gave it her attention, plucking at it slowly, as though it were important.

"Was he—"

"Yes," Harriet admitted. She sniffed and helped herself to another tissue, applying it to her raw nose. "Lissie was always complaining to me about how poor they were. Nobody was buying Simon's paintings, and she was forever getting fired from these dead-end jobs. I asked her once if their families couldn't help out, but she said her folks were gone and that Simon didn't have any family either. So that's when I told her about the sperm bank and how they paid good money to donors who qualified.''

''And Simon did qualify,'' Eden said.

''Lissie joked about it, saying something about Simon being rich in sperm, if nothing else. I think he was unwilling at first, but she finally convinced him to apply.''

''Red-gold hair and lavender-blue eyes,'' Eden murmured, and Shane knew she was thinking of her son and that learning the identity of his father must be both exciting and troubling for her.

''What?'' Harriet asked.

''Nathanial has red-gold hair and lavender-blue eyes.''

Harriet nodded. ''He got those from his father. Simon didn't suffer in the looks department. Lissie went all to pieces when he died like that.''

''A boating accident,'' Eden said. ''The court told my lawyer after the records were subpoenaed that he'd died in a boating accident.''

''I guess you wouldn't have been told that his girlfriend was in the boat with him. Lissie was badly injured. Only, that wasn't the worst of it.'' Harriet paused to blow her nose again. ''She was five months pregnant and lost the baby.''

''And this happened while I was carrying Nathanial, right?''

There was a horrified expression on Eden's face. Shane could see that the same wild possibility that had just occurred to him had struck her as well. A blow that made him want to go to her and hold her. But she wouldn't want him to do that, not when she needed to hear the rest of Harriet Krause's story.

''Lissie spent months recovering. I thought she'd start to feel better about everything once her injuries were healed. She didn't. I mean, she just never seemed to get over grieving for Simon and that baby. And when they told her she could never have another…well, that made it all the worse.''

Harriet resumed her nervous pulling at the loose thread on her robe, an occupation that permitted her to once again evade their gazes.

'''Simon is gone, Harry,''' she said to me. '''I think I could accept that if I knew he was living on through a baby I couldn't give him myself. You've got to tell me, Harry, whether there's a kid of his out there somewhere. That's all I have to know, no names or anything, just if there's some part of him that will go on.'''

Harriet looked up then from the thread, risked meeting their gazes. ''Lissie was in a bad way,'' she said. ''And I just wanted to help her, you know?''

*She wants us to understand and forgive her,* Shane thought. But there was no way to excuse what he realized Harriet Krause had gone and done. Eden's tone told him that she agreed with him.

''You told her about Nathanial.''

''Just that there was a child, a boy. Nothing more than that.''

''Not then maybe,'' Shane said harshly. ''But what about later on?''

Harriet was silent for a moment, but she must have understood she had already gone too far to turn back. That there was no way for her to avoid the rest. ''Look, it seemed to satisfy her,'' she said, the cold-induced hoarseness in her voice growing more pronounced in her effort to finish the story. ''Lissie got to be her old self. She got on with her life. And then, months later, I guess it was, she hooked up with some rock musician and left town. She was all excited about traveling with him around the country to his gigs. I didn't hear from her again.''

''But that wasn't the end of it, was it?'' Eden demanded.

Harriet shook her head. ''About a year later she turned up at my door. She was broke. The rock musician had dumped her in Savannah. She laughed about it. 'Turns out he did me a favor, Harry,'" she said. "'Guess what I learned about Simon's people while I was down there? They're not poor like he was, Harry. They're rich as sin. His daddy is, anyway.'"

"You're telling us now," Shane challenged her, "that Simon did have a family? That he lied about that on his donor record?"

"I didn't know it myself until that morning, though Lissie had known all along. 'That's the way Simon wanted it, Harry,'" she told me. "'He wouldn't talk about his folks to me, except to say his father kicked him out when he wouldn't give up painting and that he and his family were dead to one another and that was fine with him. But guess what else I heard in Savannah, Harry? Sebastian Jamison—that's Simon's rich daddy—is ailing and would give anything if his son could be with him again.' I told Lissie I knew what she was thinking and that it was wicked. That I didn't want to hear her even say the words."

"Nathanial," Eden whispered.

Shane, watching the color drain from her face, had all he could do to check his anger on her behalf. Restraint was necessary if they were to learn the whole story.

"But in the end you did listen to Lissie, didn't you, Harriet?" he accused her. "You listened to her, and you gave her what she wanted. The name and address of the woman who bore Simon's child. What else did you help her to learn? Maybe the day-care center the child attended?"

Harriet was now using the tissues, not to blow her nose, but to mop at the tears streaming from her eyes. "I didn't know Lissie was going to snatch the kid like that," she blubbered. "She swore she was going to offer his mother a deal and that all she wanted out of it was a cut of the fortune Nathanial was bound to inherit."

"And what was your share going to be, Harriet?" Shane asked.

"It wasn't like that."

Harriet clutched the collar of her robe against her throat,

a desperate, imploring look in her red, swollen eyes, her face all blotchy. Shane gazed at her without a shred of sympathy. The woman was despicable, letting a mother suffer all these years while she held her silence.

"No? What *was* it like, Harriet? What kept your mouth shut after Lissie Reardon took Nathanial and disappeared from Charleston?"

"I was scared," she cried. "I would have lost my job, never been allowed to work again as a technician. I could have gone to prison. Can't you understand that?"

"You don't want to know what I understand," Shane said in disgust. He glanced with concern at Eden. She'd made the effort to recover herself and was leaning intensely forward again in her chair.

"Did you have contact with Lissie after she left Charleston? You must have if you knew she took Nathanial."

Harriet shook her head in emphatic denial. "No, I didn't hear anything from her. And I didn't know for certain it was Lissie who took the boy. Not until a couple of weeks ago, anyway."

"What happened?" Eden urged her.

"I had a visitor. He told me some things, enough that I was able to piece together all the rest."

"Such as?" Shane pressed her.

"Lissie did go to Savannah, but it couldn't have been right away. Not from the date I was given when she turned up there. It had to have been months after she left Charleston."

Months, Shane figured, that Lissie Reardon must have used to her advantage. Probably covering her trail, maybe by cunningly traveling as far away as she could get before doubling back to this region. Seattle, for instance. He remembered Eden telling him that one of her P.I. family had investigated a sighting in Seattle that went cold.

And, of course, Lissie would have also needed that time to win Nathanial's trust, probably even his love. A two-year-old, after all, has a very short memory, and in a matter of months Nathanial could have been conditioned to forget everything in his past. Because Shane had no doubt at all what Lissie intended from the start, and from the taut expression on Eden's face, he guessed she was thinking the same. Harriet verified as much seconds later.

"When Lissie finally did go to the Jamisons in Savannah," she said, her fingers twisting the robe's collar, "it was as Nathanial's mother. Except she'd renamed him Patrick, after Simon's grandfather."

Shane, seeing Eden close her eyes in pain over the image of another woman replacing her as Nathanial's mother, stretched out an arm toward her chair. His hand found hers, squeezing in brief comfort before he released her. Turning her head, she flashed him a look of gratitude before resolutely facing Harriet again.

"And, of course," Eden said, "Sebastian Jamison must have welcomed them into his home. Why not, when Nathanial was the image of his son and, if any member of the family had demanded it, testing would prove he was Simon's child. I don't suppose they ever questioned Lissie's motherhood. That wouldn't have been an issue."

"She might have showed them snapshots of her and Simon together," Harriet said. "I know she had them, and I remember looking at this one taken when she was pregnant."

"But they had to have wondered why she'd waited almost three years before going to them," Shane pointed out. "What did she tell the Jamisons?"

"I don't know that. Maybe just that she was in need. I guess the old man didn't care. All he cared about was having the miracle of his grandson. He made Patrick one of his heirs."

"Lissie must have been in clover," Shane said dryly.

"You'd think so, but then why did she do what she did?"

"Which was?"

"The old man died about six weeks ago. Lissie took

Patrick and left Savannah. No one knows where or why. It's funny.''

"Yeah, it is," Shane said. "And I'll tell you something else that's funny, Harriet. How did you come to be told all this? Who was this guy who visited you a couple of weeks ago, and what did he want?"

"He was a private investigator. The Jamison family wants Patrick back, and they hired him to find Lissie and recover the boy. He knew Lissie had lived in Charleston, and I don't suppose it took him much digging to learn I was her neighbor and friend. But what could I tell him when I haven't heard a word from Lissie since she left Charleston?"

"The private investigator from Savannah," Eden said. "What was his name?"

There was something about the way she asked her question, maybe with a note of strain in her voice, that made Shane look at her closely.

"Charles Moses," Harriet answered her.

Shane saw Eden's mouth tighten and knew that he wasn't imagining her strain. The name Charles Moses meant something to her, just as the name Reardon had seemed familiar to him. He and Eden would have questions for each other on this subject, but this wasn't the time for them. They still had Harriet Krause to deal with.

"There's something more we need to know," Shane said to her. "This P.I.—did he ever refer to me? Or anyone that could have meant me?"

"No, he—" Her hand still on the collar of her robe, Harriet paused to clear her throat several times. "I think this cold is beginning to settle in my chest," she complained.

Shane, offering no word of sympathy, waited for her to answer him. Her voice was even more noticeably hoarse when she went on.

"He didn't mention anyone other than the people I already told you about."

"You're sure about that? How about the two gorillas who were bringing me here Saturday night?"

Harriet shook her head in vigorous denial. "I've said I don't know anything about those men. I never heard of them until you told me about them." Her anxious gaze went from Shane to Eden. "I've told you all I know. I cooperated and gave you everything you asked for. Now you've got to promise to keep me out of it, not to—"

"No guarantees, Harriet," Shane cut her off. "We'll do what we can. Right now we need to find a missing child."

Eden nodded in understanding when he sent her an un-spoken question. They were in agreement. There was noth-ing more to be learned from Harriet Krause. It was time they got out of here, breathed air that didn't smell of illness and complicity.

EDEN WAITED until they were out on the street again to express her joy.

"Nathanial is alive!" she said, turning to Shane. "He's still alive! I would never allow myself to believe he didn't survive, and I wouldn't let others try to tell me otherwise, but underneath there was always the fear…"

"That maybe you were wrong," Shane said with an un-derstanding she would have thought only a parent could know. But this man had depths that surprised her at every turn. And warmed her. "But you weren't wrong, Eden. Your boy is still out there."

Or he was six weeks ago when the woman posing as his mother left Savannah with him. But Shane didn't say that, and Eden wouldn't permit herself to think Nathanial didn't continue to be alive.

She and Shane had to talk, had to examine what Harriet Krause had unwillingly shared with them. Had to decide what to do next. But not while they drove aimlessly around the city, Eden thought with a glance at her car beside which they stood. Her taut nerves demanded action.

"Can we walk for a bit?" she asked Shane. "That is, if your leg is up to—"

"Eden, will you stop worrying about my leg? If it bothers me, I'll let you know. And if we walk too far, and I get tired—" he paused to grin at her wickedly "—well, I'll just let you put your arm around me tight and help me back."

His grin suggested a great deal more than his permission for her to assist him in the event of a crisis. There was a promise in it as outrageously sexy as the solid figure of the man who fell into step beside her.

How, Eden wondered as they left her car parked at the curb and headed in the direction of the harbor front, was she supposed to concentrate on business when she was so aware of Shane close beside her? When her feelings for him seemed to grow stronger with each hour they spent together?

And treacherous, she reminded herself sharply. He was still a man without a memory. She didn't know who or what he was any more than he did. However powerful her attraction to him, however convinced she was now of his basic decency, it could turn out that there was a dark, dangerous side to him.

So her emotions couldn't be trusted. Not when there was something so vital as the welfare of her son demanding her immediate, full attention. Shane, too, must have realized the necessity of seriously addressing this subject. The provocative tone was gone from his voice when he spoke to her.

"What do your P.I. instincts say about Harriet Krause?"

"That she's scared and probably regretting at this moment everything we threatened her into telling us. The question is, how much did she *not* tell us?"

"And is she being paid to keep her mouth shut?"

"Lissie Reardon?"

Shane nodded. "Yeah, it's possible this Lissie promised her a cut of the action when she got established with the

Jamisons. Why else would Harriet have risked her career and then kept silent all these years? On the other hand…''

Eden waited for Shane to go on. A horse-drawn carriage passed them out on the street, its driver pointing out the sights to the four occupants on the seats behind him.

''Maybe we're looking in the wrong direction,'' Shane continued. ''Maybe there's another explanation. Like Harriet lying to us about not knowing those two gorillas who grabbed me.''

''If she is involved with them, and it's not Lissie who's paying her, then Harriet is guilty of another complicity. But what?''

''And just where do I fit into this puzzle, and why can't I remember?'' Shane wondered, his frustration so enormous Eden could feel it.

Bahama Street ended at East Battery. They crossed the thoroughfare and mounted the elevated promenade along the seawall, turning to the right in the direction of White Point Gardens. On their left stretched the city's broad, sun-licked harbor. Across Battery to their right were the unbroken ranks of the historic seafront mansions that were the pride of Charleston. But today Eden was immune to their elegance. Her attention was focused on the man who strolled beside her.

''But something Harriet Krause said was familiar to you, wasn't it, Shane?'' she asked him soberly. ''I could see it in your face. The name Reardon had meaning.''

''If it did, I couldn't make sense of it.'' He stopped under a palmetto, whose leaves rattled in the gusts off the harbor, and turned to her. ''But there's one thing I am clear about. I'm the key to Nathanial. There are people who want him back, and they're convinced I know where he is.''

''Yes,'' Eden agreed with him. ''That's become more and more evident.''

They moved on again along the promenade. Shane was silent. When she glanced at his face, she saw him looking out into the distance at the tiny island that was the Fort

Sumter National Monument. But she didn't think he was seeing the island. His gaze was too intense for that.

His voice carried the same intensity when he spoke again. She listened, but she had the feeling he was talking more to himself than her. Impatiently, angrily reproaching himself for his inability to remember.

"And if I do know where he is, if the boy somehow came into my possession, where is he now? What did I do with him, and why does this brain of mine refuse to give up that secret?"

Eden had no answer for him. Her own mind was silently crying the same appeal. *You're somewhere out there, Nathanial. I can feel it. But where are you? Where?*

They crossed Battery again and stood under a live oak at the edge of White Point Gardens. Shane looked into the park at the columned bandstand with that same unseeing gaze. But this time he spoke directly to her, resolve in his deep voice.

"I don't know what I've done or why I did it, and at this point it isn't important. All that matters is finding your boy, which is why we've got to take this whole thing now to the police."

"But you've said all along—"

"I know what I said, and I'm changing my mind. We go to the police, Eden."

"No," she said. "We will not go to the police."

Her complete reversal on this issue was so decisive and so unexpected that he stared at her in surprise. "Why this hundred-and-eighty-degree turn?"

"Because I've been thinking, and it suddenly makes sense. What if you've been resisting the police all along, not for your own sake, but for Nathanial's sake? What if that locked mind of yours has been guarding him and refuses to part with him because it knows you aren't legally entitled to him and that the police would turn him over to the people who do have a legal claim to him? The *wrong* people, Shane. People who could harm him before I could establish my own legal right to my son.''

''And what if I had a mercenary agenda of my own, Eden, and that's why I took the boy and hid him? Are you prepared to risk that?''

''Yes, because I don't think I'm just speculating. I think my explanation is the right one. A man can't be bad and then turn around and be good just because of amnesia.''

''Is that how you see me, Eden?'' he said softly, his voice husky, intimate. ''As a good guy?''

He had turned to face her, and he stood so close that his virile nearness made her light-headed. He might in no way be a threat to Nathanial, but he was a threat to her. It was time to defuse the moment.

''Of course,'' she said lightly. ''You're my husband, aren't you?''

''Yeah, I'm not forgetting that. Okay, so we don't go to the police.''

''Which wouldn't be very useful, anyway, when we don't really have anything concrete to offer them. And I can't see Harriet Krause confessing to them. She'd just deny everything she told us.''

''Probably. So what are you proposing?''

''That we go on trying to find Nathanial ourselves.'' Her voice sobered again with urgency. ''There's something big at stake here, Shane. For all we know, it could be a kidnap-for-ransom plot that somehow went wrong. Whatever it is, I have this awful feeling—call it a mother's intuition—that my son is at risk and that we have to get to him before—''

Eden couldn't bring herself to say it. She didn't want to imagine the worst, though her maternal fear was very real. So strong that she knew she mustn't allow it to interfere with her judgment as a private investigator. Not if she were to save Nathanial.

She didn't have to put it into words for Shane. The concerned expression on his face told her that he understood.

And when he spoke, uttering a single word, it was all she needed to hear to know that their minds were turned in the same direction.

"Savannah?"

"Yes, Savannah," she said, grateful for his acceptance.

He nodded. "Seems the logical place to try next. We've exhausted our leads here, and since the Jamison family is in Savannah, and with Lissie Reardon and the boy having lived there…yeah, we may find the answers in Savannah."

"There's something else I was thinking of," Eden said slowly.

"What?"

"You could also have come from Savannah."

"If that's true, it could explain my connection with this situation. And if there's anything I need right now, it's an explanation, because I'm getting damn weary of this memory block."

"Then let's get back to the car and see what we can do about trying to relieve it."

Eden was anxious to be on the road. It was too late to reach Savannah today, but they could at least make a start, spend the night along the way, and reach Savannah in the morning.

Eden's mind was busy planning a quick stop at her house to collect their things as they hurried back toward Bahama Street and the parked Toyota. Shane's sudden intrusion on her thoughts startled her.

"Charles Moses," he said.

She had wondered when he would get around to that. "The P.I. who called on Harriet Krause. What about him?"

"If the Jamisons hired him to recover Nathanial, it's reasonable to suppose he's based in Savannah, too."

"Maybe."

"But you know who he is, don't you? After the look I saw on your face back at the Krause woman's apartment, I remembered what you told me out at the houseboat. About the P.I. you were supposed to marry before he ended up disappointing you and moved on. Where did he wind up, Eden? Savannah, right? This Moses is the same guy.''

''Yes, Charlie went to Savannah,'' she admitted. ''And if you're asking me whether I'm looking forward to running into him again, I'm not.''

''But a meeting with him will probably be necessary, Eden.''

''I know.'' She would deal with it when she had to, but until then...

By now, they had turned off East Battery and were on their way down Bahama Street.

''There's something else,'' Shane said. ''Harriet Krause insisted I was never mentioned when she met with Moses, but I think she was lying. I think I might not only have been discussed, but that there could be some involvement with Moses and those two—''

Shane came to an abrupt halt on the sidewalk. They had come within sight of her car. But it wasn't the Toyota that had suddenly captured his attention. He was gazing at another vehicle, a silver Mercedes-Benz that had just parked on the opposite side of the street. Or, to be exact about it, he was staring at the two broad-shouldered figures who emerged from the sedan.

A warning stirred inside Eden. This is trouble, she thought. She understood that much even before Shane, cursing savagely, grabbed her by the arm and thrust her protectively behind him.

# Chapter Eight

Eden understood now why Shane had referred to his two adversaries as a pair of gorillas. Even at this distance, more than a block away, she could tell as she peered around Shane that they were all bulk and brawn. Gorillas in business suits and driving a luxury car.

Eden had no doubt at all that these were the brutes who had captured and beaten Shane. She knew he had immediately recognized them, and his reaction terrified her. His body was tensed for action, his hands at his sides curled into fists. Fists that she realized he wouldn't hesitate to swing with the force of hammers. Courageous, but a mistake.

"Shane, no," she appealed to him, plucking at the sleeve of his jacket. "We've got to get out of sight."

"Too late. They've already spotted us."

It was true. The heavier of the two men had looked up the street, noticed them on the sidewalk, and was now excitedly alerting his companion. This second gorilla had a head of close-cropped hair so pale it was almost white, and a yell worthy of Tarzan.

His shout of discovery was still ringing in the air when Shane's hand whipped around to the back side of his belt where he still carried the pistol under his jacket. Another mistake.

"You can't!" Eden cried. "Not out here on the street!

Not when they're probably armed themselves! We wouldn't stand a chance!''

She prayed that Shane would accept the wisdom of her argument, and was relieved when his hand dropped back to his side. "You're right. A shoot-out isn't smart."

"Please," she pleaded with him, "let's get out of here."

And fast, she thought, because the two gorillas were already pounding up the pavement in their direction. She could imagine how much Shane hated the idea of turning and running, but he must have realized that Eden's safety, as well as the outcome of their investigation, depended at this stage on flight. They had to stay free if they were going to find Nathanial.

"Later, then," Shane said with cold anger, swinging around and snatching her by the hand. She knew he was promising himself a future meeting with his enemies, one in which he would confront and deal with them without the need to retreat.

How? Eden wondered as they raced back toward the waterfront. How did those two know we were here? Because it couldn't be chance that they'd arrived on the scene. Harriet Krause? Did she lie about not knowing them? Fear what we would do after we left her apartment? That we would fail to keep her out of it, and in a panic she phoned this pair of thugs, hoping they would take care of us?

Or had it been the frightened caretaker back at the Jolly Mariner motel who'd called them? Roy, who had known she and Shane would be coming here, because he had provided them with Harriet Krause's address?

But what did it matter who had contacted them? They were here and a threat she and Shane had to lose. She was worried about that, worried about Shane's leg. She didn't dare mention his leg to him, though. He didn't want to be reminded it might in any way be a problem for him, and so far he was managing, moving with an amazing speed that left her breathless as he drew her along. But the leg had already been stressed by two lengthy walks today. How long could Shane maintain this pace? Or she, herself, for that matter?

"Which way?" he asked, pausing on the corner as they reached East Battery again.

Eden glanced back. Their pursuers were still almost a block away but slowly gaining on them. She and Shane couldn't hope to outdistance them. They needed a refuge. But what and where?

Shane supplied the answer when a boat whistle sounded, signaling an imminent departure from a landing on the other side of East Battery.

"Whatever it is, let's see if we can get on board."

The thoroughfare was a busy one, but there was a break in the traffic that permitted them to streak across the street to the seawall.

It was probably one of the excursion boats, Eden thought. She knew there were several places along the waterfront that offered various tours of the harbor. Her guess proved correct when they reached the promenade and were able to look down on the craft, whose crew was preparing to cast off the lines. But the prospect of their being accepted among the passengers crowded on deck wasn't good.

"Charter buses," she said, indicating the two long vehicles parked along the promenade. "That means a private party hired the boat."

"We've just become two of its members," Shane promised her with a confidence she admired but wasn't ready to trust.

Eden cast a last anxious look over her shoulder as he hurried her to the steps that descended to the landing. Their pursuers had reached the corner but were prevented from crossing the street by a heavy flow of rapid traffic. She blessed the delay forced on them. But would it be long enough to permit Shane and her to board the vessel? To put a watery distance between them and their enemies? That is, if they were even allowed on board. Eden still had her doubts about that.

"Hang on!" Shane shouted to the crew about to release the lines. "Don't leave without us!"

Eden felt his strong arm around her waist, rushing her to the craft and practically flinging her onto its deck before scrambling after her. They had made it! And were immediately challenged.

"What's this? You're not part of our tour."

The officious young man who confronted them had a loop of tickets in one hand, a packet of brochures in the other and a scowl on his face that indicated an intolerant disposition.

"Sure we are," Shane said boldly. "Been with you from the start."

Shane's lie earned him a sneer. "Is that so? Funny that I can't recall you. And I don't imagine I'd forget any of the faces on my bus."

*He's the tour guide,* Eden decided, *and we've had it.*

Mercifully, an elderly woman nearby came to their defense. "I think I remember them, Ozzie. They're from the other bus."

"That's right, Ozzie," Shane said. "We're part of the other bus."

"Then what are you doing on this boat? You should have been on the first boat that pulled out ahead of us."

"Got delayed in a souvenir shop across the road," Shane said. "Wife here can't resist those souvenirs."

"Uh-huh."

"Aw, Ozzie, don't be a stinker," an old man in a baseball cap and thick glasses spoke up. "What difference does it make what boat they're on? There's plenty of room."

They're *all* seniors, Eden realized as she gazed at the faces around them. What had they gotten themselves into?

Not that it was important as long as this boat moved, which it hadn't yet, although its engine was throbbing. She looked frantically toward the steps from the promenade. No sign of their pursuers on them yet. They were probably dodging traffic on the street, but it could only be a matter of seconds before they appeared.

The hostile tour guide relented. "Oh, all right. Just find your seats, all of you, so we can get under way."

He signaled to the pilot at the wheel, and to Eden's relief the craft began to draw away from the landing. Their departure was just in time. At that moment the two burly figures charged down the steps to the landing.

Eden whispered a quick prayer of thanks to whatever god was looking out for them. There was a safe barrier now, widening rapidly, between the boat and the landing. The two men stood there, their broad faces wearing furious expressions as they watched their quarry escape.

Eden could see now that the heavier of the pair was also fair-haired, though a much darker shade of blond than his companion. In fact, they were enough alike to be brothers, which meant they probably were. They both had the hard looks of men who didn't concern themselves with how they got what they wanted. Or cared who they hurt. It was a realization that made Eden shiver.

Aware of her reaction, Shane murmured a quick reassurance. "It's all right, Eden. We've left them behind. Uh, I don't suppose that one of our two friends back there happens to be your Charles Moses?"

She shook her head. "Not unless Charlie acquired muscles since I saw him last, and weight lifting wasn't one of his favorite recreations."

"I didn't think so, but the idea did cross my mind. Ozzie is glaring at us. I guess we'd better behave ourselves and find some seats."

The elderly man and woman who had come to their rescue made room for them on one of the benches under the canopy that roofed the open deck.

"Got another question for you," Shane whispered when they were squeezed side by side. "Just where are we going?"

"I don't know," Eden whispered back. "Maybe out to Fort Sumter, or maybe it's just a general tour of the harbor. Shane, have you noticed? We're the youngest couple here.

No wonder the guide is suspicious. I think we've just joined a seniors' bus tour.''

"Where you folks from?" the man in the baseball cap asked them.

"Chicago," Eden replied.

"Cleveland," Shane answered simultaneously.

The old man looked puzzled until Eden hastily explained. "That's where each of us was from originally."

"Chicago, huh?" He nodded. "Used to visit cousins there."

He went on to reminisce about Chicago while the gulls swooped overhead, the boat chugged onward through the choppy waters of the harbor, and Eden tried not to mind the chill wind blowing in from the open sea. She only half listened as she tried to determine their destination. She couldn't ask, not when she was supposed to know where they were going.

Maybe Shane would have better luck with his own neighbor. He and the old lady on his side were engaged in a friendly conversation. A moment later he leaned over close to Eden and spoke softly in her ear.

"We're okay. It is a theme tour, but age isn't a requirement."

She turned her head and looked at him. There was a gleam in his eyes. She wondered if she ought to be worried about it. "Then what is?"

"Marriage. This is the Renew-Your-Wedding-Vows Bus Tour."

"You're kidding."

"I swear. It's a second honeymoon kind of thing. It all winds up at a fancy hotel where all the couples renew their wedding vows in this mass ceremony. Guess it's a good thing we bought these matching bands, huh?"

"What are you doing?"

Shane had caught her hand and was lifting it to his mouth. For a moment he was too busy to answer her. He spent several seconds nuzzling the backs of her fingers.

Then, turning her hand over, he began planting warm kisses in the hollow of her palm.

Things happened whenever he touched her like this. Things that made her go all limp and weak. Things that cost her her self-control.

"Shane—"

"Quiet," he ordered her in a low voice. "I'm playing devoted husband. Ozzie is standing over there looking at us suspiciously again. You want him to think we're not the genuine article?"

As far as Eden could tell, the tour guide was not particularly interested in them at this moment. And Shane was carrying this masquerade too far. She should have objected when, head bent over her hand once more, he resumed his attentions to her palm. But she didn't.

It was a slow, sensual affair. A thorough one that involved caresses from his lips, little nibbles with his teeth, and the tip of his tongue stroking her willing flesh. The breath stuck in Eden's throat while her head spun with the hot memories of what this same mouth had done to her back at the houseboat.

There was no telling how long Shane would have lingered over her hand if his elderly neighbor's loud, wistful sigh hadn't startled Eden into restoring her reason. She quickly withdrew her hand.

"I don't know how long you two have been married, but anyone can tell you don't need to repeat wedding vows to remind yourselves what you mean to each other." She poked the man next to her in the ribs. "Stan, why don't you ever make love to my hand like that?"

"I gave it a big diamond, didn't I? Say, how much farther is it to this Patriots Point?"

Eden and Shane exchanged glances. Now that she knew their destination on the far side of the harbor, she explained it to him in a rapid whisper. "It's a maritime museum. The navy retired four of its ships there. The aircraft carrier *Yorktown* is the main attraction."

Shane nodded. Turning away from him, Eden strained

forward in her seat, trying to measure the distance they had yet to travel to reach Patriots Point. "This is good," she murmured, her gaze on the approaching docks where the four vessels were permanently berthed. "We won't have to risk going back to that landing, because there's a visitors' center at the point. We should be able to catch a taxi there to take us back to the car. With any luck, our friends won't be hanging around Bahama Street by then."

Shane had no answer for her. When she turned to him again, the teasing gleam had gone from his eyes.

"They aren't back on Bahama Street, Eden," he said, jerking his thumb over his shoulder. "They're behind us."

Alarmed, Eden swung around on her seat. While she had been looking forward, Shane must have been checking their rear. The sight that met her gaze made her heart lurch in dismay. There was a speedboat behind them. It was still some distance away but plowing steadily in their direction. She couldn't mistake the two figures standing near its bow, legs braced apart.

Their pursuers hadn't surrendered the chase. They had managed to hire a motorboat. A fast one.

Why? Eden wondered. Why were they so determined to catch Shane again?

It was an unnecessary question. She knew the answer, didn't she?

*To force him to give up the secret they're convinced he's hiding, that's why. To make him reveal to them what he's done with Nathanial, because they don't know he's lost his memory.*

Not that she and Shane knew for certain this was their aim, but everything they had learned so far indicated as much. Anyway, there was only one question here that really mattered: why was Nathanial so important to those two that they would resort to every desperate measure to find him? Did it involve a kidnapping for ransom?

Remembering the glimpse she'd had of their brutish faces as the excursion boat pulled away from the landing, Eden was convinced their motive was not a virtuous one.

The sickening thought of either of them ever getting his hands on her son made her shake with anger.

Shane must have been aware of her agitation. He took her hand again and held it, not in any mischievous seduction this time but in comfort. She was thankful for his solid presence.

Both of them kept twisting around to check on the progress of the speedboat. It was clearly gaining on them.

"What if they catch up with our boat?" Eden whispered into Shane's ear. "What then?"

"I deal with them," he said, his voice like flint. "But I think we're going to make it."

Eden, too, could see that they were nearing their objective. The immense World War II aircraft carrier loomed in front of them. Probably less than a quarter of a mile away now. And then came a maddening delay.

The tour boat slowed to a crawl as a shrimp boat cut across its bow. Eden cast another nervous glance behind her. The speedboat was closing on them rapidly.

*Move,* she silently urged their own craft. *Please, move.*

The shrimp boat cleared them, and the tour boat gathered speed again. A moment later they were mooring at a floating landing on the harbor side of the *Yorktown*. The lines had yet to be secured, when Shane drew Eden to her feet and hurried her toward the exit.

The speedboat had also arrived on the scene, but it was forced to stand off from the small landing until the tour boat had disembarked its passengers. She and Shane could still make a successful escape. Except for one problem.

"This isn't where I expected them to deliver us," she murmured to Shane. "I assumed we'd dock at the pier around on the land side. That's where the center is and where visitors usually arrive."

"It looks like we don't have any choice but to board the carrier," he said, eyeing the hanging stairway attached to the lofty side of the *Yorktown*.

As swiftly as Eden and Shane had moved toward the exit in order to be among the first off the tour boat, there were still people ahead of them. And another frustrating delay while the tour guide, who stood beside the opened gate in the rail, handed out tickets and brochures.

Ozzie looked at them again with disapproval when they reached the gate. But all he said when he gave them their tickets and a brochure was a cool, "You have one hour to explore. Enjoy your visit."

Those who had disembarked ahead of them were already climbing the long stairway to the top deck of the carrier. There was no room to squeeze around them, though this was exactly what Eden longed to do as she and Shane followed them up the tall flight.

Looking down, she could see the two gorillas on the speedboat glowering up at them. Their impatient craft, no longer willing to wait, was jockeying for a position at the floating landing. And all Eden could do was cry a silent, frantic plea to the line ahead of them: *Hurry, hurry.*

As they neared the top, the elevation permitted them a view of the other three vessels at the point, a destroyer, submarine and Coast Guard cutter, all of them dwarfed by the enormous *Yorktown*. There was another sight directly below them, a chilling one. The speedboat had managed to nose in close enough to permit its two passengers to leap the gap from deck to landing. Eden watched them hurl themselves toward the stairway, prepared like a pair of bulldozers to shove their way through the crowd still ascending the flight.

Shane, too, had seen them. "We've still got time," he said calmly, drawing her up the last few steps.

They emerged on the flight deck where an attendant greeted the arrivals, took their tickets and informed them they could either join one of the conducted tours or visit on their own any of the areas designated in their brochures.

Shane pulled her off to one side. "Which way to the land side exit? Do you know?"

Eden had visited the *Yorktown* only once before, and her recollections weren't dependable. She certainly hadn't remembered how vast the flight deck was, its length stretching out before them like a football field for giants.

"Toward the stern, I think. Yes, I'm pretty sure of that."

"And we're up near the bow. The expanse is too long and too open. Bruno and Boris would be on top of us before we could make it. And if they pull guns with all these people around—"

"There must be security on board."

"Not enough time to call security." Shane looked around, spotting an inside companionway that descended to the lower decks. "Let's see if we can lose them below. On a ship this big that shouldn't be too hard."

We could also get lost ourselves before we find that exit, Eden thought, but she didn't argue with him as they sped through the shadow of the carrier's soaring superstructure.

They passed a group surfacing from the companionway, the guide telling his charges, "We're going to visit the bridge now before we head for the Combat Information Center. It was the nerve center of the carrier during operations. Notice the antiaircraft batteries located on both port and starboard sides as we…"

Eden looked back just before she and Shane plunged down the companionway. The two thugs had arrived on the flight deck. Had they spotted them? She had no chance to find out. She was too busy negotiating the steep companionway, which felt more like a ladder than stairs.

The stairway carried them to the next level where they paused to consider their options. They found themselves in the huge hangar bays. Visitors wandered around, examining the World War II planes that were on display and the massive elevators that had lifted the aircraft to the flight deck above.

"Still much too open," Shane said. "We'd be asking them to catch up with us. Let's go down again."

They descended to the next deck, and here the companionway ended.

"You have the brochure," Shane said. "Which way?"

Eden consulted the diagram of the carrier's layout in the

brochure. It wasn't a very adequate map. "To the left. That should take us to the rear of the ship."

They hurried along a corridor, passing facilities whose meaning was lost on Eden. But Shane seemed to understand them.

"Wardroom," he said.

"What is—"

"Officers' quarters."

How would he know that? she wondered. And then she remembered what his disclosures under hypnosis had suggested. That he might have recently served in some branch of the military. This was further evidence of that possibility.

With this area of the carrier being less interesting, there were fewer people around. But Shane wasn't satisfied, and when they came to another companionway, he took them still lower in the ship.

Their feet clanged hollowly on the metal treads. It was a lonely sound, and one that seemed to echo so loudly in the silence Eden feared their pursuers couldn't help hearing it. Not that there had been any sign of them since they'd left the flight deck, but she kept worrying that at any moment she and Shane would turn a corner and run smack into them.

Where were they now? she wondered when they paused again. She had lost count but thought this might be the fourth deck. Wherever it was, they were in the bowels of the ship. There was no one around. They seemed to be the only ones currently at this level.

Shane turned to her. "I want you to have this back before we go on." Removing the pistol from under his jacket, he held it out to her. "Just in case we get separated."

"Shane, no. It's you they want, not me."

"Damn it, Eden, don't fight me on this. I need you to have some way to defend yourself if I should get in a situation where I can't protect you. I'll be all right if I know that."

She could see he wasn't going to move until she accepted the gun, and they were losing time. She took the pistol and tucked it into her purse. But she intended for them not to be separated.

Praying to God they weren't, she followed him down a long passage. Because if they were, she was afraid they might never find each other again. The ship was like a vast maze, and she no longer knew where they were. But Shane seemed by some directional instinct to be confidently working them toward the stern of the vessel and that vital exit.

They met no one in the gloomy passage. Stacked berths in the open compartments off either side indicated these were the quarters for the crew.

Where were their enemies? she kept wondering. Far away in another part of the carrier or close behind them? It was unnerving not to know.

They turned a corner and traveled along another passage. No stacked berths here, but there were several doors that puzzled Eden. They were constructed of thick steel and had small window openings that were barred. The doors opened outward and had been swung back against the passage walls, permitting her glimpses of the compact interiors.

"Cells," she said. "They look just like jail cells."

"They are," Shane said. "This is the ship's brig."

They went on to the end of the passage, expecting it to branch off into another corridor. But the passage dead-ended in a solid wall. The heel of Shane's hand slapped its surface in frustration.

"I should have known it wouldn't run through without coming up against a bulkhead. We'll have to go back, maybe try another level."

They were losing time, Eden thought as they turned around and retraced their route. They should have been off the ship by now, not caught down here where—

Shane put a hand on her arm, bringing her to a halt. "Listen," he whispered.

And then she heard it, too. The sound of approaching footsteps from somewhere around the corner in front of them. They were followed by voices. Male voices raised in an argument.

"We're wasting our time."

"I'm telling you, that guy I asked said he'd seen a couple matching their description headed down this way."

The footsteps came to a stop.

"All right, maybe we'll have better luck finding them if we separate. You go on looking here, and I'll go back the other way. Just watch your step. This bastard is tricky, and we don't want to lose him again."

Eden didn't need to see their faces to know who they were. *And here we are trapped in this dead end,* she thought, her body rigid with fear.

Hand still on her arm, Shane drew her swiftly back the way they had come. When they reached the first cell, he motioned her inside. Pulling the door after him so that it was just barely ajar, he joined her in the cell.

In the dimness she could make out a narrow bed against the wall at a right angle to the door. In the opposite corner was a stool and next to it a sink below a mirror. Except for these, the cell was bare.

"Get on the cot," he whispered, "and make yourself as small as possible."

She could tell by the certainty in his voice that he had a plan, but there was no time to ask him about it. Obeying him, she placed herself on the bed and squeezed into the corner, legs drawn up against her breasts. Once silently settled, she reached into her purse and withdrew the pistol, gripping it tightly in her hand.

Shane had flattened himself against the wall close beside the door. His gaze was focused on the mirror opposite him. She guessed then what he intended. While she had curled into the corner on the bed, he had quickly managed to angle the mirror over the sink so that now, from his position next to the door, it gave him a reflected view through the window of the passage outside.

Eden couldn't see that stretch of passage from her own position. But she knew seconds later, by the way Shane's tall figure tensed in readiness, that their opponent was coming down the hall. More seconds passed as they waited, an indication to Eden that the lone enemy must be pausing to check out areas as he advanced.

*Come on, come on. Just get here, will you?*

As she watched in unbearable suspense, Shane's body seemed to coil like a taut spring. His timing had the perfection of a professional athlete. In one instant he was crouched there. In the next he was at the door, his body driving against it with all the force of a linebacker in lightning action.

The thick steel door burst outward, slamming into Shane's target. The blow must have been a powerful one. Eden heard a single startled yelp followed by the sound of a heavy body striking the floor. Then there was silence.

Shane shot out into the passage. Eden, scrambling off the bed, followed. She found Shane bending over the sprawled body of the towheaded gorilla.

"You can put that away," he said, indicating the pistol in her hand. "We're not going to need it."

"Is he—"

"No, just stunned. But from the looks of that nose, he's going to be feeling pretty miserable when he comes to. And probably as mad as a bull. Take a leg and help me drag him into the cell."

The burly figure never stirred as they dumped him into a corner of the cell. But from the way Shane's fists were balled as he stood over the man, Eden knew he was ready to deal with him if he regained consciousness before they left the cell.

"Can we lock him in here?" she asked.

"Probably not. They would have fixed these doors so that some tourist didn't get himself trapped inside the brig. But maybe—" His glance fell on the bed. "Let's slide the cot out into the hall."

The bed was just long enough, once they had situated it crossways in the passage, to reach from the wall on one side to the closed cell door on the other side. Its stout steel frame made an effective wedge.

"That should hold him," Shane said. "At least until a

tour wanders this way and hears him shouting his head off.''

''Can we get off this level now before the other one turns up again?''

''I vote for that.''

They made their way cautiously back to the nearest companionway. There was no sign of the towhead's companion, but Eden remained anxious about his whereabouts as they climbed the stairway to the level above them.

''Third deck,'' Shane said. ''Let's see if this one will take us to that exit.''

''Where are we now?'' Eden wondered a moment later, consulting the brochure again. ''I'm still lost, and this map is useless.''

They had entered a mammoth room furnished with long tables and benches.

''Crew's mess,'' Shane said.

He led them through the sea of tables to the far wall where a series of serving hatches, their doors raised, revealed on the other side the main ship's galley with what seemed like acres of stainless-steel equipment.

They spared the galley no more than a glance. Their interest was in the open doorway just ahead of them and the passage beyond it. Its width indicated it was a main corridor with the promise of stretching all the way to the exit in the vicinity of the stern.

They were passing the last hatch when there was a sudden eruption of noise somewhere off that corridor. It sounded to Eden like the banging of locker doors, as if someone was conducting a hurried investigation. The other thug searching for them?

''Stay here while I take a look,'' Shane said.

He was gone, moving out into the passage before she could object. He should have taken the gun with him, not left it with me, she thought. Slipping the pistol out of her purse again, she hung back by the open hatch and held the weapon in readiness in case it should be needed.

Eden's attention was on the figure of Shane prowling up

the passage. She had no awareness of any stealthy activity in the galley on the other side of the hatch. When from the corner of her eye she did finally catch a shadowy movement, it was too late. A hand lunged out over the counter, gripping her by the arm just below her elbow.

Eden cried out and then began to struggle against her attacker, whose face beneath his streaky blond hair was livid on the other side of the hatch. He wrestled her for possession of the pistol, and for a moment she was able to hold on to it. But in the end the semiautomatic leaped out of her hand and went flying off into the galley where it landed with a thunk, disappearing somewhere among the clutter of equipment.

Not satisfied with her surrender of the gun, her attacker began to drag her toward him, as if he intended to pull her through the hatch. Eden resisted but lost ground inch by inch against his superior strength.

His forearm was directly beneath the door of the hatch when Shane raced back into the mess and, with the same speed he had used in defeating their enemy's partner, caught the edge of the door and brought it smashing down on his arm.

Abruptly released, Eden staggered back from the hatch and the savage howl of pain on the other side of its lowered door. What followed was a blur of events so swift they scarcely registered with her.

Had the gorilla managed to free his arm? He must have. Then must have, from the sound of it, gotten off a wild shot that struck metal on the other side. Her gun or his own? She would never know. Nor did she even know if he had a weapon in his hand when he vaulted over the counter through one of the other hatches.

Not that his enraged performance was of any use to him. Eden had the impression of Shane being ready for him, his fist connecting with some portion of its owner's heavy body before it even landed. That same body went crashing into one of the tables with such force that it was robbed of consciousness.

The next thing Eden knew, this time with full awareness, Shane was rushing her along the corridor outside.

"What just happened?" she asked, trying to sort it out.

"Not much. You all right?"

"Dandy. I lost my gun."

"You can buy another."

Yes, she guessed it wouldn't be smart going back and trying to find the pistol. Not with a flock of people charging toward them behind an alarmed tour guide.

"What's going on back there?" the guide demanded.

"Couple of guys fighting in the mess," Shane informed him innocently. "We got out of there."

"Did one of them have a gun? I thought I heard gunfire."

"Beats me."

"I've called security. You folks stay here," he instructed his group. "And, kids, please, no more slamming of locker doors."

"This the way off the ship?" Shane asked him.

"Yes, straight ahead, but don't you think you ought to wait until you explain just what—"

Shane and Eden were on their way to the exit before he could stop them.

# Chapter Nine

"Cleveland?"

Shane, his hand protectively cupping Eden's elbow as they fled along the pier away from the *Yorktown,* turned his head and looked at her. There must have been a puzzled expression on his face, because she breathlessly elaborated on her question.

"We've been just a bit too occupied for me to ask you this until now, but on the tour boat when that old man asked us where we were from, and I said Chicago and you said Cleveland…"

"Ah, that Cleveland." He was beginning to understand. "And you were wondering if maybe it popped out of me like that because Cleveland *is* where I'm from. Sorry, Eden, it didn't mean anything. It was just a place I snatched at. At least I think that's the explanation. Look, there's a taxi pulling up. Let's see if we can grab it."

Four young sailors, eager to explore the ships that their predecessors had served on, were settling with the driver when Eden and Shane reached the taxi. The cabbie was happy to have another fare back into the heart of the city.

And Eden was equally happy to put Patriots Point behind them. Shane noticed the relieved look on her face as they pulled away from the maritime museum. But there was also a slight note of regret in her voice when, after a hurried glance through the back window, as if to assure herself they weren't being followed, she turned to him.

"I don't suppose there was any hope of getting either of those two to tell us exactly what's going on."

Shane shook his head. "I wouldn't have minded having a go at it, but security would have been on top of us before we had the chance to get anything out of them. And security—"

"Would have turned us over to the police, and we have to stay free to find Nathanial. I do wish, though, there had been time to look for my gun. If the police get it, and with it being registered to me—"

"You can explain what happened, but until then…"

"Yes, we have to go on to Savannah. Unless, Cleveland aside, you've experienced something useful."

There was a hopeful look in those fantastic blue eyes that she trained on him. He knew what she was asking him, and he hated to disappoint her again.

"I wish I could tell you that some new memories have surfaced by now. I'd give anything if they would, but they haven't, no matter how hard I've been reaching for them."

"Nothing at all?"

"Just what I told you this morning, and those shadows that came out of my session with Atlanta Johnson last night."

Shane thought about those images as the cab worked its way through the early stages of the evening rush hour traffic on its way to the Cooper River bridges. He wished the meaning of them wasn't stuck down there in the depths of his mind. Whatever they signified, a military operation gone wrong or something else, he had the persistent, bleak feeling that he'd screwed up somehow. That maybe he was to blame for lost lives.

The possibility haunted him. Made him wonder, when his memory did return, whether he would ever be able to forgive himself. Or if the torment would stay with him for the rest of his life.

There was something else. Another shadow that lurked under his consciousness. It wasn't exactly a faint image like the others, more of an impression really. But he could feel her buried in his memory.

*Her?*

All right, it was a woman, and she had once mattered to him. How much and in what connection he didn't know. Except there was one thing he was clear about. Whenever he thought of her, it was in past terms, which had to mean she was gone from his life. So, whoever she was, or had been, she was no longer a reality.

But the woman sitting beside him in the back seat of the cab *was* altogether real to him. Shane's gaze slid in her direction, resting on her in a mixture of desire and tenderness.

Did Eden have any idea how tantalizing she was? Not because she was beautiful; her features lacked the necessary balance for that. But she didn't need those kind of looks. Not when she had that incredible mouth going for her, the ivory skin framed by her dark, dark hair and those pure blue eyes and thick lashes.

He wasn't going to start on her figure. He was in enough trouble as it was where she was concerned. Had been all day, his groin tightening whenever she came near him.

No, he decided, she probably didn't know how desirable she was. In that area, if no other, she lacked confidence in herself. He wanted to show her just how wrong Charles Moses, and any other man who might have hurt her, had been not to hang on to her. Wanted to let her know all about the other qualities she possessed that had nothing to do with sensual pleasure but everything to do with a man valuing a woman for more than just her body.

Only Shane couldn't tell her these things. He had no right to tell her, not when his life was still a blank, with no identity. But there was something he could share with her, that she deserved to know if he stood any chance at all with her when this was all over. Chance? Yeah, he guessed that was just what he did want.

"I know this sounds like a line a million guys have used before me," he said, "but about those shadows…"

She looked at him, bemused.

"There's another one who's a woman," he continued, telling her all about it.

"The Beth you referred to under hypnosis?"

"Could be. Whoever she is, I want you to know I don't belong to her. She isn't waiting for me. No one is, Eden."

"How can you be sure of that? You can't be sure."

"My gut-level instincts tell me it's true. And, memory or no memory, I think I must be someone who's always relied on his instincts."

She nodded, but Shane had the miserable feeling his certainty had left her unconvinced.

CHARLESTON WAS BATHED in the ruddy glow of a vivid sunset when the taxi reached Bahama Street where they had left the car. Their major concern at this point was not to be delayed by any further encounter with the two gorillas. Though it wasn't likely, the pair might have managed to leave the *Yorktown* and return by speedboat in time to intercept them.

But that concern was forgotten when the taxi delivered them to their destination. Or as close as the driver could get to it, which was nearly a half block away from the Toyota.

"Looks like I'll have to drop you off here, folks. I'm sure not gonna be able to get through *that.*"

The street in front of Harriet Krause's building was blocked by several vehicles with flashing lights. A crowd of spectators was gathered there.

Eden prayed that the scene in progress had nothing to do with them. But she had an uneasy feeling, after she paid the driver and joined Shane on the sidewalk, that this event was no coincidence and they were in some way connected with it.

"We'd better see what's up," Shane said.

"Do you think we should risk it?"

"We don't have a choice, Eden. Your car isn't going anywhere until the street is cleared."

But Eden wasn't happy about the situation. She could see as they approached the activity that the flashing lights belonged to an ambulance and three police cruisers. Two uniformed officers were so busy holding the curious back that Eden and Shane were able to melt into the crowd unobserved.

*I don't know why I should be worried,* she thought. *The police can't be interested in us, except maybe to question us about what happened aboard the* Yorktown. *And even if that episode had been reported to them by now, it certainly wouldn't be a priority.*

On the other hand, she and Shane had yet to learn that he wasn't a wanted man, although at this moment he didn't seem troubled by that possibility.

"What's all the excitement?" he asked the man next to him.

"They're saying a woman was murdered in one of the apartments up there."

"She *was* murdered," the woman beside him insisted. "I know the neighbor who found her and called the cops. There's a detective questioning Walter right now."

"So, maybe it was an accident or suicide," the man suggested.

"Oh, *please*. Lying facedown with the back of her skull split open? I don't think so."

"Who was she?" Eden asked, fearing what was already obvious.

"I don't remember Walt saying, but she worked for one of them sperm banks. It'll be on the six o'clock news."

Anxious to prevent the possibility of their own names being included in that broadcast, Eden laid her hand on

Shane's arm and drew him out of the crowd and over to the sidewalk on the opposite side of the street.

"Harriet Krause," she murmured, hearing the shock in her voice as she faced him. She had a genuine reason now to be worried. "If we were seen entering or leaving her apartment, the police will be looking for us."

"There isn't anything we can tell them about her death."

"Except that we might have been the last people to see her alive."

"No, that would have been her killer."

"Or killers. Those two brutes who were after us…"

"They couldn't have murdered her, Eden. They'd just pulled up when they spotted us, and after that they were busy chasing us."

"But if they beat us back here…"

Shane shook his head. "Not enough time."

"You're right. Even if they had somehow managed to get back here ahead of us, all this couldn't have happened before we turned up again. Harriet's death, the neighbor finding her, the police arriving on the scene. That has to mean she was killed shortly after we left her apartment, while the four of us were playing cat and mouse. But who—"

Eden's speculation was interrupted by a swell of fresh excitement across the street. The two officers parted the crowd to allow for the passage of a gurney. Glimpsing the black body bag it bore as it was loaded into one of the emergency vehicles, Eden knew this was Harriet Krause on her way to a forensic facility. It was not a pleasant sight.

Members of the crime investigation team followed the gurney out of the building and began to make their way to their cars. Eden tensed at the sight of them.

"Relax," Shane said. "No one is looking this way. We're just another pair of gapers."

But Eden wasn't satisfied until they shrank back into the concealing shadows at the mouth of an alley just behind them. That's when she noticed something neither one of them had observed until now.

"Shane, it's missing! The Mercedes was parked just about out there in front of where we're standing now, and it's gone! Those two *had* to have gotten back here ahead of us and driven off before the street was blocked."

"There's another possibility you're not considering. A far more likely one."

Eden stared at him. And then she, too, understood it. "There could have been someone else with them. Someone we didn't see because he stayed behind in the car. And whoever it was might have gone up afterward into Harriet's apartment and—"

She didn't finish. Their attention was drawn again to the street where a path was being cleared for the departure of the emergency vehicles. Two men—probably the detectives on the case—emerged from the building, spoke to one of the uniformed officers, then drove off in their own car. The crowd was beginning to break up, drift away.

"Your ex-boyfriend, Charles Moses," Shane said to her softly. "Could he be capable of murder?"

Eden shook her head. "I don't know. There was a lot about Charlie that in the end I realized I didn't know. Do you think he was the third occupant in the Mercedes?"

"Maybe. We know he met with Harriet Krause, and if Bruno and Boris were working with him… Yeah, he might have paid Harriet another visit today, one that ended with her death."

"And then afterward fled in the Mercedes." Eden gazed at the building across the street, its upper windows reflecting the last flaming light of sunset, and felt the sudden lure of her P.I. instincts tugging at her strongly. "I'd give anything to have a look inside Harriet Krause's apartment. And that's an urge that doesn't make sense, because what could I possibly expect to find that the police haven't already turned up?"

Shane didn't answer her. He looked out at the street.

There were only a few bystanders now. A single police cruiser parked at the curb was all that was left of the crime investigation team. Its lone officer remained on watch out in front of the apartment house.

"My car isn't hemmed in anymore," Eden said. "There's no reason for us not to leave."

"Did you notice?" Shane said. "There were no women on that team. They were all men."

She had learned that Shane sometimes had an oblique way of approaching his subjects. She assumed this was one of those occasions. "What are you saying?"

"That a woman has the ability to observe useful things about another woman, or in this case her possessions, that a man can easily overlook."

"You're not proposing—"

"Sure I am."

"And just how do you expect us to get past that cop over there and inside an apartment whose door is sure to be locked and sealed with the kind of bright yellow tape that gets you in trouble if you fool with it?"

"Maybe that door isn't the only way in. Let's drive around the block and see what the back has to offer."

"Shane, this isn't smart."

"You're a private investigator, aren't you?"

It was a challenge Eden's family pride couldn't ignore, though she questioned her sanity when she found herself fifteen minutes later clambering around an ancient fire escape. And hoping neither one of them lost their footing on the iron rungs in the rapidly fading light. Not that the deepening twilight didn't have the advantage of concealing them in the shadows, should any of the neighbors happen to look out their windows.

"See," Shane whispered, indicating the door at the top of the fire escape. "There is another entrance."

"And lots of that yellow police tape stretched across it," she whispered back as they reached the landing. "Though I don't know why the tape was necessary. The last time I

saw a door this solid it was on a vault. Shane, we can't
possibly force our way in here.''

"Yeah, but look at the window over there. I think I can
reach it.''

Eden eyed the window several feet away off the side of
the landing. It had frosted glass, which probably meant it
was a bathroom window.

"It's probably locked.''

"Probably, but maybe I can pry it open.'' He fished in
his pocket, producing the screwdriver he had taken from
the glove compartment in Eden's car.

"Careful,'' she whispered, watching him as he stretched
out over the railing.

"Let's see just how locked it is,'' he said, one hand
around the screwdriver, the other tugging on the sash. To
Eden's amazement, the window lifted without an argument.
"What do you know. It wasn't locked. Here.''

He passed the screwdriver to her, leaned out even more
precariously over the railing, clamped his hands securely
over the window frame and swung himself into space. For
a breathless moment he hung there, and then with the
strength of a gymnast, he lifted himself through the opening.

Whatever he was, or had been, Eden thought with a mixture of relief and admiration, it must have required rigorous
conditioning.

Shane stuck his head out. "There's a good reason why
the window wasn't locked. The catch is broken. Hold on
while I come around to the door.''

Eden waited on the landing, looking nervously into the
gathering darkness and hoping that she wouldn't hear some
voice down below raised in a sudden challenge. But the
only sound that reached her ears seconds later was the snap-
ping of a lock on the other side of the door.

"We're in,'' Shane whispered as he drew the door back.
"Careful not to disturb the tape.''

Eden found that she had to get down and crawl through

the opening to avoid the crime scene tape. When she got to her feet again, Shane had the door closed. She had armed herself with a flashlight from the car, but she had no more need for it than Shane had for the screwdriver.

There was enough light from the living room down the hall to tell her she was standing in a small kitchen. That there was light at all in the apartment surprised her.

"You didn't go and turn on a lamp, did you?"

"There was one already on in the living room and another one in the bedroom. Don't worry, there's no one else in the place. I had a fast look to be sure."

"The police must have left them on."

Shane nodded. "Probably as a precaution. Now that it's fully dark, that cop out front would be able to tell if anyone got in and was moving around up here. We'll be all right as long as we stay away from the windows. Where do you want to start?"

Eden was the trained investigator. She ought to have been able to answer that question. The trouble was, she had absolutely no idea what they should be looking for. That made their intended search, even in an apartment this small, a monumental undertaking.

"Let's try the bedroom first. If we can find anything that connects Harriet to Charlie or those two thugs…" She left the rest unsaid because she wasn't sure what it could prove if they did discover evidence of a connection.

Talking in low tones, and only when it was necessary, they searched the bedroom, Eden taking the closet and Shane the desk. When she found nothing of interest in the closet, she began on the drawers of a bureau, hoping all the while that the police had already checked the apartment for fingerprints. Otherwise, without gloves, she and Shane would be leaving evidence of their search.

*This is a waste of time,* she thought. *If there was any worthwhile clue in the place, the police would have turned it up and carried it away. What was I thinking to suggest it?*

"Anything?" Shane asked her.

"Nothing. What about you? Tell me you found a bank-book with large deposits that has got to mean Harriet was receiving payoffs."

"All I found were the receipts from the bills she paid. There wasn't so much as a letter in the desk."

"If there had been any letters or a bankbook, the police would have claimed them. Shane, this is useless. We should be on our way to Savannah."

"Let's not give up yet. You had a P.I.'s itch to investigate the place, and I'm all for trusting that. Let's see if the living room has anything to offer."

Leaving the bedroom and its contents as they'd found them, they moved down the hall to the living room. Eden tried not to think about Harriet Krause lying on its floor with her skull split open.

"You want to take the bookshelves there while I have a go at the cupboard?" Shane suggested.

A moment later, crouched in front of the cupboard, one hand on a lower door he had opened, Shane paused and looked over his shoulder at her. "What is it?" he asked, suddenly aware that she hadn't moved, that she continued to stand in the doorway between the hall and the living room.

"Can't you smell it?" Eden whispered. She couldn't believe he hadn't noticed it. She had been conscious of the scent almost from the second they had arrived at the entrance to the living room.

Careful to get nowhere near the windows, Shane got to his feet and came over to stand beside her. She watched him as he sniffed the air.

"Yeah, now I smell it. There's a fragrance in the room. So what?"

"Shane, don't you remember? Harriet wouldn't let us in the apartment until she made certain neither one of us was wearing cologne or perfume. She was intolerant of them."

"Okay, so this fragrance wasn't hers. But the police were

in here. Either one of them, or maybe the neighbor who found her, had to be wearing cologne or aftershave.''

Eden shook her head emphatically. "All men, and this isn't a man's fragrance. It's a woman's perfume. An expensive one from the smell of it, maybe French. And I'll tell you something else. Whoever she was, she had to have been in this room for more than just a few minutes. Her scent wouldn't be lingering otherwise.''

"But if it was a strong perfume, or she'd doused herself with it—"

"No, it's too subtle for that. And any woman who can afford this scent probably has better taste than to apply it too liberally.''

She could see by the way Shane looked at her that he was impressed by her detective work. "It looks like your gut instinct was right and that mine was, too, when I said a woman could see, or in this case smell, what a man might overlook.'' His mouth widened into a grin. "Do I have a smart wife or what? Remind me that I owe you a hug when we get out of here.''

She felt herself flush with pleasure over his compliment. It was ridiculous of her to glow like this just because he had expressed pride in a wife who wasn't his wife at all. Or at the prospect of a hug she had no business anticipating. But, wise or not, this man had exactly that effect on her.

It wasn't easy getting back to business, but Eden made the effort to do just that. "Don't you see what this means, Shane? The third occupant of the Mercedes could have been a woman, not a man.''

He nodded slowly. "Who called on Harriet Krause while the four of us were busy elsewhere.''

"And whatever her visit was about, it had to have been important enough for Harriet to admit her when she was wearing that perfume.''

"So important,'' Shane said soberly, "that it could have cost Harriet her life.''

A woman, Eden thought. But who? Harriet's friend, Lissie Reardon, who had snatched Nathanial? Had she turned up at Harriet's door this afternoon? Where had Lissie gone after she and Nathanial had disappeared from Savannah? What had become of her, and where was she now?

They were fearful questions when Eden was faced by the possibility that Lissie Reardon, who had been in possession of her son, could have committed murder. Even more chilling was the realization that the Reardon name had an unknown meaning for Shane. That in some way he might not only be connected to a killer but that her son had come into his possession.

## Chapter Ten

"You'd better let me have a turn at the wheel," Shane had urged her.

There had been no hesitation from Eden about her decision in this matter. "Absolutely not. You not only don't have a driver's license, you have no identification at all, and if for any reason we should be stopped by the police—"

"I'm prepared to chance that. Come on, Eden, it's been a long day heavy with action. You need to rest."

"Well, *I'm* not prepared to chance it. And I'm not tired."

How could she be when she was driven by this urgency to find her son? When now, more than ever, she feared that Nathanial was threatened by some mortal danger she and Shane had yet to understand? And even though in one respect it might have been wiser for them to spend the night at her house in Charleston before heading for Savannah, sleep was unthinkable to her.

Besides, in another respect her house posed a risk. If those two gorillas, and whoever had accompanied them in the Mercedes, were still roaming around Charleston hunting for Shane, it wouldn't take them long to discover who she was and where she lived. Even a quick visit to her place to collect their things and reassure her friend Tia had been risky. So, yes, it was much better to go on immediately to

Savannah where, hopefully, they would learn the answers they needed.

That had been over a half hour ago, and the city was behind them now. But though the night was young, there was very little traffic on the road. That was because Eden had chosen a less traveled back highway. It was a longer road to Georgia, but she and Shane had reasoned that if their enemies somehow learned they were on their way to Savannah, they were more likely to try following them on the major route.

There had been no sign of any pursuit, but Eden remained vigilant at the wheel. Shane, too, had stayed alert. However, after a brief stop for a meal at a fast-food restaurant, she had managed to convince him that, if they were to encounter more trouble, he would be better prepared to deal with it in a fresh state.

Shane was asleep now in the passenger seat, leaving Eden with her concerns. Among them was a lingering guilt. They had completed their search of Harriet Krause's apartment without any further result, made sure the back door was locked again behind them, and slipped away into the night. Eden wasn't happy about running off without sharing what they had learned with the Charleston police.

"If we did that, they could end up holding us," Shane had pointed out. "Me, anyway."

"I know, and we have to stay free if we're going to unlock your memory and reach Nathanial."

"That's a priority, Eden. Finding Harriet Krause's killer can wait."

"But after we rescue Nathanial—" She wouldn't permit herself to believe they wouldn't.

"Then," he said, "you and I will do whatever it takes to help the police solve her death."

There had been nothing casual in Shane's words. They had been spoken with purpose and determination. He was that kind of man, Eden realized. Promises were sacred to him. Whatever she had learned about him, which was a great deal considering the short span of time she had known him, this was one of the hallmarks of his character she most valued.

*Careful, Eden. If you don't watch yourself, you'll be in over your head. Anyway, how can you be so sure he's a man who'll go to any lengths to keep a promise?*

She just knew, that's all. The same way she knew that the deep, rich timbre of his voice had the capacity to leave her with an aching longing. That the mole high on his lean, bronzed cheek intrigued her. That and the proud, erect way he carried himself, which might or might not have a military origin, stirred her senses.

*He's gonna do things to you. Things that are gonna squeeze the life out of your heart and soul.*

Atlanta Johnson's parting words to her at the houseboat came back to mock her. Joining that warning were the memories of her own suspicions about the man who called himself Shane. Those fleeting but potent feelings of mistrust she had experienced as recently as the moment in Harriet Krause's apartment when she had been shaken by the realization that Shane might be associated with a killer.

The headlights of a car behind them illuminated her hand on the steering wheel. A gleam of gold briefly caught her attention before the car turned off on a side road. The wedding band on her finger. It already felt familiar, as if belonged there. As if she *wanted* it to belong there.

Here was another disconcerting awareness; this marriage of pretense. It was turning out to be far more emotionally difficult than she had anticipated.

She glanced over at Shane. The light from the dashboard was sufficient enough to reveal the shadow of the day-old beard on his square jaw. Now why should that be so sexy?

His hands as he slept were locked across his middle. A man's strong, capable hands, the left one wearing the wedding band that matched her own ring. The sight of it jolted Eden. That's when she understood that none of the warnings, either from Atlanta Johnson or herself, meant a damn.

She was in love with Shane.

How could that be? How could she be in love with a
man she had met only two days ago? *Two* days. But so
much had been crowded into these past forty-eight hours
that it seemed a lifetime. She supposed people did fall in
love in even less time than that. Still, to be in love with a
man who was a mystery to both himself and her...

*You know the important things about him, Eden.*

Did she? Yes, she did. She knew he had a sense of humor
in even the toughest of situations. That he was instinctively
protective of her. That he operated by a code of honor that
convinced her that whatever his involvement with her son,
he would never harm Nathanial, would have done all in his
power to safeguard him. All qualities any woman would
prize, especially when they came wrapped in a package as
virile as Shane.

*It's too late, Atlanta. He's already taken control of my
heart and soul.*

That realization should have left her with nothing but a
sense of elation. Then why was her joy shadowed by a
sudden bleakness? Because she feared that Shane might not
return her feelings? After all, there was no reason why he
should be in love with her just because she was in love
with him. It didn't work that way. At least it hadn't for her.
Hadn't she already learned that painful lesson?

*You can handle this. You have to. Just get yourself
through this whole thing, find Nathanial, and then if Shane
turns his back and walks away...well, you'll survive. As
long as you have your son, you'll survive.*

It had begun to rain, a thin, persistent drizzle that in the
glow of the headlights cast a sheen on the highway. Maybe
it was the rain that accounted for her now dismal mood.
She wanted to think this was the explanation.

The rain continued to fall, making halos around the headlights of the oncoming cars. The combination of those au-
ras, the flat, ruler-straight highway that stretched out in
front of her and the rhythmic swish of the wiper blades on

the windshield was mesmerizing. She found herself struggling to keep awake, to concentrate on the road.

Eden had no awareness of nodding off at the wheel, of the Toyota starting to drift into the left lane. It was the warning shrill of a horn from an oncoming car that shocked her back into full alertness. Understanding the situation with a gasp of alarm, she corrected the position of the Toyota in time to avoid a collision. The other car swept on by, its horn still wailing.

Shane must have jerked awake at the first sound of the horn. That, together with Eden's sudden action, had him immediately conscious of what had happened.

*Or almost happened,* Eden thought, angry with herself.

"Pull over," he said.

He was calm about it, but there was a quiet authority in his voice that permitted no objection. Eden eased off the highway onto the gravel shoulder and brought the car to a stop.

"I'm sorry," she apologized, turning to him. "I could have killed us."

"It's as much my fault as yours. I should have stayed awake to keep you company. This settles it. License or no license, I'm taking the wheel, and you're coming over on this side where you will close those sweet blue eyes of yours and not open them again until *reveille.*"

"When is that?"

"Sunrise."

So he did have a military background. Not that this was the time for them to try to probe that likelihood. Eden obeyed him without an argument, though she didn't think she could possibly fall asleep now. Not after their near-fatal accident, not when her mind was active again with all those anxious thoughts.

THERE WAS A RED GLOW in the sky when Eden awakened. It took her a moment to realize the car was stopped, the radio was on and tuned in to a country-music station, and it was still raining. Not until she sat up did she comprehend the red glow was not the sun coming up but a nimbus of light from a neon sign outside the car.

"Where are we?"

"The parking lot of the Sea Breeze Motel, though as far as I can figure out, we're nowhere near the sea. Not that it matters as long as they have an available room."

"What time is it?" It couldn't be anywhere near morning. The sky was still black above the roof of the motel.

"After ten. I think we're close to the Georgia line."

"Then why are we stopping with Savannah so near?"

"Eden, it doesn't make sense getting there at this time of night. There's nothing we can do until morning. Besides, I'm having trouble myself keeping my eyes open." He nodded in the direction of the radio. "Even Dolly Parton isn't working for me."

"*Reveille* then for both of us?"

"Yeah, *reveille.*"

Taking their things and locking the car, they went into the motel's office where the attendant behind the desk offered them a double.

Since Shane had neither identification nor funds of his own, it was necessary for Eden to register and pay for the room. He said nothing, but she could tell by the little frown he wore that it bothered him to have to rely on her not only for tonight's lodging but the food he ate, the clothes he wore, even the wedding band on his finger. It was evidence of an old-fashioned male pride. She liked him for that.

There was a great deal more that Eden found herself appreciating about him once they were behind the locked door of their room. Shane wasted no time, or modesty, in stripping down to a pair of snug briefs.

She had already seen that superb body the night she and Tia had removed his clothes and cared for his injuries. But he had been unconscious then and helpless. Now there was something vital, riveting about the way those long limbs, sleekly muscled shoulders and powerful chest looked as he moved around in the soft light from the bedside lamp. Even the scars he carried had the raw, elemental appeal of a warrior.

Finding herself wanting what wasn't hers, what she might never be entitled to, Eden escaped from the impossible complications of her longing by fleeing into the bathroom, where she brushed her teeth and changed into a nightie.

When she emerged, Shane was in his bed and already asleep. Quelling a pang of disappointment, trying to convince herself she was relieved, she turned off the lamps, left the bathroom light burning and the door ajar so there would be some form of illumination to guide them if one of them awakened in the night, and crawled between the sheets of her own bed.

It had been a long, exhausting day and what sleep she'd had in the car was insufficient. She should have dropped off immediately. She didn't. Instead, she lay there listening to the drip of the rain off the eaves outside. It was a sad sound. It made her feel lonely. Lonely for the son she had missed for three years. Lonely for the man in the bed next to hers.

Another sound finally comforted her. The steady, reassuring rhythm of Shane's breathing, which eventually lulled her to sleep. But sometime in the night her peaceful rest was invaded by a nightmare.

Eden found herself in a maze of dim corridors. The *Yorktown?* Was she back on the *Yorktown?* Wherever it was, she was hunting for something she had lost, chasing frantically down one long gallery after another. There! Far ahead of her was a small, forlorn figure calling out to her.

"Mom, help me! I need you!"

"Hang on, Nathanial! I'm coming to get you!"

But she couldn't get to him. He wasn't alone. There was the tall figure of a man with him, someone who was no more than a shadow. He kept drawing Nathanial away from her, farther and deeper into the maze until she could no longer locate them, until her son's appeal was nothing more than a distant echo.

*Nathanial, where are you?*

It was a plea torn from the depths of a mother's wildest fears. So intense in its silent cry of desperation that it thrust her out of the dream into a bewildering reality.

Eden found herself awake. She was cold and trembling all over, her face wet with tears. She must have been sobbing in her sleep.

"The door is locked," said a voice that was deep, raspy. "You and I are alone here."

Turning her head on the pillow, she saw his tall figure looming over her like a threat. He was no more than a dark, faceless form against the subdued light from the bathroom behind him. A menacing shadow like the one in her nightmare.

He spoke again. "Eden, it's all right. You were shouting like you were being attacked, but you're safe."

Then her cry hadn't been a silent one. She cleared her head with an effort. Shane, of course. It was Shane standing over her offering reassurance. Not the figure in her nightmare who had been holding Nathanial, fleeing with him.

But suppose that dream shadow had represented Shane. What if, unknown to him in his present state of amnesia, he had in actuality stolen Nathanial, was hiding him from—

No! She was in love with him. He couldn't be that man. He *couldn't.*

"Bad dream, huh?" Shane said, understanding what had happened. His words were gentle, but his voice was still gruff from sleep. "Want to tell me about it?"

She briefly described her nightmare. She didn't tell him about her fear that the man in the dream might be him. "It was so real," she whispered with a shudder.

"The worst ones usually are."

"And I'm so cold."

He didn't hesitate. "Move over. I'm coming in."

She hadn't meant her complaint as a form of invitation.

There were, in fact, several reasons for her to object when he slid his long body into her bed, most of which involved a mistrust of her own emotions. And every reason for her to welcome that hard, hot body pressed close to her side. Eden decided to go with the latter argument, wisdom be damned.

"I promised you a hug back in Harriet Krause's apartment," he reminded her, his arm going around her, drawing her against him in a snug embrace. "Consider this the first payment on the debt."

His protective bulk was warm, comforting. But she couldn't forget the nightmare.

"Shane?"

"Yes?"

"I've got a feeling we're getting close to the answers. To finding Nathanial. But I can't shake this fear that I could lose him before that happens. I think that's what my dream was all about. That I could lose him again, maybe this time forever. And I couldn't bear it if—"

"It's not going to turn out that way," he said fiercely, his arm around her tightening. "We're not going to let it turn out that way. We're going to see to it that your kid is back with you where he belongs."

Nathanial. She and Shane shared Nathanial. They had bonded over the subject of her son. Was that what her love for this man was all about? But it had to be more than that to be real and meaningful, a great deal more. She wanted it to be everything.

"That's my guarantee to you," he said.

He was talking about Nathanial. But Eden knew that nothing was a guarantee. And that loving Shane was a risk. Maybe that's why she stiffened when he urged her over on her side and turned his own body so that they were facing each other.

Aware of her resistance, he murmured a soothing, "Nothing is going to happen here that you don't want to happen."

That might be true, but his self-control was already in serious conflict with his body. The evidence was there when he made contact with her bare thigh below her hiked-up nightie. She could feel his arousal straining against his briefs.

She was in equal jeopardy with her whole length welded like this to his. The feel of his strong, naked flesh was incredible. She no longer shivered with cold. The heat of him banished even the memory of being cold.

"There's a place I want to touch," he confessed in a low, husky voice. "Something that's been driving me wild since that first morning in your apartment." He paused and then amended himself. "All right, so most of your anatomy has been driving me wild, but this spot tops my wish list. Permission?"

She hesitated while he waited hopefully. Yes, she decided, she wanted him to touch her. Treacherous or not, she wanted it. "Feel free," she said. "No pun intended."

She expected his hand to travel to an intimate area. Her breasts, her hips, or the juncture of her thighs. To her complete surprise, his forefinger came to rest on the tip of her nose.

"Ah," he said, gently caressing the spot as if it were an erogenous zone.

"That's it? That's what turns you on? I've heard of things like foot fetishes, but—"

"It isn't your nose. It's this little valley here at the bottom of it."

Eden groaned. "You would go and pick out a flaw. Even as a little girl this dent you're so fascinated by gave me grief."

"Yeah?"

"Yeah. I can remember Pop taking me on his lap after I was teased about my nose. Saying something about God being so pleased with his work after he finished making me that he placed his thumb on the tip of my nose. The little depression it left was a mark of his special favor, and

I should be proud of it. I wonder how many fathers have told their daughters that.''

"You should have listened to him. He was right. It *is* special." Shane demonstrated his conviction by placing his mouth where his finger had been and tenderly kissing the tip of her nose.

Eden sighed. "Where were you when I was in high school?"

"What needed kissing then?"

"My whole body. I put on pounds whenever I so much as looked at food. Kids can be cruel about things like that. I no longer have that problem, though I still have to fight weight gain. But then most women do."

It was a revelation of an old vulnerability that didn't come easily to Eden, and something about the way she said it had Shane drawing back to gaze at her solemnly in the dimness.

"Charles Moses wasn't the first guy to hurt you, was he?"

"No," she admitted. "There were others before him."

"No wonder it's so hard for you to trust. Is that what you think I'm going to do, Eden? Hurt you like the others hurt you?"

"Not willingly, but maybe in the end you won't be able to help yourself."

She didn't have to name it. He understood the concern that lingered with her. "What I said earlier in the taxi, I meant it. There is no one." He paused a beat before adding a fervent, "Only you."

"Shane—"

He silenced her by placing the forefinger that had been touching her nose against her lips. "Let me kiss something else that's had me on fire since day one."

"Like what?"

"This quivering bottom lip of yours. It's sexy as hell."

Replacing the finger that had been resting against her lips with his mouth, he kissed her. It was the kiss of a man who was in no hurry, who took time to express his sensual nature by pausing to nibble at the bottom lip that intrigued him, then soothing it with the tip of his tongue.

"I thought," Eden managed to croak when he finally released her mouth, "you said nothing was going to happen that I didn't want to happen."

"I lied. And, anyway, we're doing something important here."

"Such as?"

"Building confidence in yourself as a desirable woman."

"I guess I do want that to happen."

"Let's work on it then."

When he kissed her now, he was far less leisurely about it.

His performance was eager, deeper and more thorough. This time it was the kiss of a man who might have been branding the woman he had chosen as his lifetime mate.

Eden lost herself in the kiss, inhaling the masculine aroma of him, savoring the clean taste of him in her mouth. Her lips and tongue were as busy as his. And so were her hands as they learned the contours and textures of him. The battle scars he wore on his body, the wound across the bridge of his nose that was nearly healed now, the stubble on his jaw. They were all material for her sensitive fingertips.

She was so occupied she was scarcely aware of what his own hands were doing. Not, anyway, until she realized he had lifted her nightie to permit him access to her breasts. That his palms were stroking the heavy fullness of her exposed breasts, massaging the peaks into hard buds.

And where his hands went, his mouth followed, suckling each breast in turn as she gripped his lowered head, her fingers digging into his scalp beneath the thatch of his sunbleached hair.

She was so inflamed by then she would have abandoned all caution without hesitation. But Shane managed to hang on to his last shreds of reason for both of them, though his ragged breathing betrayed his massive effort at self-restraint when he finally lifted his head and stared into her eyes.

"You have to say if it stops here, Eden," he said, and there was nothing playful in his manner now. "Because there's no turning back if we go on."

For a moment she didn't respond. Then, with a catch in her voice, she pleaded with him for the moral right to lower the last barrier between them. "How can you be so positive there's no one waiting for you?"

"I can't be positive. You know there's no way I can be." He paused to choose his words with care. "All I can tell you, Eden, is I've been thinking about this since the night I landed on your doorstep. Wondering, just like you, why I was so convinced the first time I laid eyes on you that I'd come home to my wife."

"There is a simple explanation, you know. After all you'd been through, you badly needed a connection that was familiar. Not that I was, of course, but since I was there on the spot, I qualified. Something like that."

"No," he said, shaking his head. "I think it went much deeper than that. I think it was because I recognized you."

"Shane, we'd never met before, and if you're talking about reincarnation—"

"Nothing like that. But, yeah, it was an immediate connection for me. The kind of thing that happens when—" He paused again and then continued in a voice raspy with defiance. "All right, so it sounds sappy, but I just knew that on some level I'd recognized my soul mate in you."

It wasn't sappy. It was beautiful, an admission spoken from the heart, and Eden loved him all the more for it, especially when she knew that expressing such a sentiment couldn't have come easily to a man like him.

"I'm going to start blubbering here if you go on," she warned him, "and that wouldn't be at all romantic."

"How about going on with action then instead of words?"

She hesitated only briefly. "I'm all for it."

But Shane understood her better than she understood herself. He knew what that hesitation meant. That a part of her was still torn by guilt. The fear that she would never be able to forgive herself if they went all the way and it turned out he was committed in some form to another woman.

"You can't bear to hurt her, can you?" he said quietly.

"Who?"

"The girlfriend I don't have, the other wife who doesn't exist. Even yourself if we take the chance and it turns out I'm wrong."

"Shane, no. I want us to make love."

"I know you do, maybe even as desperately as I want it, but it's not going to happen."

He released her, drew away from her a scant few inches. But the loss of his embrace felt like miles to her.

"I'm making the decision for both of us," he said. "We're going to wait until I recover my memory. Until we can be together with no shadows between us. It's all right, sweetheart. Fooling around with you was as good as sex would have been with any other woman. Better. I can imagine how spectacular the whole nine yards will be. Definitely worth waiting for."

Eden couldn't deny the emotion that seized her, a sense of relief under her disappointment. And a profound gratitude to Shane for making the choice she'd been unable to make, though she knew by his raging arousal she'd felt just before he let her go what it must have cost him.

"Go to sleep," he murmured, leaning toward her just far enough to plant a chaste kiss on her forehead. Then he turned over on his back again and closed his eyes.

His even breathing seconds later told her that he'd managed to conquer his frustration and was sleeping soundly. Eden, wide awake beside him, unable to overcome her own frustration, listened to the patter of rain at the window.

Shane had told her he'd recognized his soul mate in her. But he hadn't told her he loved her. Was one possible without the other? If not, why hadn't he declared his love? Maybe he had decided this, too, had to be withheld until his memory was restored. That unless he had an identity, he didn't deserve her. And if he never recovered that identity—

It was a cruel possibility. It left her aching inside. Forced to remind herself that Shane wasn't her husband, just pretending to be, and that she might never be the wife to him she now longed to be in reality.

"I SUPPOSE WE ARE taking a risk in being here," Eden admitted.

Shane didn't answer her, which didn't surprise her. He knew she was already aware of his feelings on this issue. They had discussed plans before their arrival this morning in Savannah.

Being a man of action, he had wanted to tackle Charles Moses first. To go directly to the private investigator's office and demand answers. That is, if Charlie was even in Savannah. He could be anywhere on a case, perhaps off somewhere still trying to locate Nathanial on behalf of the Jamisons. He might even be back in Charleston.

What Shane didn't want to do, Eden knew, was to lurk here in the shrubbery like this. He must regard it as a useless endeavor. Staring at a house that could provide them with no explanations.

How could he possibly understand this wasn't just a building for her. It was the house in which her son had spent the last three years of his life. She'd needed to see it, had to try to imagine Nathanial's existence here. Had he been loved, happy?

"I hope the cops in Savannah are sympathetic," Shane said, "because they're sure to turn up if anyone in there spots us spying on the place."

Eden was fairly confident there was no danger of that. Being that much farther south, Savannah's vegetation was even more luxuriant than Charleston's. It was particularly lush in this square, one of the many historic old squares the city was famous for, where she and Shane were concealed behind a mass of early azaleas. They were just beginning to flower, and through their blooms Eden could see the Jamison house that dominated one end of the square. It was an imposing Italianate mansion behind cast-iron railings.

"Hell," Shane said, tempering his impatience, "I suppose we did have to start here. If looking at the place gives you any kind of connection at all to your kid, that's important."

He *did* understand.

Eden turned her head to gaze at him. It didn't matter that the Jamison mansion failed, after all, to offer her either the comfort or reassurance she'd sought. It was enough to have Shane's support.

"What about you?" she asked him. "Does anything here stir up any kind of recognition at all?"

"Eden, there isn't anything in this whole town that looks vaguely familiar to me."

This was a disappointment. They had hoped that Savannah would hold some memory for Shane, that if Nathanial *had* come into his possession he might even have originated from here.

"Look," he said softly, drawing her attention back to the house. "Someone is coming out."

Eden peered again through the azaleas. The front door had opened. A figure appeared and came down the steps. He stood there, looking expectantly up and down the street.

"Surprise, surprise," Shane muttered.

It *was* a surprise, Eden thought. The figure turned out to be the burlier of the two blond brutes who had been after them back in Charleston. And he wasn't alone. Another man emerged then from the house and joined him down on the sidewalk. His towheaded partner.

"What are these two characters doing here?" Shane wondered.

"Well, they couldn't have followed us to Savannah, not as careful as we were. And they don't know we're in the city, and yet they're here themselves and just walked out of the Jamison house—"

"Yeah, they're working for the Jamisons. Maybe. And wouldn't I just love to know."

Eden could sense Shane's anger. Knew he was itching to confront the two men. But it would be a mistake to reveal themselves. She laid a restraining hand on his arm, fearing he was about to charge recklessly across the square.

"Wait. They're both looking up and down the street. They're expecting something."

"No, someone. And he's here."

A sleek, silver Mercedes-Benz rounded the corner and pulled up in front of the house. It looked like the same car that had arrived in front of Harriet Krause's apartment building back in Charleston. The driver stepped out and spoke to the two men.

He was thinner than she remembered and much better dressed, as if funds were no longer a problem for him. But she immediately recognized him.

"It's Charlie," she whispered.

"Then whatever this whole thing is all about, it seems like Moses is somehow in on it with them."

"And that he could have been somewhere in Charleston at the same time they were. They're going."

Charlie had climbed behind the wheel again. The other two joined him in the sedan.

"Let's try to follow them," Shane urged.

"Shane, it's too late. They're already rolling. We'd never get back to my car in time to catch up with them."

"Damn. And there's no point in going now to Moses's office when he isn't there."

"No, but there is something else I would like to do. Research."

"Do I hear a P.I. talking?"

"Arming yourself with information is the best thing an

investigator can do to solve a case. The Jamisons are a prominent family in this town. There must be all kinds of material on them in the public library, and if we could hunt down one solid lead, maybe even something that would trigger your memory…''

Shane agreed to her plan, though he didn't look happy at the prospect of digging through endless records for something that might not be there.

One of the trolleys that conducted tours through the historic district of Savannah was parked at the other end of the square to permit its passengers to take photographs of a fountain. The trolley's driver supplied them with directions to the main library.

Within minutes of their arrival in the building on the other side of town, a resource librarian had them in front of a pair of microfilm readers situated in an alcove.

''Not computers?'' Shane had asked.

Eden, whose work as a P.I. made her familiar with this kind of research, had explained it to him while they'd waited at the desk. ''The local newspaper is always the best way to start. In most cases, the subjects of their stories are indexed online but not the stories themselves. You have to go to microfilm for that.''

''In other words, start looking, huh?''

Seated side by side in front of the two machines, that's exactly what they were now doing.

''How are you making out?'' Shane asked her fifteen minutes later.

''Well, there's no shortage of stories on the Jamisons. They seem to be a pretty active family socially. Or they were before Sebastian Jamison's death.''

''Amen. It's going to take us forever to plow through this stuff.''

Eden went on scrolling the microfilm the librarian had loaded into the machine for her. Many of the accounts she read dealt with projects the wealthy Sebastian had helped to fund. It seemed that Nathanial's grandfather had been

something of a philanthropist. It was all interesting, but
Eden could find nothing useful in it where she and Shane
were concerned.

At some point she became aware that he was being aw-
fully quiet. Curious, she turned her head to look at him.
And discovered him sitting there in a frozen silence, staring
rigidly at the screen.

"What is it? Have you found something?"

Shane didn't answer her. She got up from her chair, feeling a mixture of excitement and uneasiness, and went to
look over his shoulder at the image on the screen.

It was a photograph of a silver-haired Sebastian Jamison
attending a charity benefit. Beside him, a startled, reluctant
expression on her face, as if the camera had caught her off
guard, stood a woman who was probably somewhere near
Eden's age. She was slender, light-haired and attractive.
The caption identified her simply as the mother of Sebastian's grandson.

Eden swung her gaze from the face on the screen to the
face of the man in front of the microfilm reader. He continued to be mesmerized by the woman who stared out at
him.

Eden could see it this time. It glowed from Shane, a light
of recognition. There was something else she could see.
The wall that had blocked his memory was crumbling at
last, its bricks tumbling down one by one.

"It's her," Eden whispered. "It's Lissie Reardon. And
you know her, don't you?"

"She's Beth," Shane said slowly, his voice raspy with
emotion. "She's my Beth."

# Chapter Eleven

"I can't look at this anymore," Shane said, shoving back from the microfilm reader, surging abruptly to his feet. "I've got to get out of here. I need to move."

Limp or no limp, his gait was so swift as he headed for the exit that Eden could barely keep up with him. She tried to ask him about Nathanial, whether he knew now where Nathanial was. But he wouldn't talk to her about any of it, kept telling her to wait until they were outside.

And all the way out of the library, beneath her need to know about Nathanial, Eden was miserable. Their research had been successful. It had released his memory. And she was miserable.

*My Beth.*

Shane had called her *his* Beth. There had been a tenderness in his voice when he said it, the kind of tone you used when someone mattered a great deal. When they meant everything to you. Eden had lost him, and the only way she could deal with it was to think about her son. He was the only real urgency now.

By this time she was aware of her surroundings again. She found herself in an unexpected setting. Shane had led them through the iron gates of a cemetery across the street from the library.

Like the rest of Savannah, the old graveyard had an exotic flavor with its moldering tombs and mossy, crooked headstones. In the absence of a park, Eden supposed it was as good a place as any to exercise both your body and your mind.

Shane had slowed his walk by now, as if he had reached a vital destination and could breathe again. They paced among the grave markers under a canopy of live oaks.

"Nathanial," she reminded him.

"Give me time. They're still coming in."

His memories, she thought. He's talking about his memories. She restrained herself, trying to be patient while he pieced them together. Nothing had ever been so difficult for her. But then this had to be equally tough for him.

Minutes passed. He finally stopped on the path and turned to her. "I know who I am now. I'm Michael Reardon."

*Reardon.* She stared at him, her heart breaking. But it wasn't right for her to be anything but happy for him now that he had regained his identity. She made herself smile, made herself say to him softly, "Hello, Michael."

"Don't," he said. "I may be Michael to myself and the rest of the world, but to you—"

"You'll always be Shane."

"Yeah. Let's keep it that way. I like it."

"And what about the other Reardon? Lissie?"

"Beth," he corrected her. "She was never anything but Beth to me. Think about it, Eden. Lissie, Beth. They're both forms of Elisabeth, and that was her given name."

"Only somewhere along the way she started calling herself Lissie."

He frowned. "I'm not surprised. Beth would have been too old-fashioned for her, too ordinary. She liked to be hip about everything, always ran with that kind of crowd."

"Harriet Krause said she was a free spirit."

"Yeah, that was Beth all right."

There was a little smile on his mouth now. It was the smile of a man remembering someone who mattered to him a great deal. Eden was suddenly afraid to hear what Shane would tell her. And even more afraid of what he might be unable to tell her.

He must have noticed her fear. Cupping her chin in his hand, he gently stroked her jaw with his thumb. "You look unhappy. I like it that you look unhappy. It must mean that you're worried about Beth and me."

"You lost her. That was what you told Atlanta and me under hypnosis." He had actually told them he had twice lost Beth, which had yet to make any sense.

"And you think now I've found her again. That I was wrong about the wife I was so sure I didn't have."

"You share the same name. You called her my Beth."

"She was my Beth."

*Was.* She was aware of it now. How he had been referring to Beth in the past tense.

"And we share the same name, Eden, because she was my sister." His hand fell away from her chin. "Let's walk," he said.

She fell into step beside him. All she could feel as they strolled aimlessly again under the oaks was a guilty relief. She knew she ought to be experiencing other deep emotions, but for the moment there was nothing but this sweet relief. His sister. Not his wife or his lover, but his sister.

He began to tell her about Beth. "I loved her, but we never had much in common. Different interests, and I was much older. She was always a little wild, and I didn't have much patience with that either."

"Where was this?"

"Richmond. That's where we grew up. Richmond, Virginia. Beth and I were all each other had after our parents died when I was in my late twenties. We should have been closer, but we'd already drifted apart by then. She had her own life, and I was totally focused on my career."

Eden caught a note of bitterness in his voice when he referred to his career, but she didn't remark on it. She let him go on.

"The service was all I ever wanted. Or thought I wanted. I was an officer, a major in the Army Rangers."

And that explained his alertness, his ability to deal with difficult situations. Being a member of a Special Forces unit, he would have been trained in such skills.

"It's easy to become a loner when you live with danger as I did, when you're always moving on to the next operation. I used to tell myself there was never any time for a permanent relationship. I think that must be why I was so certain I had no woman waiting for me. And to be honest about it, I never wanted that kind of attachment."

*Until now.* Eden waited for him to add those two precious words, hoped for it. But she was disappointed he failed to do that.

"I was out of the country on assignments so much of the time that I didn't know where Beth was living or what was happening with her. I realize now what a poor excuse that was."

He had lost track of his sister, which was what he must have meant under hypnosis by losing Beth. That would account, anyway, for his first loss of her. And the second? Eden was eager to hear about that, praying it would provide her with all that she desperately needed to know about Nathanial. But she didn't want to rush Shane. Not when she could see he was looking even more troubled than he had a moment ago.

"Out of the country," he repeated softly, a faraway expression on his face.

"What is it?" she prodded him gently. "Something more you've remembered?"

"Yeah, something more. My last mission as an Army Ranger." He began to tell her about it in a mechanical voice. "The U.S. was working with the Colombian government to take down this drug lord. Only he couldn't be eliminated until he'd been disarmed."

"Weapons?"

"Something more powerful than that. Human hostages.

He'd grabbed four American tourists and was holding them. He threatened to kill them if his compound was attacked. I was in command of a force sent to rescue the hostages.''

"And it all went wrong," Eden said, remembering the scene he'd relived so painfully under hypnosis.

"There was this informer our people were using. It had been arranged for us to meet him at a rendezvous in the jungle. He was supposed to show us a way to sneak inside the compound. I didn't trust the little bastard. I'd heard rumors about him, but our people in charge insisted he was okay, and orders were orders.''

"So you went to the rendezvous.''

"It wasn't a rendezvous. It was an ambush. It was bad, but it could have been a lot worse if I hadn't been alert for trouble. As it was, I lost two of my men before we got out of there with our wounded.''

"Among them yourself," Eden said. "That is right, isn't it?''

"Yeah, that's how I ended up with this leg and an end to my career in the Rangers. Well, I could live with that. What I couldn't live with was the knowledge that I'd led my men into a trap.''

"But it wasn't your fault," she defended him. "You were obeying orders, and if you hadn't been the leader you were, your whole force would have been wiped out.''

"That's what I've tried to tell myself all these months, Eden. That it even came out all right in the end. The hostages were eventually freed, the compound raided, the drug lord and his gang defeated.''

But he still suffered from the torment of what he perceived as his failure to save two of his men. She could hear that in his voice, unemotional though it had been throughout his account.

He was silent now, and that's when she realized they were no longer strolling through the cemetery. At some point she didn't remember, they had settled side by side on a sun-dappled stone bench under one of the ancient oaks.

Head turned to gaze at him, she wished she could heal his anguish. But she feared not even all the power of her love for him was capable of that. That in the end it was something he must do for himself.

There was a wry smile on his mouth when he turned his own head to meet her gaze. "I may not have relieved myself of that guilt," he said, "but at least I don't have to live anymore with the fear that I might have harmed your son."

"Yes—Nathanial. Please tell me you know now what happened to him."

"Beth brought him to me about five weeks ago. I was on extended medical leave with this leg and living in Arizona. Holed up in a small house out in desert country that I'd bought as a retreat years ago."

Which explained his bronzed look and the western-style garb he had been wearing the night he'd collapsed on her piazza.

"It was a good place to be while I tried to figure out what I was going to do with the rest of my life when the army officially let me go. And not being in any state for even my own company, much less a sister's I hadn't laid eyes on in years, I wasn't exactly happy when Beth turned up at my door out of nowhere."

"How did she know you were there?"

"She'd managed to contact one of my army buddies, a guy she'd dated in the old days back in Richmond. He told her where she could find me."

"So you took her in."

"She was family. What else could I do? Besides, there was the boy with her, Patrick. Sorry—Nathanial. It's a little hard to think of him now as—"

"My son and not hers?" Eden challenged him, unable to help the sharp edge of anger in her voice.

"Eden, I swear I didn't know he was anything but her own kid. And if it's of any comfort to you at all, she was devoted to him. Maybe because she was no longer the old

Beth, all spunk and defiance. I figured motherhood must
have changed her. Only it was a lot more than that. She
was thin and worn out. I wanted her to see a doctor. She
wouldn't.''

"Ill? Is that why she came to you?"

"It was more than that. She was scared."

"For herself?"

"For Patrick. He was safe when his grandfather was
alive, she said. But now that Sebastian was dead, she didn't
trust the Jamisons."

"Why?"

"According to Beth, the old man had made Patrick his
chief heir. She was afraid the other Jamisons meant to see
to it Patrick didn't live long enough to collect the fortune
that was supposed to have been theirs. 'Then you should
have gone to the police,' I told her. 'Not taken him and
disappeared without a word.' 'You don't understand,' she
kept insisting. 'The Jamisons are a powerful family in Savannah. The police would never listen to me. I had to turn
to you, Michael. There was no one else.'''

"Did you believe her?"

"I wasn't sure then, and I'm not now. I think there may
have been something else going on, something she refused
to discuss. I tried asking Patrick about it, but he clammed
up. I think he was scared, too. That, whatever it was, Beth
had warned him never to talk about it to anyone."

"But, Shane, if she came to you for help, what on earth
did she expect you to do?"

"I was family, remember? And when you're in trouble
or need, it's instinctive to turn first to family. Also, she
figured with my training I would be able to protect Patrick
if the Jamisons learned where she had taken him and tried
to get their hands on him."

It was hard for Eden to hear Shane still calling her son
Patrick. But that was who Nathanial had been for him, so
she didn't bother to correct him.

"And that was all Beth wanted from you?"

"I thought so, until—"

"What?"

"She did something funny a few weeks after she arrived. She had me drive her and the boy into town where she had the local photographer make a portrait of Patrick. One wallet-size picture. That's all she wanted."

"What on earth for?"

"That's what I wondered. But she wouldn't tell me. Not until a few days ago. I said she didn't look well, and it turns out she *was* ill."

"How ill?"

"Much sicker than I imagined. She'd been functioning on sheer will. That's what the doctors told me after she finally let me take her to the hospital a couple of weeks back. By then it was too late for her. It was probably already too late for her when she first came to me, though Beth would have refused to accept that."

Shane was silent for a moment. There was a vault in front of the bench where they sat. Mounted on it was the marble sculpture of an angel with bowed head and folded wings. He stared at it, while Eden, her insides churning with conflicted emotions, waited for him to go on.

"Cancer," he said. "Beth admitted to the doctors that she was being treated for it back in Savannah. She'd left a hospital bed there without anyone's knowledge to flee with Patrick. Since then the cancer had accelerated. There was nothing they could do for her but make her as comfortable as possible."

Shane turned his head, gazing at her solemnly. "She was responsible for a mother's worst nightmare. She stole your son, Eden, left you with the anguish of not knowing whether he was dead or alive. You're entitled to hate her. But there's one thing you should know. At the end there was no mercenary motive, only her love for Patrick. She'd sacrificed her own survival for his. All she cared about was his safety."

"Did she tell you that?"

"No. In those first days in the hospital all she wanted to do was remember her life with Patrick's father. I don't know, maybe because that was the happiest time for her. She'd talk to me about Charleston, what it was like and the scenes there that Simon had painted. I think now it's why Charleston seemed familiar to me when I came to you that night, why I knew what a single house and a piazza were. Things like that."

"And that's all?"

"Until the end when she understood there was no longer a hope for her. That's when she gave me the photograph of Patrick and your business card. As dog-eared as it was, she must have had it from the beginning. 'Put them in a secure place, Michael,' she said. 'Don't let anyone see them but the woman on that card.'"

"She told you about me? That I was Nathanial's actual mother?"

Shane shook his head. "My promise. That's all she would talk about then, nothing else. My promise to her that after she was gone, I would take Patrick to you in Charleston. 'Don't let them get him, Michael,' she kept saying. 'Just take him to Eden Hawke. Eden Hawke will know what to do.'"

Eden was astonished. "And you never understood she was sending him home to his mother? You made that promise without—"

"What else could I do? She was dying. I figured you would explain it all to me. The card said you were a private investigator, and maybe that had a lot to do with why Beth trusted you."

"But Nathanial wasn't with you when those two gorillas grabbed you, which means you *weren't* bringing him to me."

"Don't look at me like that. Do you think after all of Beth's fears I was going to just hand Patrick over to you? Believe me, I had every intention of checking you out thoroughly before I let you get anywhere near him. Beth knew

that. That's why she gave me his photograph to show you.
If you hadn't connected with that picture, I wouldn't have
trusted you.''

''So you—''

''Buried a sister in Arizona before I could do anything
else.''

*Even though they hadn't been close, that couldn't have
been easy for him. Just as it couldn't have been easy for
Beth to finally admit to herself she was dying. To have
made the monumental decision then to return Nathanial to
me, not just because I was a P.I. who would know about
security but because I would safeguard him against all
threat with the ferocity only a mother could possess. At
least, that's what I imagine must have been Beth's conclusion.*

She wouldn't have supposed she could ever feel any
sympathy for the woman who had taken her son away from
her, hadn't thought it would be possible to forgive her. Now
she wasn't so certain. In any case, all that mattered at this
point was recovering Nathanial.

''And after you buried Beth, what then?''

''I took Patrick—Nathanial, that is—and boarded a plane
for Charleston.''

She leaned toward him eagerly. ''So where is he, Shane?
Where did you hide him until you could check me out?''

He gazed at her in a long, abject silence. The look in his
eyes made Eden feel as though a fist had closed around her
heart.

''I don't know,'' he finally muttered.

She stared at him in dismay. ''What do you mean you
don't know? You *must* know.''

''I wish I did. But there's this gap between the time the
plane landed and I was forced off the road.'' His voice was
gruff with the effort it cost him to admit that his memory
suffered this last, agonizing blank.

''But how is that possible when you've remembered all
the rest?''

"I wish I could explain it to you. I can't. Maybe it's a kind of defense mechanism, a corner of my brain guarding Nathanial by refusing to give him up to anyone. Maybe this subconscious instinct is even the explanation for why I've had a need all along to avoid the cops. Whatever it is, it's not talking to me."

"Why didn't you tell me this at the start? Why did you let me assume—"

"I know. I'm sorry," he apologized, the haunted expression still in his eyes. "I should have warned you, but I thought if I held off while I told you all the rest that this last blank would fill in. It hasn't."

Eden fought a rising despair. To be this close to finding Nathanial, and have him still out of her reach, was worse than maddening. "But what could you have possibly done with him before you drove off alone in that rental car?"

"Whatever it was," he tried to reassure her, "I wouldn't have just abandoned him in the airport. I must have made certain he was absolutely safe, out of harm's way."

Eden tried to believe that, but she was afraid. If Beth had been right and the Jamisons were a threat to Nathanial, her son could be in danger wherever he was. They had to find him before the Jamisons did! "What are we going to do, Shane?" she pleaded with him. "What *can* we do?"

He was silent for a moment, his gaze fixed again on the marble angel atop the vault. There was something intense about the way he looked at the figure.

"What is it?" she demanded. "Have you remembered what you did with—"

"Not that. I was thinking about stone sculptures."

"Shane, what are you talking about?"

"The newspaper reports on the microfilm reader. One of those stories I came across was about a tribute to the late Sebastian Jamison. A sculpture honoring him for his public work is going to be unveiled this afternoon at a memorial ceremony in the Savannah Art Museum. All of the Jamisons are scheduled to attend."

Eden recalled scanning a similar account on her own microfilm reader. "All right, I saw the story, too, but what's that got to do with us and finding Nathanial?"

"I say it's time we had a look at that family, and this would be the opportunity for it."

"Why? What good will it do?"

"For one thing, it will give me the time I need to dig into my mind for the last missing piece of my memory. But I also think the Jamisons could still be our key to Nathanial. Research, remember? You said it yourself."

Eden couldn't deny it. Information from as many sources as possible was vital to any investigation. It was also valuable to know your enemy, especially when that enemy was so desperate to have Nathanial returned to them they hired thugs to locate him. Who were these people, and just why did they want her son?

Yes, Shane was right. It was time to look at the Jamisons. She prayed that view would produce a result. It wouldn't be easy, though, when her need to reach Nathanial demanded action, not a visit to the local art museum.

"It's a plan," she agreed. "But there's a problem. The paper said this ceremony was to be by invitation only, and those invitations were being issued mainly to representatives of prominent organizations Sebastian supported."

"Then there's sure to be a crowd. We'll manage to slip in somehow."

Eden shook her head. "Not without those invitations. The security will be tight, because there's also a Vermeer collection on loan from the Netherlands, and they won't be taking any chances with that."

"There must be a way."

"Maybe there is." She had remembered something. "Let's go back to the library for a minute. There's something I want to check out on that microfilm reader."

WHATEVER HER mysterious errand, Eden was in too much of a hurry to stop long enough to explain it to him. Shane was willing to wait. He needed the opportunity, anyway, to tackle his thoughts as he accompanied her out of the cemetery and across the street to the library.

Some of them were wild thoughts, and they could use taming. Not surprising after the emotional upheaval of having his identity back along with most of his memory. That was good, especially the relief he'd felt when he'd been able to tell Eden without hesitation that there was no other woman waiting for him.

He sure as hell never wanted to repeat the kind of restraint he'd had to exercise last night in the motel. Though he had respected her need for them not to make love until they could be certain he wasn't already married, it had nearly killed him to withhold himself when he'd ached to bury himself inside her sweet softness. He longed for that ultimate joining even now.

There was something else he yearned to do. He wanted to tell Eden what she had come to mean to him in these last couple of days. That he had fallen in love with her. But this was neither the time nor the place for such a declaration, not when their energies had to be focused on the urgent matter of Nathanial.

Anyway, Shane was afraid to open his mouth. Eden might not feel that way now, but when she had time to think about it, maybe she wouldn't be able to get past the knowledge he was the brother of the woman who had taken her son away from her. And if she was unable to forget that, if it threatened always to be there between them, then this marriage of theirs could never be more than what it currently was—a masquerade.

That worry, along with his frustrated inability to restore the last essential piece of his memory, was still with him several minutes later as he stood behind Eden at the microfilm reader and watched her scroll through the microfilm.

"There!" she said, finding what she'd been searching

for. "I wasn't wrong. It *is* one of the organizations invited to the ceremony."

"Which one?" he asked, peering over her shoulder at the list on the screen.

"The African-American Society." He must have looked thoroughly mystified, because she added a quick, "Never mind, I'll explain as we go."

"Where?"

"Outside. I need to use my cell phone."

A moment later they stood beside the Toyota while Eden dialed a number in New Orleans. Shane had learned by then she was calling her sister, Christy, who was also a private investigator. Her motive remained a mystery to him.

"Chris? Yes, it's me. I know, we haven't talked in ages, and I can't talk now. I'm in Savannah, and I need a favor. It's important. Didn't you tell me Denise took a job with the African-American Society here? So she still works for them? Great. Look, this is what I need you to do…"

Seconds later, the phone still to her ear, Eden spoke to Shane. "I'm holding while she calls Denise."

"Uh, I don't suppose it matters, but who exactly is Denise?"

"She was Christy's assistant at her office in New Orleans. Chris lost her when Denise married a man from Georgia and they moved here to Savannah, but they've remained friends. I just hope—" She interrupted her explanation as her sister came back on the line. "She will? Wonderful! Bless you and Denise. Yes, I've got it. Washington Square in half an hour."

Eden rang off and turned triumphantly to Shane.

"We're in! Denise has agreed to meet us on her lunch hour. They received three invitations, but only one of them is being used. We can have the other two, but we have to be careful her boss doesn't find out about it."

Which could be a problem, Shane thought, since he and Eden were obviously not African-American. But Eden was so excited by now over the potential of this undertaking that he didn't point that out to her.

There was something else she'd failed to remember, which was understandable considering this morning's rapid events with its storm of emotions. Nor did he choose to remind her. She was already frantic enough about Nathanial. But Shane wasn't forgetting. Harriet Krause had been murdered, and with what they now knew about the Jamisons, it was possible her killer was a member of that family.

THE SAVANNAH ART MUSEUM was an immense, classic building that sprawled along the bluff above the Savannah River. Visitors were streaming through its front doors when Eden and Shane arrived on the scene.

They joined the noisy throng in the vast entrance hall, many of whom were interested only in the Vermeer collection. But most of the crowd was queuing up in front of the two gates that would admit them into the setting for the memorial ceremony.

"You were right," Shane observed. "The security *is* tight."

Eden nervously eyed the uniformed guards carefully checking each visitor through the post-and-rail barriers. Their invitations were genuine, so there was no reason that she and Shane should be challenged, but she'd feel a whole lot better once they were beyond those gates.

"Stick close," Shane had instructed her.

It was good advice, except they were unable to manage it in the crush. She found herself soon separated from him and being squeezed toward one gate with Shane headed in the direction of its neighbor. It didn't matter. Each of them had an invitation in hand, bearing the name of the organization to which it had been issued.

Maybe what happened was because of that, since Eden hardly qualified as African-American. Or maybe it was because she was dressed too casually for the occasion in a cotton sweater and a pair of slacks that hadn't traveled well.

Whatever the explanation, the guard, when she reached him, wasn't content with a mere glance at her invitation.

"Open your purse, please."

Eden complied and was thankful for the first time that her pistol had been lost aboard the *Yorktown*. The guard poked through the contents of her bag with his pencil and was satisfied. "Thank you. Enjoy the ceremony."

Eden passed through the gate. Her relief was short-lived. When she turned around to look for Shane, she found him faced with a more alarming problem at his own gate.

"May I see some identification, sir?"

Shane had no identification, only the invitation! They hadn't anticipated this.

"Look, I'm sorry, but I went and left my wallet at home."

Eden acted swiftly, placing herself in front of the suspicious guard with her own wallet open to her driver's license. This time she was ready with a credible lie. "It's all right. He's my husband. We both work in promotion on behalf of organizations like the African-American Society."

The guard, a petite woman, hesitated, looking uncertain.

"No, really, I am his wife," Eden insisted. She grabbed Shane's hand and held it out together with her own hand. "See, matching bands."

Glancing first at the wedding rings and then at the line waiting impatiently for their own turns at the gate, the guard nodded. "Okay, pass."

Shane joined Eden on the other side of the barricade. "Fast thinking," he congratulated her in an undertone. And then he grinned at her. "Comes in handy, doesn't it?"

She knew he was referring to their pretend marriage. Once again it had saved them. But there was no time to dwell on the possibility of that arrangement being anything more than a fantasy.

"Looks like we go this way," she said.

Following the crowd along one of the exhibition halls,

they reached the open setting for the ceremony. Most of those in front of them poured through French doors into a spacious courtyard situated at the heart of the museum. Eden and Shane didn't join them.

"My boss is gonna be seated down front," Denise had cautioned them when she'd given them the invitations, "so you'd better find a spot on the upper level."

Her suggestion suited Eden and Shane, who needed to see without being seen. They climbed a stairway on their right to an arcaded gallery that framed the courtyard below on all four sides. The gallery was already filled with standing spectators, which was also to their advantage. Able to blend in with the crowd, they found places for themselves next to a column in the dimness under an arch.

Aisles of folding chairs had been placed in the flagged courtyard beneath them, nearly all of them occupied. Sebastian Jamison must have been a much admired benefactor to draw an audience of this size, Eden thought.

A harpist played softly at one end of the sunlit courtyard where pots of flowers rimmed a fountain. A low stage had been erected at the other end. Down in front of it was the tall memorial sculpture shrouded under a cloth cover.

"Reserved for the family, I imagine," Shane said, indicating a row of chairs on the platform.

That family hadn't appeared yet. The chairs were empty.

"Here we go," Shane murmured as a tall, silver-haired man with the bearing of a senior statesman mounted the platform. The harpist fell silent, the audience hushed.

"Good afternoon, ladies and gentlemen." He introduced himself as Edward Harris, director of the Savannah Art Museum, then went on in a more solemn tone. "We're here today to pay tribute to one of Georgia's extraordinary citizens. Joining us are our five honored guests. Please welcome the family of the late Sebastian Jamison."

The audience applauded politely as two women, followed by three men, stepped through a doorway on the left and filed across the stage to the chairs that waited for them.

Eden gasped and clutched Shane's arm. From the tenseness of his muscles under her hand, she could tell he was as shocked as she was. The two women had yet to have identities for them. But the three men were all too familiar.

"No wonder they came out of that house and have been driving around in a Mercedes-Benz," Shane muttered at her ear.

And no wonder those two thugs are here in Savannah, Eden thought. They must have come back for the ceremony. And if they'd managed to learn Shane had left Charleston, there would have been no point in their hanging on there, anyway. But members of the Jamison family? That was surprising enough. Even more startling was the presence of Charlie Moses on that same stage.

"For those of you who may not already know them," Edward Harris said, "let me introduce our guests. Sebastian's wife, the much respected Dr. Claire Jamison."

She was slender and elegant, with ash-blond hair. Probably somewhere in her early fifties, Eden judged, but carefully preserved. She smiled and nodded to the audience.

"Sebastian's daughter, Irene Jamison Moses."

Charlie's wife? That explained his connection to the family. Charlie had done all right for himself. Irene had the same stunning, red-gold hair as her late brother, Simon. Nathanial's hair, Eden thought with a pang.

Irene sketched a little wave. The director moved on to the three men. "Irene's husband, Charles Moses. Sebastian's stepsons, Bryant and Hugh Dennis." He indicated first the darker of the two blond brothers, then the lighter.

Claire's sons from a first marriage, Eden assumed. For, of course, she must have been Sebastian's second wife and not the mother of Simon and Irene. Had the old man cared for any of them? Even Claire? He must have had a good reason for deciding to make Nathanial his chief heir. And just how much would those five people down there have resented that? Enough to kill?

The family had seated themselves on the five chairs. The

director began to extol the virtues of Sebastian Jamison. Claire sat quietly, her hands folded in her lap. Irene looked bored. She toyed with a pair of designer sunglasses. Charlie and the two brothers looked equally restless. Eden was prepared to duck behind the wide column, and guessed Shane was ready to join her if any of them started to cast a gaze in their direction. But none of them glanced up at the packed gallery.

"And now I'd like to ask Dr. Jamison to join me on the floor, where she'll unveil the sculpture dedicated to Sebastian Jamison."

Offering his arm, Edward Harris conducted Claire from the platform and down to the waiting sculpture.

"To the memory of my husband," she announced in a proud, cultured voice, tugging at the cord her escort indicated.

The cloth covering dropped away, collapsing the flags to the applause of the audience. Beneath it was an obelisk mounted on a temporary carousel. The shaft began to revolve slowly, revealing on each of its four sides a series of reliefs carved into the stone.

Claire returned to her chair on the platform. The director addressed the gathering again.

"The reliefs you are admiring, ladies and gentlemen, depict the projects here in Savannah, as well as elsewhere in Georgia, that Sebastian Jamison helped to endow. This museum is among them, which is why it is so fitting that the obelisk should be installed permanently tomorrow here in the courtyard."

Other speakers from the various charities Sebastian had funded in his lifetime followed, all of them praising his support.

At some point in the dry proceedings, Eden became aware of Shane's long silence. Looking at him, she saw that he was no longer paying any attention to the ceremony. His gaze was fastened on the obelisk that continued to turn in the sunlight.

"What is it?" she whispered.

He shook his head. "I'm not sure. There's something…"

He fell silent again and went on staring at the tall shaft. She had seen that same little frown on his face before, that same transfixed look in his eyes. Hadn't they always preceded an awakening of another memory? Her heart began to beat rapidly in anticipation.

## Chapter Twelve

A few minutes later the ceremony ended. The crowd began to depart from the courtyard. A photographer asked the Jamison family to pose around the obelisk for a few shots, and then they, too, left the scene. The gallery was also emptying, but Eden and Shane remained back in the shadows behind the arch.

"Something on that thing has jarred your memory, hasn't it?" she asked him hopefully.

"Maybe," he admitted. "Except I can't imagine how anything Jamison was connected with could be familiar to me."

"What are we going to do?"

"I need a closer look," he decided.

That might present a risk, Eden thought, but they couldn't afford to overlook any possibility. They waited until the gallery was clear, and then they descended to the lower level and checked the courtyard from one of the open French doors. It was deserted now except for two workmen who were taking down the folding chairs and loading them into a cart. The obelisk was no longer revolving on the carousel.

"Why don't I wait for you out here in the hall," Eden said. "It wouldn't hurt for me to keep a lookout."

Shane considered her suggestion. "I don't know that I

like the idea of us being separated with those Dennis brothers somewhere out there on the loose.''

"We were careful not to be spotted. They don't have any reason to be hanging around, not when they have no idea we're in Savannah.''

"Then why do you have to keep watch?''

"It's just a precaution.''

She could see Shane still wasn't satisfied by her answers, but they were wasting time. "All right," he agreed, "but you holler if you need me. This should only take a couple of minutes.''

She watched him start across the courtyard in the direction of the obelisk. The two workmen were still banging chairs and didn't bother to question his presence.

Turning away from the doorway, Eden moved out into the hall a few paces where she had a view in both directions. On her left, the broad corridor stretched off toward the back of the building. It was currently empty of visitors. The view on her right, equally deserted, ended a couple of yards away where the corridor turned a corner on its way back to the main entrance.

*Just a precaution.* But why? Why should it even cross her mind that the two-man crew in the courtyard could in any way be interested in Shane's errand? Or that if a museum guard happened to wander this way he might challenge them? Why should he when they were just another pair of visitors?

There was no reason for her concern. Except she *was* concerned, because the Jamisons had a great deal of influence in this town. And she was beginning to fear that anything was possible with that family.

Eden learned several seconds later she had good reason for her uneasiness. The silence was broken by a sudden conversation. It came from somewhere around the corner, close enough that she could clearly overhear it.

"Doing your rounds, Jerry?''

Eden went rigid. She knew that voice!

"Actually, I'm just on my way out front for a break. Thought you folks had all gone."

"My wife is missing her sunglasses. She thinks she may have left them behind on the platform."

"Be happy to go back and help you look for them."

"No, Jerry, I'll find them if they're there. You go ahead and take your break."

"Guess I'd better if I'm gonna get one. I have to relieve another guard in twenty minutes over in the wing where the Vermeers are on show."

Eden made a fast decision. She could either race back to the courtyard and warn Shane that trouble was on the way, or she could remain here and risk a bold confrontation with the man who had once meant everything to her. It was vital Shane have sufficient time to examine that obelisk, the key that could unlock the rest of his memory and lead them to Nathanial. She knew she had to stall Charles Moses.

"Have a good day, sir."

The guard must have departed. Eden steeled herself. A second later Charlie came swinging around the corner. And halted abruptly as they came face-to-face.

"Eden! What are you doing here?"

She gazed at him without reply. He had always been good-looking, with almost perfect features and a head of midnight-black hair, and that hadn't changed. If anything, he was even more handsome than when they had been together. And all she could do was stand there and wonder how she could ever have loved him when she could see that, even with those spectacular looks, he wasn't a fraction of the man Shane was.

"It's been a while, Charlie, hasn't it?" she said with a careless smile.

Her friendliness didn't fool him. His gaze left her face, searching the area behind her. She knew he was looking for Shane. "Where is he?" he demanded.

"Who?"

"Don't pull that innocent act on me, Eden. You know

who I'm talking about. The guy you've been on the run with."

"Oh, you mean Michael Reardon." Charlie wasn't quick enough to hide his surprise. "That's right, he knows now who he is. Funny thing though, Charlie."

"What is?"

"The way you looked just now when I told you he'd recovered his identity, as if you knew he'd lost his memory. And you couldn't have known that unless you, or someone close to you, had learned it from Harriet Krause just before she died."

"I don't know who you're talking about."

"Sure you do. You visited her a couple of weeks back, and she told you all about Lissie Reardon. I think she must have also told you that Lissie had a brother, and you figured there was a good chance Lissie had gone to him. It took you a while to track him down, but, being the able P.I. you are, you must have eventually located him in Arizona. That's about the way it went, didn't it, Charlie?"

"So what? The family was worried. We had a right to know where the boy and his mother had gone."

"*I'm* his mother, Charlie, but I guess you already know that by now. I guess Harriet would have told you. Or whoever visited her there at the end."

He stared at her without a response.

"So what happened in Arizona?" Eden pressed him. "You were too late when you got there, I bet. Lissie was dead, and Michael was already on his way to Charleston with my son. So what did you do then, Charlie? Contact your wife's stepbrothers to intercept him? Turn those two brutes on him with their dirty methods?"

"Reardon had no legal right to Patrick," he ground out. "He's no better than a kidnapper."

"No right to bring the son of the woman he'd married back to his own mother?"

"What's this?" Charlie sneered.

"It's true. Michael is my husband. See?" She held out her left hand, showing him the wedding band.

She knew Charlie would soon figure out Shane wasn't her husband, that nothing he had learned about Michael Reardon could have hinted at the possibility of a wife. But if it put him off for now, bought Shane a few more minutes in the courtyard, then the ruse was worth it. And to be honest about it, she enjoyed the astonished expression on Charlie's face. It gave her the momentary satisfaction of letting him know that, although he'd once dumped her, another man had wanted her.

"Anyway, if you were convinced Michael is such a villain, then why didn't you let the police handle it? What are you all hiding?"

Charlie's surprise vanished and was immediately replaced by something else. He advanced on her, his eyes narrow now with anger as he loomed over her threateningly. "You're not being smart, Eden."

She held her ground. "No?"

"I recommend that you tell me where Reardon is."

"And I recommend," said a cold voice behind her, "that you back away from her."

She and Charlie had been so involved in their verbal duel that neither one of them had been aware of Shane's sudden arrival on the scene.

"Because if you were even thinking about touching her," Shane warned him, "I'm going to tear you apart piece by piece."

Charlie's startled gaze shifted in Shane's direction. Swinging around, Eden saw the savage look in Shane's eyes. Charlie hesitated. Then, apparently realizing he was no match for Shane, he dropped back, turned and strode away swiftly in the direction of the entrance hall.

"He's going for help," Eden said.

"Yeah, and with the clout that bunch he married into seems to have in this place, there'll be security swarming all over this wing. Not to mention the Dennis brothers, if they're still hanging around out front waiting for Moses.''

She dragged at Shane's arm. "Then we'd better get out of here. But which way?"

"Let's see if we can find an exit at the back."

Praying it wasn't sealed off before they could get there, Eden fell into step beside Shane as they hurried along the corridor toward the rear of the museum.

They had broken no law. There should have been no reason why they couldn't simply walk out the front door. But if the Jamisons had enough pull to have them held and questioned, Shane possibly charged with abduction, the delay would give the family the time they needed to find Nathanial. She and Shane couldn't risk that. It was more imperative than ever now that they stay free. Her maternal instincts sensed that Nathanial's very existence depended on them reaching him first. But was that possible?

"The obelisk," she questioned him breathlessly. "Were you able to—"

"Yeah, I recognized one of those reliefs. I know the place, Eden. Looking at it finally kicked my last missing memory into place."

"Nathanial?" she asked, striving to control her excitement.

"He's nearby. And he's in safe hands. I'll tell you all about it when we get out of here."

Shane was right. They needed to conserve their breath, concentrate on finding an exit. She would have to be content for now knowing that her son was secure and they were on their way to him.

This section of the museum was devoted to Eastern culture, with things like samurai swords and tribal masks from New Guinea. They were no more popular than the art photos in the other wing. Eden and Shane met no one. Not even a guard was evident.

They were rapidly approaching the end of the corridor when Shane decided to share another discovery with her.

"There was something else about that obelisk. Or at least in the air around it."

She slid a sideways glance at him. What was he talking about?

"Perfume," he said. "I could catch a whiff of it still hanging in the air. No way to be sure, but I'd swear it was the same stuff we smelled in Harriet Krause's living room."

The Jamison women! They had both stood there close beside the obelisk posing for photographs. "If you're right, that means either Claire or Irene were in that apartment before Harriet died." And could have killed her, Eden thought.

Shane nodded. "Something more for us to look into."

And that, also, would have to wait until they got out of here. Which didn't look promising, Eden realized when they reached the end of the corridor. There was no exit here, only one of the museum's few windows.

Shane muttered a curse when he looked out, trying to determine their position. Eden could understand his chagrin when she joined him at the glass. They were no longer at ground level. The bluff dropped away at the back of the building, putting this floor at the height of a second story.

The corridor, however, was not a dead end. It branched off both to the left and to the right. "Which way now?" Eden wondered, glancing first in one direction and then in the other.

"That way," Shane decided, nodding to the right. "Looks like stairs down there."

It was a stairway to the first floor, but they were unable to descend it when they reached the flight. One of the uniformed guards stood at the bottom, his head lowered as he spoke earnestly on his hand radio.

"Wanna bet we're the subject of that conversation?" Shane whispered as they backed quickly away from the landing before the guard had the chance to look up and spot them.

Eden feared he was right and that the guard was being told to look out for them. Worried that he would mount the stairs and catch sight of them before they could take cover, she kept checking over her shoulder as they rushed back the way they had come.

Their only choice now was to try the left branch of the corridor and hope it would somehow lead them out of the building. In the meantime, they had to leave that guard far behind them as swiftly as possible, a need which Shane didn't seem to appreciate when he brought them to a halt again just as they started past the window.

"Hold on a second," he said. "There's something I want to check."

"Make it fast," she urged, puzzled by his sudden interest again in the view from the window.

"Yeah, I was right. Look at that other window across there and what's just below it."

Eden saw what he meant. Away to their left, in the same direction they were now headed, a short wing projected from the back of the building. On this side of that wing was a ground-floor utility extension with a flat roof. The second-story window Shane indicated was located directly above it.

"If we can get through that window," Shane said, "we'll be on the roof."

"And then what?"

"I think there's an easy way down. See the pair of iron handrails there curving up over the edge of the roof on the river side?"

"A fire escape?"

"No, a permanent ladder for servicing the roof and all that ventilation equipment on top of it. There are probably metal rungs attached to the wall just below those rails. Let's go."

He gave her no opportunity to question his intention. But why should he? He had been an Army Ranger, Eden reminded herself as she trotted after him. This kind of stuff was probably no challenge for him.

Eden kept thinking there had to be an easier way down and out. However, a quick look at a museum map they passed, posted under glass on the wall, indicated there was no other stairway in this section of the building. It would have to be the window, after all.

But the window proved to be even more difficult than she'd feared. To begin with, they had trouble finding it. When their route finally turned into the shallow wing, its sharp right angle making the guard somewhere behind them less of a threat now that they weren't visible from the other corridor, they found themselves in a gallery exhibiting Native American artifacts. There was no window in sight.

"It's got to be along here somewhere," Shane insisted. "I'd judge it to be just about— Uh-oh."

They had reached a closed door on the right. Presumably, the window was on the other side of it. And that could be a bit of a problem, Eden thought, considering the door was marked Women.

"Maybe it's empty," Shane said.

This was a strong likelihood. They had encountered no one in this wing but a father and his two children wandering along the glass cases of relics. But there was sure to be another guard somewhere in the vicinity, and if they didn't hurry—

"Let me be sure," Eden said.

She spread the door inward. Behind it was an L-shaped rest room. There were sinks directly in front of her, with the window they sought between them. And off to the right, in the base of the L, was a row of stalls, their doors all open.

"It's clear," she reported to Shane hovering behind her.

Except it wasn't clear. Eden hadn't thought to look behind the door. And not until they were both inside the rest room, with that door swung shut behind them, did she see the alcove with a full-length mirror on its wall. The alcove's occupant was a tall woman with a startled expression on her face.

"Um, sorry," Eden hastily apologized. "I have this medical problem, so I need my husband with me to help out whenever I—well, you know."

The poor woman nodded, as if she understood, but Eden knew that she'd probably spend the rest of the afternoon wondering what medical problem could possibly require a husband's presence with his wife in a rest-room stall. Scooting past them, she fled from the place.

"Our marriage just keeps getting better and better, doesn't it?" Shane observed with a wicked grin.

There was no easy way for Eden to respond to that one. Her emotions on the subject ran too deep by now. *Is our pretend marriage nothing more to you, Shane, than what it started out to be? A masquerade to facilitate our search for Nathanial?* That's what she wanted to ask him. And then she would have followed it with a heartfelt: *Because for me it's come to mean more than that.*

*A lot more.*

But she didn't say any of those things. There was no time for them. Nor was she certain she had the courage to hear what he might tell her. So, instead, she replied with a very ordinary, "Our marriage isn't going to rescue us where that window is concerned. Look." She pointed to the alarm high on the wall above the frosted window.

"Yeah, with that roof out there, it figures it would be wired to go off if anyone tries to get in or out this way." He dug into one of the pockets of his jacket. "Ah, I still have it," he said, producing the short-handled screwdriver he had armed himself with back in Charleston, and which he hadn't bothered to return to the glove compartment of Eden's car.

"It can't be that easy to disconnect the alarm."

"It shouldn't be, but if you know what you're doing…"

His Special Forces training.

"Keep watch," he instructed her over his shoulder as he crossed to the window.

Eden posted herself at the door, opening it a crack and ready to warn him if anyone approached the rest room. Nothing should have been on her mind but her vigil and the tense hope that Shane would succeed with disarming the device, but an unexpected question intruded into her thoughts.

How did Sebastian Jamison die?

She suddenly realized that Harriet Krause hadn't told them that, probably because she hadn't known. Nor had she and Shane learned the cause of the old man's death when they searched the newspaper files. They'd begun with stories of the family in the society pages, but Shane had recognized his sister in that photo before either of them had the opportunity to move on to an obituary.

So they didn't know how Sebastian had died. Was the cause important? Quite possibly it was, and, if so, this was something more for them to inves—

"Somebody deserves to be shot."

Shane's muttered complaint put an end to her speculations. *He didn't have any luck with the window,* she thought, her hope sinking as she released the door and turned around to see for herself.

The window was wide open.

"But you've done it! So why—"

"It was too easy," he grumbled, slipping the screwdriver back into his pocket. "There's no excuse for an antiquated security system in a place like this. And the bathroom window back at Harriet Krause's apartment, that's another example. She should have had that broken catch repaired. And since she didn't, certainly the police ought to have seen to it before they left the apartment."

"Shane—"

"Yeah, I know, all this can wait. It's given me an idea, though. But that's for the future. Come on, let's get out of here."

Shane helped her through the window and onto the roof, then scrambled through the opening after her. He made no effort to close the window behind them.

"A guard will check the bathroom before closing," he said. "Let them see they've got a problem that needs to be corrected."

Eden held her breath, fearing an angry shout behind them as they made their rapid way through the ventilation equipment to the metal service ladder at the far edge of the roof. They reached it without a challenge.

"The rest should be a piece of cake," Shane said.

Thankfully, it was. Minutes later, they were back inside the Toyota and headed away from the museum. And at last Eden was able to learn from Shane what she had longed to hear from the moment he had emerged from the courtyard.

"OF COURSE, they got away. He's too smart for all of you. He has been all along."

Claire Jamison gazed lividly at her family gathered around her in the empty courtyard. Charles had just rejoined them to report there was no sign of Eden Hawke or Michael Reardon and that an open window in one of the rest rooms indicated they had probably fled the museum by that route.

Claire's calculating green eyes, in a delicate face that belied an inner strength, came to rest on her two sons. More brawn than brains, just like their father whom she had divorced years ago when she'd realized that the widowed Sebastian Jamison had a great deal more to offer her.

"Why did I ever trust either of you? If you hadn't bungled it from the start by not being there at the airport when Reardon's plane landed, none of this would have gotten out of control."

"It's not our fault that the weather and traffic delayed us," Bryant spoke up in defense of himself and his brother. "Or that his flight got in ahead of schedule."

"And I suppose it's not your faults that you went and

lost him again in Charleston, and then you come back here with your tails between your legs.''

Claire made a sound of disgust, her gaze shifting to Charles. Unlike Bryant and Hugh, Charles wasn't stupid. She had expected better from him, but he, too, had failed her. ''You were a fool to alarm the guards like that. Telling them that lie about Reardon threatening the family when you knew how vital it was to keep everything as quiet as possible.''

Charles shrugged. ''What was I supposed to do? Let him get away?''

''He *did* get away,'' she reminded him sharply, ''and we still don't have Patrick.''

But she would before she was through, Claire promised herself. Because she had enough brains for all of them, and something even more important than that: a ruthless determination. She had proved that both here in Savannah and up in Charleston where Harriet Krause had supplied her with useful information before she died. Claire had learned Eden Hawke was Patrick's biological mother and that the man calling himself Shane had amnesia and didn't know what he had done with the boy.

''Now you hear me, all of you,'' she told her family severely. ''What I've done before, I can do again if I have to. But I'm not in this alone. We're all of us in it together, and you know what we'll lose if any of us forget that.''

''Then why are we standing here talking about it?'' Claire's stepdaughter challenged her. ''What are we doing back in the courtyard, anyway?''

''Think about it,'' Claire said, addressing not just Irene but the others as well. ''We don't know why Reardon and the Hawke woman came to Savannah. But we do know, from what Eden Hawke told Charles, that Michael Reardon's memory is restored.''

''If that's true,'' Irene said, ''why would they bother turning up here at the museum?''

''Exactly.'' Claire paused, brushing her hand impatiently

across the side of her stylish ash-blond hair as she looked at each of them in turn. But none of them could see the obvious. "Don't you understand? If Michael Reardon had fully regained his memory, then he and Eden Hawke would have the boy by now and would probably be back in Charleston talking to the police."

"Are you saying," Charles asked her slowly, "that Eden lied to me, and Reardon hasn't recovered his memory?"

"They wouldn't know his name if that were true. But more often than not, the memory of an amnesiac returns in fragments," Claire explained, speaking from her knowledge as a doctor. "And if his mind had yet to restore the last of those fragments…"

"Yes," Charles said, finally comprehending. "You're telling us there's a good chance Reardon remembered everything but where he put Patrick."

Claire nodded. "And he was here in the courtyard when you came back to look for Irene's sunglasses. You're sure of that, Charles?"

"Yeah, he marched out of here while Eden was talking to me in the hall."

"Then it makes sense. There's something he felt was important enough to risk his appearance here in the courtyard."

"What?" Irene demanded.

Claire didn't answer her. The two workmen had returned to the courtyard with the cart. They were preparing to load the last of the folding chairs for storage, when Claire crossed the flags to speak to them.

"I wonder if you gentlemen could help me. There was a man here about a half hour ago."

Charles had joined her to offer a description. "Tall guy with a slight limp. Were you in the courtyard then?"

The elder of the two workmen nodded.

"Did you notice what he was doing?" Claire pressed him.

"Looking at the obelisk over there."

"Any part of it in particular?"

"I didn't notice."

"I did," the younger of the two spoke up. "He looked at the back side of it. Stared at it for a long time, and then he got this kind of excited expression on his face. I figured the guy was really into sculpture, you know."

"Thank you, gentlemen." Claire dismissed them sweetly before either of them could start asking questions.

They went back to loading chairs as she hurried toward the obelisk, her family trailing behind her. Circling the monument to its back side, she spent several moments shrewdly studying the reliefs. There were four of them carved into the length of the obelisk.

"One of these," she said with growing certainty, "gave Michael Reardon the last missing piece of his memory."

Neither the one on top nor the third one down qualified as possibilities. They depicted the art museum itself and a children's playground in Savannah. But the second and fourth reliefs were of considerable interest to her.

"It's either this one or this one," she said, her hand fingering the raised representations of a lighthouse on the coast and an antebellum plantation house in rural Georgia. They were both of them restoration projects Sebastian had helped to fund.

"You telling us one of those places is where Reardon stashed the kid?" Bryant asked, a sneer in his voice.

"It's a hell of a long shot," his brother, Hugh, agreed with him.

Claire rounded on her two sons. "You listen to me, both of you. This could be our last chance, and you're not going to screw it up this time. Hugh, I want you and Charles to take the plantation. Bryant, you're coming with me to the lighthouse. I'm convinced Patrick is near one of them, and we're not coming back without him."

Reardon or not, she promised herself fiercely, the boy had to be found and dealt with. Everything depended on it.

# *Chapter Thirteen*

"Palm Island Lighthouse," Shane said.

Eden was eager to hear the rest, but she had to concentrate first on getting them out of Savannah. She pulled up behind a tourist trolley at a traffic light. A decision was necessary before the light turned to green.

"Which way?"

"Straight ahead."

He gave her the number of the route they needed. Moments later they were out of the historic district and headed in the direction of the coast.

"Now tell me," she urged him.

"It's one of the Atlantic seaboard's early lighthouses, and it was in bad shape when I knew it as a teenager. There was talk then of restoring it. Jamison must have funded a large portion of the project, and that's why a carving of it ended up on the obelisk."

Shane wasn't making sense. "Nathanial is at a lighthouse?"

"No, but nearby. I used to see the light every day off in the distance on this point where it stands. It's a familiar landmark, which is why I finally recognized it."

"Wait a minute. Didn't you tell me you grew up in Richmond, Virginia?"

"That's right, but I spent my high-school summers down here working for a couple on Palm Island."

Palm Island. Eden didn't recognize the name, but that wasn't surprising. There were countless barrier islands all along the Carolina and Georgia coasts.

"Estelle and Victor DuBois," Shane said. She could hear the affection in his voice as he went on to tell her about the couple. "Victor and my father were professors at the University of Richmond, but he and Estelle had a summer home and rental cottages on the beach on Palm Island. I used to help them run the place. Now Victor's retired, and they live there full-time."

Eden understood at last. "Nathanial is with this couple."

"I contacted them from Arizona, and they met me at the Charleston Airport and took Nathanial home with them, where I knew he'd be safe while I checked you out. Estelle and Victor are like family to me. They're good people, Eden," he assured her. "I would never have trusted Nathanial with them if I hadn't been certain they would care for him like he was their own."

Eden didn't doubt him, but the situation being what it was, she remained anxious. Shane understood that without her need to express it.

"I'll call them," he said, helping himself to her cell phone. "They ought to know we're on our way."

Eyes on the road, she listened closely as he phoned the island and spoke to Victor DuBois, explaining the whole situation.

"Everything's fine," he reported moments later after ending the call. "Patrick—Nathanial, that is—is safe and happy. No one's been near the house or asked about him, but they promised not to let him out of their sight until we get there."

Eden nodded and checked the rearview mirror. She knew that Shane had also been keeping an eye on the road behind them. There was no sign whatever that they were being followed, but it paid to be vigilant.

Satisfied for the moment, Eden relaxed. There had been no opportunity before this to ask Shane what she had been hungering to know ever since he had told her that Beth had entrusted him with Nathanial. But now...

"It's been three years since I lost him," she said, her voice thick with emotion. "He must have changed a lot since then. You spent time with him, Shane. You can tell me what my son is like now."

"I've never been around kids before, Eden. I don't know whether he's a typical five-year-old or not."

"Please, I have to know."

Shane was thoughtful for a moment. "He's a good-looking little boy, but you know that already from the photograph. As for the rest...well, I think you'll be proud of him. He's intelligent, loves animals, but he's shy with people."

"Lively? Is he at all lively? Most boys that age are."

"Sometimes. He'd be playing hard, and then—"

Shane hesitated. She knew he was reluctant to tell her anything that might worry her, but she had to hear it all. "What?" she pressed him.

"He'd turn suddenly quiet, withdraw into himself."

"Because he was missing the woman he knew as his mother? Is that why?"

"I think it was more than that, Eden. I think he was remembering something he wanted to forget and couldn't."

She nodded. "Something that frightened him. The thing, as you said before, he wouldn't talk about and probably the reason why he and Beth left Savannah."

Dear God, what could her son have seen that had traumatized him like that?

Sensing her concern, Shane made an effort to comfort her. "He's going to be okay, Eden. He's a tough kid underneath it all, and with time and patience he'll come around. You'll see."

She flashed him a look of gratitude and then gave her attention entirely to the road again. She didn't want to risk any further glances in his direction, didn't want to tempt herself with the potent sight of him. There was too much uncertainty in that.

They would soon reach Palm Island, claim Nathanial and return with him to Charleston where his true identity would be established, her legal right to him secured. The police would handle everything after that, including any investigation of the Jamisons and their involvement.

She and Shane would have finished with what they had set out to do. What then? Would he go out of her life as suddenly as he had entered it? Return to Arizona and his own existence? She hadn't dared let herself think about that before, and she didn't want to think about it now. The idea of losing him was unbearable.

It was a subject, however, that sooner or later would have to be addressed, but at this moment Eden preferred to avoid it. She was almost grateful that she had something else to distract her. For some time she had been aware of the sky. It had darkened and was looking increasingly threatening in the southeast, the direction in which they were headed.

"I guess there's a reason why the traffic is so light," she said. "The weather doesn't look good."

"Yeah, I know. There's a storm brewing off the coast. I've seen them come up like this before in this part of the country, and they can be pretty bad."

She might have been alarmed, except his tone was so mild. But he was silent after that, his gaze fixed on the menacing sky. *He* is *worried,* she finally realized. *And he doesn't want me to know.*

"Shane, what's wrong? This isn't hurricane season, so I don't know why—"

"There's no bridge, that's what's wrong."

"I don't understand."

"Palm Island isn't connected to the mainland by a bridge, like so many of the barrier islands are. It depends on a small car ferry, and if the weather is too wild..."

"Are you saying there's a chance we won't be able to cross?"

"Maybe it will be all right. Maybe we can beat the storm."

But they didn't. Even though Eden increased their speed, the storm broke over the flat, marshy lowlands while they were still miles from their destination. The wind and rain were so severe over the open country that Eden was forced to slow the Toyota to a crawl. It was either that or risk being blown off the highway, which she could barely see through the sheets of driving rain.

The torrent had eased some by the time they reached the ferry landing. But the wind was still a gale, so fierce that her heart sank when she glimpsed the intercoastal waterway frothy with whitecaps. Was she to get this close to Nathanial, only to learn she wasn't able to reach him?

"Sit tight," Shane instructed her, "while I find out what our chances are."

Sliding out of the car, he dashed through the rain toward the snub-nosed ferry sitting at the dock. He was back in a moment, wet hair plastered to his scalp as he rejoined her in the car.

"We're in luck," he reported. "Pilot said he's making this the last run of the day. Said he's crossed in worse, though he wouldn't be attempting it if the island wasn't the ferry's home base and he doesn't want to spend the night on this side. Are you up to it?"

If it had been necessary, Eden would have swum the broad sound to reach her son. "Of course," she said without hesitation.

But it was a rough crossing, the vessel wallowing in the swells like a sick animal as it chugged through the rapidly failing light. She was relieved when they finally crawled into the quiet waters of the harbor and coasted to the dock.

It was nightfall by the time they crossed the island where Shane directed her along a road edging the oceanfront. Her whole body was thrumming with anticipation when they turned into a driveway and arrived at a long, low brick ranch house situated in a grove of tall pines. Welcoming lights glowed in the windows.

It was still raining, the wind so strong that great rollers piled along the beach. But Eden was oblivious now to the weather and scarcely noticed the sweeping beam of the lighthouse off in the distance as they left the car and made their way to the front door. All she could think about was Nathanial somewhere inside this house.

Her tremulous bottom lip that Shane seemed to find so intriguing must have betrayed her nervous state. As they stood under the light on the covered stoop, waiting for their ring to be answered, he leaned down and placed a light kiss on that lip. It was an act of reassurance that moved her. Told her he understood the emotions that were churning inside her.

"It's going to be okay," he said. "He's going to learn to love you all over again."

She could have kissed him back for that. And would have if the door hadn't opened in that second. They were ushered inside with smiles of greeting, and Eden found herself being introduced to the African-American couple who had been caring for her son.

Estelle DuBois was a small woman, all warmth and gentleness. Her husband, Victor, who towered over his wife, bore himself with an innate dignity. Eden immediately liked them.

She must have looked more eager than she realized, her gaze casting around the entrance hall where they stood for a sign of Nathanial. Victor understood. "He's in the family room with Spice," he said in a bass voice that must have commanded attention in his classrooms.

The couple led them through a comfortable living room, across a dining room whose table was laid for dinner, and into the spacious family room off the rear of the house.

Spice turned out to be a lively spaniel tugging at the end of a towel in the hands of the boy who was playing with him on the floor. He was unaware of their arrival, probably because of the blaring television set.

Estelle crossed the room and lowered the volume. "Look who's here, Patrick."

He lifted his gaze then, and even with the width of the room between them, Eden could see the lavender blue of those wonderful eyes that had haunted her every dream for three years before tears blurred her vision. She had been waiting for this reunion all that time, longing for it, and suddenly she was scared. Praying for his acceptance of her.

But she was a stranger, after all. Shane wasn't. Dropping the towel, the child scrambled to his feet and raced across the room. "Uncle Mike!"

Man and boy shared a fierce hug.

"Hey, buddy, you didn't think I wasn't coming back for you, did you?"

Watching them together, Eden could see that Shane had minimized their relationship. He and her son had clearly bonded, and that pleased her. It also made her a little jealous.

Getting to his feet, his hands on her son's shoulders, Shane turned him in Eden's direction. "Patrick, I've brought a very special lady to meet you. Her name is Eden Hawke."

There was no recognition in the shy gaze that examined her. How could there be when he must have forgotten her long ago? Eden wanted to embrace him as Shane had embraced him, but she didn't dare. That kind of familiarity would have frightened him. Nor could she tell him she was his mother. That, too, would have alarmed him. She blinked away her tears.

It would take time and patience, a great deal of both, before he was ready to hear the truth. All she could do now was to smile down at him and offer him a very ordinary, "Hello, Patrick. I hope we'll be friends."

"'Lo," he mumbled.

She went on smiling, the sight of him tugging at her.

Would he, she wondered desperately, ever call her "Mom" again? Or would he forever belong to the woman who had stolen him from her?

EDEN FOUGHT A BATTLE with herself at the dinner table. She couldn't keep her eyes off Nathanial, and that wasn't good. She knew her repeated glances had him a little worried about her. But it was hard not to look when she wanted to familiarize herself with all the changes in him, to catch up with everything she had missed. In the end, it was Shane's hand squeezing hers under the table that gave her the courage to restrain herself. That and a concern that took her mind off her son.

The subject that had troubled her ever since the art museum couldn't be mentioned, though, until Nathanial finished his dinner and went back into the family room to watch television. Now that the adults were alone at the table, she was prepared to ask Estelle and Victor if they knew anything about it. Though she and Shane had had no opportunity to discuss it, the same subject must have been on his mind as well because, much to her surprise, he spoke first.

"Victor," he said in an undertone, leaning toward their host, "I imagine the island is too far removed from Savannah for you and Estelle to be interested in the news there. But since Sebastian Jamison helped to fund the restoration of the lighthouse here, I thought maybe the local paper might have carried his obituary."

"If it did," Victor replied in his deep voice, "I don't remember reading it. Estelle?" His wife shook her head.

"So you don't know how he died?" Eden asked them earnestly.

Victor shook his head. "No, but I know someone who might. Bud Pruitt over on the other side of the island was chairman of the restoration committee and used to meet with Jamison in Savannah. Let me give him a ring."

Victor went into the kitchen to use the phone there. He

was back in a few minutes. After glancing in the direction of the family room to make certain that Nathanial couldn't hear them, he settled again at the table and told them what he'd learned.

"Bud said the old man suffered from arthritis complicated by angina, and toward the end was pretty much of an invalid, confined either to his bed or a wheelchair."

"Did he have a fatal heart attack, then?" Eden asked.

"His heart did fail, but it was the result of a fall down a flight of stairs."

Eden and Shane traded swift glances, and she knew he was thinking the same thing. Victor didn't miss their exchange. What's more, he was shrewd enough to guess their suspicions.

"It doesn't work, people. Bud said Sebastian's wife is a doctor and that her husband was under her care. She demanded a police investigation and got it. It turns out the old man was alone in the house that night except for Patrick, who was asleep in his room, and Patrick's nanny, who'd nodded off while sitting in the chair next to his bed. The staff and family were all elsewhere and with solid alibis. No one knows why Sebastian tried to go downstairs on his own or why he didn't call for the nanny if he needed something, which is what his wife instructed him to do before having to leave him for a few hours, but in the end everyone was satisfied the fall was an accident."

"About this nanny," Eden wondered.

"No motive there," Victor said, understanding the possibility she was suggesting. "Apparently, she was as devoted to Sebastian as she was to Patrick. Even blamed herself for falling asleep."

The police might be satisfied by this explanation for Sebastian Jamison's death, but Eden wasn't. Nor, if his grim expression was any indication, did she think Shane was either. But any further inquiry in that direction would have to wait until they got Nathanial safely back to Charleston. And that, much to her frustration, couldn't happen before tomorrow when, hopefully, the weather would have improved sufficiently to permit them to leave the island.

Getting to her feet, she helped Estelle to clear the table and load the dishwasher in the kitchen where she had the opportunity to thank the woman for caring for her son. The couple's kindness didn't end there, as she learned when she returned to the dining room.

"Estelle and I were discussing it earlier," Victor explained, "and if you want it, we'd like to offer the three of you one of the beach cottages for the night. It would be a chance, Eden, for you to get to know Patrick away from all of the distractions here."

The idea of her and her son and Shane playing family, even if it was only for one night, appealed to Eden. On the other hand, they would be on their own in the cottage. She trusted Shane to look out for them, just as Victor would look out for his wife and himself here. But if any of the Jamison family *was* in some manner responsible for Sebastian's death and it involved Nathanial…

Anxious about his welfare, her gaze drifted in the direction of the family room where he was stretched out on the floor, the spaniel beside him. Her concern, and the reason for it, must have been evident to Shane.

"The weather has locked down the island for the night," he reminded her. "No one from the mainland can get here now, even if they did have any idea of where we are, and that isn't likely."

That was true, Eden thought. And she and Shane hadn't been followed. They'd made certain of that. Besides, the DuBois house could be no more safe than the cottage, and since they had to stay somewhere for the night…

"I think I would like that," she said, accepting Victor's offer.

"I should point out to you," Victor said, "that the Lincoln cottage, which is the only one made up for guests at this time of the year, has just two bedrooms, so if that's a problem—"

Shane cut him off with a confident, "I think we can manage just fine with the sleeping arrangements, don't you, Eden?"

Was that an eager gleam in his eyes? Yes, definitely a gleam. It told her he was probably far more interested in a game of man and wife in that cottage than in playing family. Did she have an argument with that? She couldn't think of any. Not a single one.

IT HAD STOPPED raining by the time the three of them piled into the Toyota with their things and drove a quarter of a mile down the road to the Lincoln cottage nestled under the pines close to the shore. If there were any palms on Palm Island, and Eden figured there must be some, she had yet to see one.

The storm clouds had cleared away, leaving a sky spangled with stars, but the wind still blustered off the ocean. She could hear the high surf booming on the beach. The sound of it, together with a phosphorescent glow from the waves, made the cottage seem isolated, almost ghostly.

There was something else that contributed to that mood. Out on a spit of land, which must have been several hundred yards away, she could just make out in the starlight the bulk of some massive, crumbling structure. The ocean pounded at the feet of its broken walls.

"Those are the ruins of the old Fort Lafayette," Shane said. "Used to be a great spot for bringing girls when I was a teenager."

*I bet,* Eden thought with a little smile.

They left the car parked under the trees and carried their gear into the cottage. The place lost its eerie spell for her once the lights were on and the electric heat was turned up to take off the chill. In fact, it was invitingly snug, and she was glad they were here. Nathanial was partly responsible for that. He was excited about spending the night here. It was an adventure to him.

"Like camping out," he said.

"That's right, buddy," Shane told him. "Only you get a comfy bed instead of the hard ground, and the clock says it's time you were in that bed."

Eden envied him his ease with Nathanial. She felt awkward and helpless with her own son, standing around uselessly while Shane took charge and saw Nathanial settled in his room.

She was in their own room, changing into her nightie after brushing her teeth and trying not to gaze with anticipation at the queen-size bed they would share tonight, when Shane returned.

"Is he asleep?"

"No, but he's in his pj's and trying to keep his lids from drooping. Why don't you go to him and tuck him in for the night."

Eden longed to do just that, but she was uncertain. "Do you think he'd let me?"

"He's your kid, Eden. It's time you started playing mother."

Shane was right. If she was ever to reestablish a mother-son relationship with Nathanial, she needed to overcome her constraint. Quelling her nervousness, she went along the hall to the tiny bedroom on the other side of the small cottage. She was disappointed to find him already in bed. There would be no ritual of tucking him under the covers, of making sure he had the stuffed elephant he had treasured as an infant. She supposed he had no memory of that elephant.

"I came to say good night, Patrick." The name didn't come easily to her. Would she ever be able to tell him his real name? And would he ever accept it?

"'Night," he responded.

Should she kiss him? She wanted to. No, better not. It might make him uncomfortable. "Would you like one of the lamps left on in here?"

He shook his head.

"Well, if you wake up and need anything, just call. We'll be right here."

"All right."

He was waiting for her to go. She hated to leave it like this, but she had no reason to linger. Not, anyway, until she started to back away and noticed the books ranged along shelves against one wall. Some of them were books for children.

"I could read you a story before you go to sleep. That is, if you'd like me to."

He considered her offer. "Okay."

She selected an anthology of classic tales. "This one looks good."

He allowed her to perch on the edge of his bed. She turned to the story of "Dick Whittington and His Cat" and began to read. He was asleep long before she was able to finish the tale. Never mind. They had shared a few private, precious moments. It was a beginning.

Fearing even now she would wake him if she risked a kiss on his forehead, she turned out the lamp and slipped out of the room. She had closed the door softly behind her, her mind occupied with her satisfaction, when she trod on something under her bare feet.

Startled, she look down. What in the name of—

Flowers. Artificial flowers of every hue and variety. She remembered there had been an enormous mixed bouquet stuffed into a basket on the table in the living room. The flowers were no longer in that basket. They were strewn along the floor in a deliberate trail that led to the other bedroom. It was an unmistakable invitation.

Eden followed the trail back to the bedroom where she discovered Shane waiting for her impatiently. He was seated cross-legged in the middle of the bed, wearing nothing but a pair of snug briefs, a sprig of lily of the valley tucked behind one ear and a wicked grin.

Her breath stuck in her throat at the sight of him. He was awesome. The sculpted muscles of his arms, chest and long legs glowed in the soft light of the single lamp on the bedside table. What those briefs concealed was something she didn't even dare think about... Except she found herself doing just that.

"I left you a message," he said.

"Yes, I found it. And understood it, I believe," she added, noticing that the flowers were scattered in a path all the way to the side of the bed. Closing the door, she gestured in the direction of the sprig behind his ear. "Nice touch."

"Yeah, I thought so." He removed the lily of the valley and sniffed it. "No scent, though. Too bad. I was kind of hoping to rekindle the fragrance you were wearing the night I stumbled in out of the rain. You know, the one that had me thinking of wife and home."

"I remember."

"Damn seductive, that scent. Makes a man imagine the wildest things. Uh, I don't suppose—"

"Sorry, I'm not wearing any of my Lily of the Valley perfume."

"Yeah, but they say traces of a fragrance can linger long afterward on the skin."

"I've heard that."

"You just have to get close enough to detect it."

"Really?"

"That's what they say."

"In that case..."

Eden crossed to the bed, placed one knee on it to support herself, and leaned toward him, offering herself for his sensory examination. Shane tossed the sprig to one side and buried his nose in her throat, inhaling deeply.

"Anything?"

He drew back, shaking his head. "I'll need more exposure than this."

Eden accommodated him, drawing the nightie over her head and kneeling now in front of him with both legs on the bed. "Enough?"

"Better, but I'll need even more to be sure. A lot more."

He left her no choice. Slipping off the bed, she removed her bra and panties and went to him again. This time his arms went around her, hauling her against his heat and hardness. For a long, tantalizing moment both his nose and mouth were occupied with the flesh between her breasts.

"Lily of the Valley?" she said raspingly.

"Something much better than that," he rumbled. "Woman. All woman."

She was able to savor an aroma of her own after that. *His* aroma, clean and masculine. Her nostrils filled with it as his mouth settled over hers in a long, blistering kiss. Her other senses sharpened when she tasted his tongue involved in a searing contact with her own. When she felt his powerful arousal strained against her belly. When she heard the primitive sounds of passion deep in his throat.

He gave a gruff voice to those groans when his mouth finally lifted from hers. "If memory serves me, sweetheart, we have some unfinished business from last night."

He was referring to their aborted lovemaking in the motel. "I think you're right."

He went rigid then as something suddenly occurred to him. "Unless Patrick—"

"Sound asleep. He let me read to him, so it was either the story that worked or I have a voice like a lullaby."

Shane grinned with relief, his hands cupping her breasts. "The body of one, anyway. So, just where did we leave off last night?"

"Somewhere between ecstasy and frustration."

"Good enough. Let's pick up from here." His head lowered to her breasts, his mouth closing around one nipple, giving it his full attention, and then turning to tug at the other while she clutched at him in mindless rapture.

"And here," he said, his mouth moving on down to her belly and finally settling between her parted thighs where his tongue worked a miracle of enticement.

She was in a fever of wanting him inside her when at

last he shucked his briefs, sheathed himself with a condom and covered her with his eager body, his swollen arousal burying itself in her wet, welcoming softness.

It was a lush joining, their rhythms alternately slow and rapid, gentle and fierce. And in the end consumed by an urgency that carried them, each in turn, to a blinding release.

Rolling to one side, Shane gathered her close against him. He kissed her tenderly, his mouth cherishing her lips before he settled his head back on the pillow with a deep sigh of contentment. There was silence then.

Eden thought he had gone to sleep, but a few moments later he eased away from her and off the bed. She gazed at him in surprise as he dragged on a pair of jeans.

"What are you doing?"

"Thought I would sit up awhile in Nathanial's room."

He said it carelessly, as if not wanting to worry her, but she *was* suddenly worried. "You're planning on keeping watch over him, aren't you? Why, if you're so certain none of the Jamisons have any idea where we are, and couldn't cross to the island tonight even if they did?"

"It just seems like a good idea."

He was right. No matter how safe they were here, they needed to exercise every caution. "All right, but you're not keeping any all-night vigil on your own. You take the first shift, and I'll relieve you in a few hours."

"Deal. Now get some sleep." Drawing the cover over her, he leaned down and dropped a kiss on her mouth. Then he was gone, shutting the door behind him.

Eden lay there, unable to close her eyes, already missing him, thinking about what they had shared in this bed. Their lovemaking had been everything she had wished for, rich and satisfying, fulfilling all her fantasies. Except for one thing. He had expressed no commitment, no words of his love for her. She tried not to be disappointed, tried not to yearn for what he might not be capable of delivering. Hadn't she known the risk?

After a moment she reached out and turned off the bedside lamp. She listened in the darkness to the breakers surging on the shore below the cottage. She reminded herself she had her son back. That was all that was ultimately important, all she had asked for. Wasn't it?

IT WAS NO LONGER dark in the bedroom when Eden opened her eyes. The moon had risen, casting its glow through the single window. Its light must have awakened her. What time was it? Switching on the lamp, she checked her watch and found it was long past midnight. Time to relieve Shane.

Crawling out from under the blanket, she recovered her nightie from where it had landed on the floor and pulled it over her head. The cottage had cooled, so she added her robe and slippers against the chill before leaving the room.

Shane hadn't bothered to turn on any lights elsewhere in the cottage. They weren't necessary when the moon was sufficient illumination. She met him out in the hall returning from the living room.

"Just checking the doors and windows," he explained. She knew he had made certain just after their arrival that both outside doors and all the windows were locked. "Everything's tight. Wake me around three, and I'll take another turn. And, Eden?"

"Yes?"

"If you hear anything, you call me."

But she heard nothing except the wind in the pines and the surf rolling on the beach after he disappeared into their bedroom, closing the door behind him. She went into Nathanial's room and found him as she had left him earlier, peacefully asleep.

Taking up her post, she curled into an easy chair in the corner. It was a bad choice, much too comfortable with her robe wrapped around her warmly. She must have dozed, because when she lifted her head, the pattern of moonlight on the carpet had shifted.

Leaving the chair before she nodded off again, she went

and stood beside the bed, tenderly gazing down at her son. Then, unable to resist the temptation, she leaned over and brushed a light kiss against his forehead. When she straightened up, there was a gun at her back.

# Chapter Fourteen

"Don't move, don't speak," whispered a gravelly voice so close behind her that she could feel his hot breath in her ear. "Not a muscle, understand, because if you do the kid will suffer for it."

Eden remained perfectly still. Or as still, anyway, as her trembling body would permit.

He was apparently satisfied. Although the gun remained pressed against her back, she no longer felt his breath close to her ear when he spoke again. The direction of his whisper indicated he must have turned his head.

"It's clear now. I've got her covered."

Eden heard no movement behind her, but she knew instantly that someone must have joined them in the bedroom. The scent of an expensive perfume invaded the air, the same fragrance she had detected in a Charleston apartment. It was a chilling reminder of what had happened to Harriet Krause.

Eden caught the sound of the bedroom door closing softly behind the new arrival, and then the gunman issued another command to her in that same loathsome whisper.

"Turn around. *Slowly,* and keep your hands in front of you where I can see them."

Eden obeyed him. What choice did she have with that gun trained on her? When her son was threatened?

She had no trouble recognizing them once she was facing

them. The moonlight from the window was bright enough to identify them as the brutish Bryant Dennis and his mother, Dr. Claire Jamison. How long had they been lurking in the darkness out in the hall? And how had they gotten into the cottage without either Shane or her hearing them?

But what did any of this matter when Claire Jamison was confronting her with a lethal expression on her elegant face? "Listen to me," she addressed Eden in an undertone. "I want you to wake the boy, but do it carefully. Make certain that he doesn't cry out. Not a sound from him."

They didn't want to rouse Shane, Eden realized. Why? Did they fear he had a gun of his own, or did they have another motive for this furtive activity?

"Is that clear?" Claire demanded.

Eden jerked a nod and turned to the bed. She was sick with fear, but it was mostly for her son. She was also angry. Angry that they were forcing her to wake him. He would be terrified. And she was angry with her own helplessness.

Bending over the bed, ready to cover Nathanial's mouth with her hand while hating the possible necessity of such an action, she spoke to him as soothingly as possible. "Patrick, you have to wake up. Can you hear me, sweetheart?"

He didn't at first. She had to call to him twice more in a low voice and then gently shake him. There was a bewildered expression on his face when he opened his eyes. She laid a finger against his lips.

"Shh, it's all right, sweetheart."

It was anything but all right, and Claire made it worse when she murmured to him from the shadows. "Hello, Patrick. Have you missed me?"

Alarmed by her taunt, by a silky voice he must not have wanted ever to hear again, Nathanial shot up against the headboard, his eyes wide. To his credit, he remained silent. Eden didn't. She turned her head, whispering fiercely. "You're scaring him!"

"Enough, I hope, that he does what he's asked without

a single word from him. Now get him into his robe and slippers.''

They mean to take him out of here. But where? She was afraid to guess the answer to that question. But wherever it was, she wouldn't let him go without her. Nathanial clung to her trustingly as she helped him out of bed and into his robe and slippers. In any other circumstances, she would have welcomed that trust. But not now. Not when his life was in danger.

And all the while she longed to call out to Shane, but she couldn't. Not with that gun in Bryant's hand. Because if Shane was startled out of a solid sleep and came bursting in here, Bryant Dennis wouldn't hesitate to shoot him, maybe her as well. And she had to stay alive for Nathanial's sake.

Eden did the only thing she could do. She made an effort to stall them, praying that the delay would permit Shane to wake on his own. To understand something was wrong and take an action that wouldn't cost all of them their lives.

''Why?'' she asked. ''Can you just tell me that? *Why?*''

It was a simple question, and Claire understood it. ''Money, of course. It's a wonderful thing. If you have enough of it, you can buy anything. Like the services of a local fisherman willing to risk his boat to carry you across from the mainland in rough waters. And having him tell you where you can find the child you're looking for. Not so surprising he would know about a boy of his age and coloring staying with an African-American couple on an island this size. It can even buy the silence of such a man.''

''But not a car,'' her son complained. ''Had to walk all the way from the landing, or we would have been here long before this.''

''Ah, but in a car we might have missed the sign for the DuBois cottages here and the sight of the Toyota with its South Carolina plate parked outside.'' Her mood abruptly shifted again. ''That's enough. Get moving now, both of you. Outside, and not a sound from either of you.''

That's when Eden understood their intention. They didn't want Shane alerted, didn't want to be forced to shoot anyone, though they would do so if it became necessary. But something that wouldn't look like murder, that could be explained as an accident—

"You heard her," Bryant growled. "Move!"

Her arm protectively around Nathanial's shoulder, Eden guided her son out into the hall and across the living room. She could feel him shivering against her side, and his fear refueled her anger. But what could she do, other than to continue to hope that Shane would somehow rescue them?

But that possibility seemed increasingly unlikely when there was no sign of any stirring behind the closed bedroom door. He had to be unaware of what was happening to them.

They had reached the front door where Eden paused, surprised to see the door ajar. Bryant nudged her in the back with the barrel of the gun. She couldn't help it. She lost her temper then.

"Stop that!"

"Then move!"

"Patience, Bryant," his mother whispered. "She's just trying to understand how we could possibly have gotten inside without their hearing." Claire leaned toward Eden, friend to friend. "You'll have to forgive my son. I'm afraid he isn't as smart as I'd like him to be. But he does have a talent for breaking and entering that grieved me when he and his brother were in their teens and forever in trouble. As it turns out, though, it's very useful." She pulled the door all the way back, holding it open for them. "Shall we go?"

Eden hesitated, knowing that once they left this cottage there would be little chance of surviving whatever Claire Jamison and her son planned for them.

"*Now,*" Claire insisted.

The gun was in Eden's back again. No option about it. Taking Nathanial's hand in her own, she led him out into the night where the wind still howled, tossing the tops of the pines, and the moon swam brightly overhead.

Their captors drove them down the lane, turning them in the direction of the old fort. Its bulk loomed in the moonlight.

"Beautiful, isn't it?" Claire's mocking voice said behind them. "Who could fail to understand how a small boy, waking up in the middle of the night and catching sight of it from his bedroom window, would be unable to resist its fascination. And how the woman, who finds him gone and has raced after him, loses her footing in her effort to rescue him from one of those high walls and carries them both into the ocean."

*Where we wouldn't survive the frigid, raging waters,* Eden thought. It would look like a tragic accident, and no one could prove that Claire Jamison and her son were ever here. That's why they had been so careful not to disturb Shane. They were a cunning pair. And absolutely ruthless.

This was intolerable. She had to do something. But what? *What?*

Nathanial tugged at her hand. "Uncle Mike will come for us, won't he?" he whispered to her bravely.

"Yes, darling," she told him, wanting it to be true, still hoping against all reason that it would be true.

WAS IT THE nightmare again?

Except for his recent session under hypnosis, Shane hadn't experienced it in a long while. Hadn't gone back to that damn jungle and the horror of battling to save his men.

But, no, he was sure he hadn't been dreaming this time. Then, what had suddenly awakened him out of a sound sleep? He didn't know.

Maybe there'd been a noise in the cottage. A warning that had penetrated his unconscious state. Lifting his head from the pillow, he listened. Nothing. If anything, it was too quiet in the cottage. Like the silence of desertion. Could that kind of stillness make a man uneasy in his sleep?

Shane didn't like it.

Throwing off the blanket, he swung his legs over the side of the bed and got to his feet, intending to check on Eden and Nathanial in the other bedroom. He never reached the door. There was a movement in his peripheral vision that stopped him in midstride. Something that came from outside.

Whipping around, he went to the window and looked out. What he saw seized him with a dread deep in his gut. They were headed down the lane toward the road, four figures in the sharp moonlight. Eden and Nathanial were out in front, their two captors directly behind them, urging them forward with a gun.

Yeah, he recognized them all right. That bastard, Bryan Dennis, and his mother beside him, her blond hair pale in the moonlight.

No!

A fury exploded inside Shane's head, along with a determination that galvanized him into action. There was no time to wonder how they had managed to get inside the cottage and snatch Eden and the boy. No time to reproach himself for failing to be aware of their arrival, for going back to bed when he should have remained on watch all night.

All that mattered was his fierce need to recover Eden and her son. Dennis and the Jamison woman couldn't have them. They belonged to him, were everything to him. The family he no longer had. Without them, nothing meant anything. Why hadn't he understood this hours ago when he and Eden had made love?

And all the while, along with his hollow feeling of loss was a blind rage that had him moving swiftly around the room. He dragged on a pair of black jeans, pulled a dark sweatshirt over his head and slid his feet into a pair of equally dark sneakers. Colors that would blend in with the night.

Without consciously being aware of it, Shane had auto

matically slipped back into commando mode. His training as an Army Ranger continued to serve him when he raced out of the cottage, stopping just long enough to scoop up a handful of wet earth from a flower bed beside the door. Smearing the mud over his face and hands in a further effort to camouflage himself, he checked on his targets.

They had reached the main road, were turning in the direction of the old fort. Cutting diagonally across the lawns he had once mowed as a teenager, Shane went after them. Hugging the shadows, sprinting from tree to tree, dodging behind shrubs whenever one of the enemies started to look back over his shoulder. He had his cover, but what he wouldn't give for an assault rifle. Or, for that matter, any weapon. Never mind, he would figure out some way of saving Eden and her son.

But save them from what? Fairly certain now that their destination was the fort, with those murderous waters beneath its high, sea-facing walls, Shane was beginning to have a sick understanding about what Dennis and his mother planned for them. Could he overtake them in time? Even though he was using a shortcut, they were still better than a hundred yards off, and with this damn leg of his slowing him down…

Eden had suddenly halted at the approach to the fort, had swung around to confront Dennis and the Jamison woman. Concealed by an azalea hedge wet and drooping from the storm, Shane watched through a gap in the foliage as she argued with them heatedly, refusing to go on.

They were too far away for him to hear what she was saying, but it didn't matter. The important thing was she was stalling them.

"Good girl," he whispered.

The delay permitted Shane to work his way rapidly in a half crouch along the length of the hedge, which rimmed the road. But there were no more gaps in the screen, and when he emerged from behind the hedge close to where they had stopped, the four were gone.

Dennis and his mother had forced their captives to move on. The four of them were already nearing the bridge over the dry moat on the landward side of the fort. The distance between Shane and the fort offered no further cover for him. Not caring now whether he exposed himself in his need to reach Eden and her son, he trotted across the open road.

By the time he gained the bridge, they were across the moat and disappearing into the sally port. He went after them on swift, silent feet, stopping for a necessary reconnaissance in the blackness of the deep tunnel that entered the fort through the gorge wall.

The four had emerged from the other end of the sally port and were starting across the broad expanse of the parade ground, picking their way with care over the broken paving. The fort was pentagonal in shape, with masonry stairs situated in the angle of two of its front walls. They were making for the stairs that rose through three levels, the tiers carried on massive brick arches, to the open terreplein high overhead.

Shane no longer questioned the intention of his objectives. Eden and Nathanial would be shoved over the parapet to certain death in the thundering sea below. What were his chances of rescuing them before that could happen? Nonexistent if he tried to charge across the parade ground. Dennis would shoot him before he got anywhere near them.

But if he could somehow get above them without their knowledge, manage to ambush Dennis from overhead—

There was only one way, and Shane didn't hesitate to choose it. Formidable challenge though it was, he would have to scale the outside of the gorge wall.

He could do it, he promised himself. Hadn't his training included climbing the faces of sheer cliffs? He *had* to do it. And do it in time to intercept the enemy.

Even before he fully reached this decision, Shane had retreated from the sally port, vaulted over the sagging railing of the bridge, and was attacking the thick rear wall of the fort.

Swarming up that steep precipice wasn't easy, but it wasn't impossible either. The onslaught of time and weather hadn't been kind to the long-abandoned fort. Its brick walls had suffered fractures that offered Shane cracks for his hands and feet.

In other places, where the bricks had crumbled away, vegetation had sprouted in the gaps. Some of it was rooted deeply enough to bear his weight. And where the wall hadn't opened up, or there weren't missing bricks, there were often narrow gun ports that had once bristled with cannon fire and now provided Shane with ledges to grip.

His only serious problem was the wind. On the ground it had been his ally. Its wail, together with the boom of the surf, had masked any sounds that might have betrayed his presence. But up here it was his enemy, becoming more of a threat the higher he climbed. At one point, the gusts were so severe they threatened to tear him away from the wall to which he clung with grim determination.

It was this absolute will that drove him upward. His urgent need to reach Eden and the boy. It was all he permitted himself to think about. Getting them back, telling Eden what he should have told her long ago. That he loved her, that she meant everything to him, and without her—

*You won't lose her. It isn't an option. Do you understand that, soldier? It* is not *an option.*

What seemed like a slow, frustrating ascent was actually something he managed in the space of a few minutes. But they were vital minutes, and Shane feared what they might have cost him when he finally hauled himself over the parapet. Scrambling to his feet, he cautiously checked on the position of his targets.

To his relief, he found them down on the second level almost directly across from where he stood. Their progress had been stalled by great chunks of fallen masonry blocking the stairway to the third tier. He could hear Dennis spewing curses.

"Go on," he commanded Eden. "Take the kid and climb over the stuff."

Drawing back out of sight before any of them could look up and glimpse him, bending low and keeping close to the parapet side of the terreplein, Shane swiftly worked his way around the perimeter of the fort. Within seconds, he had located himself above the stairway.

The three levels of the ruin, all of them missing their railings, rose like the layers of a wedding cake, wider at the bottom, narrower at the top. From where he placed himself at the edge of the third level, Shane was able to look down on his objective—Bryant Dennis, gun in hand, urging Eden onward, his mother below him on the second flight.

Shane would need a distraction if he was going to disarm Dennis. With the deterioration everywhere around him, this was no problem. He armed himself with a chunk of brick that he silently scooped up from the litter at his feet. Ready for action, he took aim and fired his missile. It struck the paving behind Dennis with a loud clatter.

Alarmed, the gunman swung in that direction. And that's when Shane launched himself. He slammed into Dennis with a force whose impact carried both of them to the floor of the level where they struggled for possession of the gun.

There were cries. Whether they originated from Eden, Nathanial or Claire Jamison below them, Shane didn't know. He was too busy using every technique he had ever learned to disable his opponent. He permitted himself no diversion except to shout, "Eden, get out of here! Take the boy and run!"

He had no opportunity to learn whether she obeyed him. Bryant Dennis was proving to be an equal match for him in their battle for the gun. Shane redoubled his efforts, landing punches in several vulnerable areas. It was an old-fashioned, ferocious fist to the jaw that finally defeated his opponent.

Stunned, the bastard relaxed his grip on the pistol long enough for Shane to wrest it from him. But when he sprang to his feet, weapon in hand, he found himself backed up to the perilous edge of the tier. Dennis had also leaped to his feet, and before Shane could level the pistol at him, Dennis rushed at him with a savage howl.

Shane sidestepped the charge. Unable to check the momentum of his attack, Dennis sailed out into space. Shane heard a yell followed by a thud. When he managed to recover his balance and swing around, he saw Bryant Dennis sprawled silently below him on the floor of the parade ground. The angle of his head indicated a broken neck.

Where were Eden and Nathanial? Or, for that matter, Claire Jamison? Shane lifted his head, his anxious gaze searching for them. There! Around on the other side!

He could see Eden. She must have taken Nathanial with her when she'd fled in that direction, but he was nowhere in evidence. At one time there had been another brick stairway over there. It was no more than a mound of rubble now, which meant they had been unable to get down.

Eden must have hidden Nathanial then in one of the numerous compartments that had once quartered the garrison and the fort's stores of ordnance. With her son safely out of sight, she was now bravely, but foolishly, on her way back to help Shane.

"No, Eden!" he shouted to her. "Go back!"

She wasn't alone over there. Claire Jamison, having reached the second tier, was in pursuit of her quarry. From his angle, Shane could see her lurking at the side of a pier out of range of Eden's vision. There was something else he could see glinting in the moonlight. Something neither he nor Eden had anticipated. Claire had drawn a gun of her own from her shoulder bag.

Even from this distance, Shane could swear he saw the vicious expression on her face when, alerted by his shout, she turned and fired at him. He fired back. She seemed to hover there for an instant, and then she crumpled to the floor and lay still.

It was only then that Shane felt the burning in his chest and realized he had been hit. He tried to go to Eden, thinking she might still have need of him. But his legs carried him no more than a few faltering steps before he sank to his knees, his hand clutching his chest.

It was his left hand, the one wearing the wedding band. But he couldn't see the ring. It was soaked in blood. And then he couldn't see anything. The moon went black.

## Chapter Fifteen

Eden couldn't stand it. This endless vigil with no definite word had her half out of her mind. If she had to sit here much longer in the waiting room without knowing, she would lose the other half of her mind.

Her inability to see him was almost as bad as not hearing whether there was any change yet, any sign of improvement. Absolutely no visitors, she had been informed. All they would tell her when she checked periodically at the nurses' station was he was still unconscious, still on a ventilator and IV drips in the intensive care unit, where he had been moved yesterday morning after spending hours in surgery.

What if Shane didn't make it? Eden didn't want to think that, didn't want to even consider it, but she knew it was a very real possibility. The surgeon had been candid when he had explained everything to her.

"The bullet tore a hole low in his right lung, causing a rib fragment to puncture his liver. We've repaired those, but there was a massive amount of bleeding."

Eden shuddered over the memory of how much blood Shane had lost as she'd huddled over him before the paramedics arrived, after which he'd been airlifted to the nearest hospital on the mainland. She had the DuBoises to thank for that. Victor had heard the shots when he'd let the dog out into the yard, and while Estelle had phoned 911, he'd raced to the fort where he had stayed with Eden, doing whatever he could to help.

"Transfusions have replaced the blood," the surgeon had continued, "and a chest tube is draining off the fluids, but his condition is critical."

"Will he…" Eden couldn't bring herself to say it.

The surgeon had tried to be encouraging. "He's a strong man, and he was in good health before this happened. Those factors are very much in his favor. It's a matter of time now." He'd paused before adding a kindly "A few prayers wouldn't hurt."

Eden had been silently doing just that ever since. But she was all out of prayers now and able to do nothing except wait. That and try to keep herself from imagining the yawning black hole in her life if the worst happened. To go on without Shane and her love for him was unthinkable.

*She couldn't lose him. She couldn't.*

"Any news yet?"

Eden looked up from her chair as her father strode into the waiting room. Both of her parents had flown in from Chicago to offer their love and support, and there had been concerned phone calls almost hourly from either her sister or one of her three brothers. It was a demonstration of how the Hawkes closed ranks in a family crisis, and Eden didn't fail to appreciate it.

She shook her head. "Nothing. Did you deliver Ma?"

"Only as far as the ferry landing, where I was instructed to come straight back here and not leave you. Victor DuBois was meeting her on the other side with his car, so I imagine by now your mother is with her grandson."

Nathanial was once again in the care of Victor and Estelle. Eden was no longer worried about her son's safety. Not now, after Shane had eliminated the threat to him. But, dear God, at what cost?

Eden's father stood there regarding her, a worried expression in his blue eyes. Unlike his three sons, he was a short man, with strong features and liberal amounts of gray in his dark hair. His size and easy smile were misleading. He was a tough P.I. and, when he had to be, a tough father. He demonstrated that now with his daughter.

"Honey, you look like hell."

"I feel like hell."

"Come on," he ordered, "let's you and I take a walk. You could use the exercise."

"Pop, no. I'm not stepping foot out of the hospital until—"

"Who said anything about going outside? There are miles of hallway in this place. Let's use some of them, at least on this floor. They'll find you when they have something to tell you. You can let them know at the nurses' station where we'll be."

Her father was right. The waiting room was beginning to suffocate her. Leaving word at the desk, they struck out along the nearest corridor. It felt good to pace something besides the confined area of the waiting room.

"How about filling me in now," Casey Hawke suggested. "You've already told your mother and me the essentials, but I'd like to know all of it. You can start with how this Lissie Reardon ended up in Savannah with Nathanial, passing herself off to the Jamisons as his mother."

"While maintaining the lowest possible profile the whole time she lived with them," Eden added. "She never wanted either Nathanial or her photographed or written about, if she could avoid it. Nathanial was the grandson of a wealthy man, and publicity could make him vulnerable to kidnapping. That was her plea, anyway, and Sebastian agreed with her. It was an excuse, of course. What she really feared was exposure."

"You learned all this from the police, I suppose, when they came here to interview you?"

Eden nodded. "Charlie Moses, his wife and the surviving Dennis brother have been arrested and charged. They were all in on the plot. Charlie and Hugh Dennis aren't saying much yet, but Irene told the police everything, hoping it will save her when they go to trial.''

They moved over to one side to avoid a gurney being wheeled off the elevator. ''So, what's the rest of the story?'' Casey urged when the gurney had passed.

Eden knew that her father's interest was genuine. But she also realized he was using it in an effort to occupy her mind with something other than her anguish over Shane. As if anything could distract her from that. But she did her best to satisfy her father.

''Beth—Lissie, that is—lied to Shane when she told him Sebastian had made Nathanial his chief heir. I suppose she figured, if she exaggerated that part of it, she stood a better chance of enlisting her brother's support. Because, without any evidence, Shane might not believe the actual danger to Nathanial.''

''So, the old man hadn't—''

''No, but he was about to. He no longer had any patience with his family and their greed, including his wife. And if he rewrote his will, Nathanial would get not just a share of his fortune as in the present will, but nearly everything. Claire couldn't let that happen. Something had to be done before Sebastian changed his will. It was her scheme, but the others were in on it with her.''

''Murder?''

''Yes, but cleverly choreographed to look like an accident. Claire arranged for every member of the family, including herself, to have a sound alibi. She chose a night when the staff was off and everyone out of the house except for Sebastian, Nathanial and his nanny.''

Eden paused for an announcement over the P.A. summoning a staff member who wasn't responding to his pager. Then she continued her account.

''It was no secret that Claire's two sons loved to gamble. She sent them to Atlantic City with instructions to remain visible all evening at the tables in one of the casinos. Charlie Moses was down in Brunswick on a case, and Irene was with him. Claire was scheduled to attend a charity costume ball several blocks away from the mansion.''

''And Lissie Reardon was in the hospital,'' Casey remembered. ''So who killed Sebastian?''

''Claire, of course. No one else had the guts for it. She made dinner that night, which she usually did when it was the cook's night off. Though she never ate desserts herself, her chocolate mousse was a favorite with the whole family. Only this time she dosed it with something guaranteed to put them all pleasantly asleep without leaving any evidence they'd been drugged.''

Casey nodded. ''Which wouldn't have been any problem for a doctor with access to drugs. Okay, so after she sees them settled in for the night, she goes off to her party. Right so far?''

''Yes.''

''Then she must have come back later and killed Sebastian. Only how did she manage that without being missed at this ball?''

''She used Irene.''

''Who was supposed to be elsewhere with her husband.''

''In Brunswick with Charlie, yes.''

They had reached the end of the long corridor where they stopped at a window overlooking the parking lot two floors below. It was already dark outside. Eden could see that the pavement was wet with rain, glistening in the headlights from arriving and departing cars. It was a dreary scene. She tried not to let the sight depress her, tried not to think of Shane down the hall struggling for his life.

''When Charlie and Irene checked into the hotel in Brunswick,'' Eden continued, ''she complained of a sinus headache. They had the desk send up something for her to take, after which she went straight to bed. When Charlie ordered room service for himself, he made certain that the waiter who arrived with his meal, and another one who collected the tray long afterward, caught glimpses of his wife asleep in her bed. What they actually saw in that dim room were pillows under the covers, along with just enough of a wig showing that matched Irene's memorable red-gold hair to convince anyone it was her.''

"Except Irene wasn't there," Casey realized. "She was—"

"Racing back to Savannah on the interstate. She and Claire exchanged places at the party. It wasn't difficult. By then Irene was wearing an identical costume, wig and mask. The switch needed to last only long enough for Claire to tear back to the Jamison mansion under the cover of darkness in a long black coat."

"So she arrives and finds…what?"

"Nathanial in his bed, his nanny in a chair beside him and asleep over the book she'd been reading to him before he drifted off, and Sebastian asleep in his own room down the hall and still in his wheelchair, although Claire had the police thinking he must have gotten out of bed on his own after she'd seen him settled in it for the night."

"No witnesses."

"And no problem for Claire to wheel her husband out to the landing, push him in the chair down the flight of stairs, make certain he was dead and slip out of the house and back to the party where she relieved Irene."

"Who was able to return to the hotel in Brunswick with no one the wiser," Casey figured. "So what went wrong?"

"My son."

Eden and her father were on their way back along the corridor now, which was suddenly busy with the traffic of dinner trays being delivered to patients in their rooms. They dodged the stream of servers as Eden continued the story.

"Claire was so busy the next day playing the grieving widow and dealing with all the details connected with a prominent husband's death, which the police were satisfied was the result of a tragic accident, that she had no thought for Nathanial, who was the responsibility of his nanny, anyway. It wasn't until the afternoon when the woman came to her in tears that she realized something had gone very wrong.''

''Which was?'' Casey asked.

''Nathanial and Lissie Reardon were missing. When Claire questioned the nanny, she learned that Nathanial had gone to bed the night before with an upset stomach after throwing up his dinner. That, together with his grandfather's death, had him so distraught and so frantic to see his mother, the nanny decided the only way to settle him down was to take him to the hospital, where Lissie sent her out of the room. When she came back later to collect Nathanial, both mother and son were gone.''

''So Claire knew she had a problem.''

''One that alarmed her,'' Eden said, ''because if Nathanial had vomited the chocolate mousse before the drug it contained had time to be absorbed into his system, it was possible he had awakened after she'd checked on him. And it was just as possible that he'd cracked his door open, maybe because he'd heard the sound of the chairlift Claire had summoned to the top of the stairs so it would look like an accident had occurred while Sebastian was trying to lever himself from the wheelchair onto the lift. If so, that meant Nathanial could have seen her push Sebastian's wheelchair down the flight of stairs.''

''Which,'' Casey said, ''as you mentioned to your mother and me earlier, Nathanial has finally admitted is what happened.''

''And why he was so scared, and Lissie so terrified of the consequences she fled Savannah with him. Her action convinced Claire that Nathanial *was* a witness. He had to be found and silenced.''

''She almost succeeded,'' Casey said angrily, ''but Claire Jamison won't be a threat anymore to my grandson.''

No, Eden thought soberly, she and her son died in that windswept fort, victims of their own avarice. But if it hadn't been for Shane… Oh, if she could only see him, touch him, let him know just how much he mattered to her!

Her frustrated need must have been evident to her father, because he stopped her on their way back to the waiting room, renewing his effort to turn her mind in another direction.

"What about this Harriet Krause? Did the police explain her death to you?"

"Yes, Irene gave them the details about that, too. Charlie had paid Harriet to tell him everything she knew about Lissie, including the existence of a brother. That was why Bryant and Hugh Dennis were taking Shane that night from the motel to Harriet's apartment. They wanted her to tell Shane in person what his sister had done and that Lissie hadn't been entitled to Nathanial. They hoped shock might accomplish what force had failed to do and that Shane would reveal what he had done with Nathanial."

"I suppose Harriet would have been paid for that, too."

"Yes, and to keep quiet about all of it. But she was scared after Shane and I visited her, and when she phoned the Dennis brothers to let them know we'd been there—"

"But they couldn't have murdered the Krause woman, not when they were busy chasing you."

"No, it was Claire who killed her. She'd arrived in Charleston furious with her sons after they called to tell her they'd lost Shane. Then, when Harriet phoned threatening to go to the police to save herself, Claire went up to the apartment to offer her more money. But Harriet was in no mood to be bought off this time."

"So Claire made sure she wouldn't talk."

"With a heavy object that turned out to be a brass bookend from Harriet's—"

Eden broke off, checked by the sight of a young woman headed toward them with an expression of urgency in her gait. Eden recognized her. She was one of the ICU nurses. Eden felt herself go rigid with fear as her father's hand closed around her arm to steady her.

It wasn't until the nurse got closer that Eden realized she was wearing a smile. A smile almost as good as her cheerful words when she reached them.

"Good news, Ms. Hawke. Mr. Reardon is awake."

"Does that mean—"

"He's rallied, yes. He's also asking for you and making such a fuss about it that the doctor is afraid he'll have a relapse if he doesn't permit you to see him. You can have fifteen minutes with him."

Eden was so overjoyed with relief she was incapable of movement until her father squeezed her arm. "He's waiting for you, honey. Go."

And Eden went.

The nurse conducted her to the ICU, leaving her outside Shane's cubicle with a firm "Fifteen minutes. No more."

Eden nodded and went eagerly into the cubicle, catching her breath at the sight of Shane in the elevated bed. He was no longer on a ventilator, but he still wore a blood pressure cuff and IV drips. Bandages swathed his naked chest.

He looked awful, his sun-streaked hair rumpled, a stubble of beard on his jaw, his face all hollow and drawn. Awful and at the same time wonderful. And she had never loved him more than in that moment.

His brown eyes were alert, though, the golden lights in them full of energy. They turned immediately to her, following her every movement as she entered the cubicle and slid into a chair at his bedside.

"So, you were worried about me, huh?" he said, his voice hoarse from both the anesthetic and the ventilator.

"Maybe a little," she admitted.

"That much?" He was still capable of a wicked grin. "You shouldn't have been. This body of mine is already so battered, what's one more hole in it?"

She would have kissed that hole if it had been available to her. Instead, she reached for his hand and held it lovingly, all the while feasting her eyes on him.

"Is that all I get?" he demanded.

"Until you're stronger, and then we'll see what else can be managed."

"Well, listen—" He grimaced, evidence he was still in pain as he shifted into a more comfortable position. Eden was immediately on her feet and leaning over him, but he waved her back onto the chair. "No time for that. We've got to talk. They're only giving us twenty minutes."

"Fifteen," she corrected him.

"Okay, but there's a lot that needs to be said."

"Shane, do you think you should be making this kind of effort?"

"Oh, yeah, definitely. See, I've been thinking about those two windows."

What on earth was he talking about? Was he delirious?

"You remember," he said. "The window with the broken catch in Harriet Krause's apartment and the one in the art museum that was too easy to open. They gave me this idea. About my future, that is, when the army and I finally part company."

"You're planning your future?"

"I have to, now that I've put the past behind me. No more anguish over the ambush in South America. You led me out of that jungle, Eden."

"I did?"

"By believing in me, yeah. Well, that and what I've come to feel for you. A good marriage will do that for a man."

He gave Eden no opportunity to ask him exactly what he did feel for her or to remind him that their marriage had been no more than a pretense. He was too busy telling her about their future.

"Anyway, I was thinking that with my training, I'd be a good protection specialist. You know, a security consultant for both private and public enterprises. And you being a P.I. makes it perfect."

"It does?"

"Yeah, a team operation. That's what I was thinking. So, what do you think?"

"You'd have to settle in Charleston."

"Where else. The thing is…"

"What?"

"I'd really like to make this more than just a business proposition."

"What did you have in mind?"

"Something more than a marriage of pretense. I was kind of hoping for a marriage for keeps. Unless…"

"Unless what?"

"Being married to the brother of the woman who stole your kid, even though he is crazy in love with you, is something you couldn't handle."

"That's not an issue. I've already forgiven her. You're in love with me?"

"Absolutely." Shane was relieved, but she still hadn't said she loved him. "Then if you're ready to move on, and if you feel for me even half of what I feel for you, maybe…"

The rest was up to her. He watched her anxiously, hopefully, as she sat there and pondered his proposal. What if she turned him down? Shane didn't think he could deal with that.

Hell, he'd been a loner for years, needing and wanting nothing else but the army. He saw now how sad that was. And no longer true. Eden Hawke had come into his life, this wonderful, precious woman, and if he lost her—

"I'm going to have a relapse here if you don't say something," he teased.

"I was just remembering something myself," she said softly. "What you asked me that night you came to me out of the storm. 'Am I home?' I have the answer for you now, Shane. You are home."

"Yeah?" he said happily. "Man-and-wife kind of home?"

"Man and wife as well as mother and father for Nathanial. This time for real. But I won't have you settling for halves," she warned him. "Because when it comes to loving you, I feel more than that. Much, much more."

He grinned at her meaningfully. "I'm feeling much stronger now, sweetheart."

The nurse chose that inopportune second to poke her head into the cubicle. "Time's up."

"Don't look so disappointed," Eden said to him, getting to her feet with a promise in her smile. "We have a whole lifetime for kissing ahead of us."

# *Epilogue*

*You have no right to be anything but supremely happy.*

Eden kept repeating this reproach to herself as she stood in the vestibule of Saint Michael's. The historic church with its pure, classic style ranked as one of the most beautiful in Charleston. A choice setting for any occasion.

In a few moments, the doors in front of her would be opened by the ushers, the organ would thunder into the wedding march, and she would glide down the aisle on the arm of her father. Meanwhile, Eden's attendants, who included her friend Tia, fussed around her, making last-minute adjustments to her wedding gown.

*You have no right to be anything but supremely happy.*

The matron of honor, her sister, Christy, stepped back to survey her. ''Gorgeous,'' she pronounced with satisfaction.

Eden knew it was a spectacular gown, a strapless confection of elaborately embroidered antique satin. The kind of special dress a bride dreamed about wearing in surroundings that boasted masses of flowers and flickering candles. And Eden *had* dreamed about such a wedding ever since she was a little girl. A grand affair, unlike the simple ceremonies of her sister and three brothers. Today that dream was a reality.

*You have no right to be anything but supremely happy.*

What on earth was the matter with her? she wondered, impatient with herself. She had everything to be thankful for. She was about to marry the man she loved and who loved her. She had her friends and family around her. Even the cascading bouquet she clutched with its mixed crimson and golden blooms was perfect.

*You have no right—*

The litany failed when her gaze went to her son standing beside her brother Devlin's daughter. Livie was to be their flower girl, Nathanial the ring bearer. Handsome in a miniature tuxedo, he fidgeted with excitement.

Eden, watching him tenderly, knew what was wrong, had known all along what troubled her. In these past six weeks, while Shane had mended, recovering his full health, she and her son had forged a union of their own. Time and patience had taught him his true identity, and he now accepted both his name and his relationship to her. But he had yet to address her in any maternal form, and Eden was beginning to fear he never would.

She was being ridiculous, of course. She had no right to her longing, especially today of all days. No reason to be anything but totally grateful she had her son back. That was all that really mattered, except—

"Are we ready?" Casey demanded, impatient with the holdup. "Honey, your bridegroom is going to be the most envied man in Charleston when they catch sight of you in there. So, if we're all in place now, let's go. Deep breaths, everyone."

"Wait, wait!" Nathanial cried, breaking out of line and racing to Eden's side. "There's something I forgot to do."

"What is it, sweetheart?" she asked as she leaned down to him, hoping it wasn't a visit to the bathroom.

Looping his arms around her neck, he gave her a quick hug. "Have a good wedding, Mom," he wished her cheerfully before turning and dashing back to his place in the procession. "Okay, we can go now."

"Don't you dare cry!" Christy warned her sister as Eden came slowly erect. "You'll ruin forty-five minutes of creative makeup. Oh, damn! Somebody go down front and warn them there will be a slight delay while we perform damage control here on the bride.''

''No time for that, we're on,'' Casey said as the doors were folded back and the organ swelled into the wedding march.

Eden didn't care that the tears were welling in her eyes as she and her father progressed slowly down the center aisle. They were the evidence of her complete happiness. Through them she saw the familiar, smiling faces of her mother, her three brothers, their wives and children, and friends like Estelle and Victor DuBois.

And then they were eclipsed by the tall figure, incredibly good-looking in his dress uniform, waiting for her at the altar. His was the only face Eden saw now. A face that registered his pure pride and admiration in her.

When she reached him, when her father released her with a quick kiss, and she joined the man who would always be ''Shane'' to her at the altar, he turned to her. For a long second they simply gazed at each other. And then he winked at her. It was the kind of outrageous wink only he could deliver. A loving wink that promised a lifetime of joy.